CULTS OF DEATH AND MADNESS

CULTS OF DEATH AND MADNESS

The Book of Ancient Evil

JOHN HAAS

WFP
WORDFIRE PRESS

EBook ISBN: 978-1-68057-233-9
Trade Paperback ISBN: 978-1-68057-232-2
Hardcover ISBN: 978-1-68057-234-6
Casebind ISBN: 978-1-68057-330-5
Library of Congress Control Number: 2021940620
Cover design by Janet McDonald
Cover artwork images by Adobe Stock
Kevin J. Anderson, Art Director
Published by
WordFire Press, LLC
PO Box 1840
Monument CO 80132
Kevin J. Anderson & Rebecca Moesta, Publishers
WordFire Press eBook Edition 2021
WordFire Press Trade Paperback Edition 2021
WordFire Press Hardcover Edition 2021
Printed in the USA
Join our WordFire Press Readers Group for
sneak previews, updates, new projects, and giveaways.
Sign up at wordfirepress.com

DEDICATION

To my two greatest supporters, my sons Jack & Oliver. None of this would be possible without your constant support.

AUTHOR'S NOTE

I walked a fine line with *Cults of Death and Madness*, between keeping everything accurate from a historical perspective and with making stuff up to conveniently suit the story. Mostly I kept to the facts where I could find them.

Some events take place in real places of late 1800s India, such as Bombay (now Mumbai) and Hyderabad. I hope any reader who lives in these places or just knows better will forgive any inconsistencies. Keep in mind this is an alternate reality and will have differences from the India of our own world. The city of Bandagar within Hyderabad, for example, is as fictional as the story itself.

Cults of Death and Madness is a prequel to my novelette "Damned Voyage" which appeared in *Writers of the Future Volume 35*. One reader of that story suggested I was guilty of giving in to the "great white saviour" character where Shaw and Singh's relationship was concerned. I have done my best to address that in this prequel while still keeping the elements of racism and white privilege from that time period historically accurate. To this end I have had friends of Indian background review the story and provide feedback. In the end it is up to you, the reader, to say if it's been handled well.

Take this kiss upon the brow!
And, in parting from you now,
Thus much let me avow—
You are not wrong, who deem
That my days have been a dream;
Yet if hope has flown away
In a night, or in a day,
In a vision, or in none,
Is it therefore the less gone?
All that we see or seem
Is but a dream within a dream.
I stand amid the roar
Of a surf-tormented shore,
And I hold within my hand
Grains of the golden sand—
How few! yet how they creep
Through my fingers to the deep,
While I weep—while I weep!
O God! Can I not grasp
Them with a tighter clasp?
O God! can I not save
One from the pitiless wave?
Is all that we see or seem
But a dream within a dream?

—"A Dream Within a Dream" (Edgar Allan Poe)

CHAPTER ONE

BOMBAY, INDIA—APRIL 10TH, 1878

Dear Mother,

The HMS Agincourt is close to completing its journey, bringing me across the no-man's-land—or ocean as it were—between England and India, old life and new. Incredible to think a mere decade ago this voyage would have taken months rather than weeks. There is surely no better symbol of modern man's ingenuity than the Suez Canal—I do know I've gone on at length about that subject earlier so shall curb my enthusiasm accordingly.

Currently I stand on deck watching the shores of India draw closer. In less than an hour I shall disembark in Bombay and begin this first great adventure of a lifetime, though I admit to a certain amount of trepidation mixed with the excitement. The usual unease which comes from facing the unfamiliar. I know little of this country other than what is reported in the papers, and from the boys' adventure stories I devoured as a child. In truth I question the accuracy of both and must allow my own experiences to inform me.

Leaving London and all I've ever known was the first great step on this journey but walking down that ramp onto foreign soil will be the *greater. There is a finality in the action, an emphasis on the fact that home is far away and it will be years before I see England again. When I do I suppose the shores on that end will have become the foreign ones.*

An interesting thought, comforting somehow.

In any case, everything has led to this point. Medical school. My officer's commission. Uncle Freddy's invitation. In short order I can begin serving God, Queen, and country in my station as doctor. This is where I shall make my mark in life and distinguish myself. I feel that.

I'd best close this letter, Mother, if I hope for it to make the return voyage aboard the Agincourt. *Tomorrow I shall start a new correspondence along with my new life. Which seems most appropriate.*

I miss you greatly, Mother.

Your son,

Doctor Archibald Shaw

With a deep inhale of humid air Shaw disembarked from the ship, hot Indian sun beating down though it had barely begun its journey into the sky. Early morning and the day held a promise of great heat and greater mugginess.

A single bead of sweat—the first of many—rolled down one side of his face.

On the dock the thick traffic of people going about their regular business buffeted him on all sides, like a ship on the ocean. All around they spoke in a rapid dialect of which he couldn't understand more than a word or two, and that only while focusing intently.

Deep breaths, he counseled. *Keep taking deep breaths.*

The salty tang of seawater and stronger smells of fish from nearby market vendors filled his nose. Women passing, carrying the catches of the day in huge bowls and baskets balanced on their heads, brought the smells that much closer.

It was a near claustrophobic experience.

With one brisk, semiconscious motion Shaw smoothed his uniform jacket, forcing those fruitless emotions away with the same movement. A train traveled from here to his final destination in Hyderabad province—or so he'd been told before departing England—but he was at a loss on how best to find it. Signs should have indicated a direction, or would have back in London, at least. Following a group of like-minded people headed in the same direction was also out, with people moving in every possible direction.

Should have asked on the ship.

Now he would need to interrupt one of the people rushing past, and hope someone could give directions. A second problem presented itself, pushing the first aside: How exactly was he to retrieve his luggage and transport the heavy trunk from ship to train?

Fish out of water, that inner voice whispered. *Fish out of water.*

It was an anxious reflex from the uncomfortable fact of not knowing what came next, or even the best way to discover those next steps. It hadn't occurred to him to ask about these details in his correspondence with Uncle Freddy and now—

"Shaw?" A voice called from the sea of people. "Doctor Shaw?"

A man, ten years or so senior to his own twenty-seven, appeared from the crowd as if he'd always been there, navigating without any apparent effort. He was tall, thin, and wore the same blue doctor's uniform Shaw had dressed in that morning. Only where Shaw wore the full uniform, including helmet, sabre, and sidearm Tranter revolver, this man wore none of those fixtures and stood much more natural and at ease.

No doubt Shaw presented a picture of the far too eager, green recruit, which was all true. There was little point denying the lack of experience, or that he was indeed eager to make his mark serving as doctor in Her Majesty's foreign army overseas. When Uncle Freddy had offered the position to replace a doctor at the outpost he commanded Shaw had jumped at the chance. Being a new doctor, and new officer to boot, meant there wouldn't be a lot of other opportunities coming along. This was better than anything that could honestly be expected.

"Yes, I'm Archibald Shaw."

The man held out a hand, lopsided grin splitting his craggy features. It was obvious he'd been in the country for some time, judging by his tanned skin and the ease with which he weathered the passing mob. Even wearing his army uniform among all the dhotis and saris didn't seem out of place. Meanwhile Shaw felt as if a shining beacon were on him.

He shook the man's hand, returning the smile.

"Lawrence Lassiter," the man said. "Don't mind the alliteration. My mum was a fan of the romances, thought it would make me into some sort of latter-day Mr. Darcy. I'm afraid she was a tad disappointed to find I was bereft of any suave flair. Poor woman had to settle for her son being just a doctor. Crushing disappointment, I'm sure."

Shaw's head swam at the amount of information in that one phrase and struggled for some reply. "You're ... from the base?"

"Well, we call it an outpost, though I've heard some of the newer lads call it a station. Take your pick. I suppose base would work as well if you could get others to adopt the naming."

"Umm ..."

"To answer the question though, yes, I am from the outpost. A doctor like yourself, in case the uniform wasn't a giveaway. The commander himself asked me to come meet you."

"Unc—?" Shaw broke off, realizing by Lassiter's raised eyebrows it was too late.

"Ah, so Commander Armstrong is your uncle then?"

Shaw gritted his teeth but nodded. Uncle Freddy had stressed in his final letter against letting it be known any relationship existed between them, but there was no sense denying it now. He'd violated that in his first ten minutes off the ship.

"Not an actual uncle. More an honorary title for a family friend. He and my father grew up together."

"Ah, I have a couple of those myself. Sadly none that were able to lend much of a hand in life. Well, your secret is safe with me. It does explain why a young doctor and new officer, with limited experience as either, was given a position here."

A protest perched on Shaw's tongue but he swallowed it knowing Lassiter was correct. He had to wonder on the man's ability to guard that secret though. It appeared every thought which popped into his head came out his mouth … Then again, Shaw could hardly throw stones on that matter himself just now.

"No need to look so glum. I've got nothing against nepotism, providing the person being nepotized can do the job." Lassiter gave a wink. "I'm assuming you've actually had medical training?"

"Of course!" Shaw glared.

"Well then, there we go." Lassiter let loose a braying laugh, closer to donkey than human. It matched his gregarious personality.

Shaw relaxed again, even managing a smile in response. He'd been drawn in by Lassiter's effortless camaraderie and without realizing had been put at ease among the crowds and unfamiliar surroundings.

Lassiter pulled out a watch, glanced down, and returned it to his pocket. "Plenty of time to get to our train, but still, best be off."

Shaw's eyes darted toward the top of the ramp which he'd descended minutes ago. The ship's stacks billowed clouds of steam which dissipated in seconds.

"Oh, your luggage will find its way to the train as if by magic. No need to worry about that, Archie."

Shaw opened his mouth to protest the use of so odious a

nickname, then noticed Lassiter's teasing grin. This was the sort of man who pushed a point to see if he could get a rise out of someone. Not through any malice or ill will, but a joker nonetheless. Mischievous. Years of experience in boarding schools told Shaw the usual way to deal with a character such as Lawrence Lassiter was to simply ignore him, but given he was embarking on a new life he threw caution to the wind.

"I want to thank you for meeting me here. Larry."

"Larry is it?" Lassiter let out another braying guffaw and clapped him on the back. "Oh, we'll get along just fine I think. Come on now, this way to the train."

Lassiter led a route through the crowd with ease, casting occasional glances back to make sure Shaw hadn't been lost in the sea of people. Every couple of minutes he would beckon to Shaw with his right hand, the left casually inside his jacket pocket.

How could this man be so comfortable? Lining either side of the street were vendors selling fruit, nuts, and spices. Animals, including one unhurried cow, wandered among the pedestrians. Newspaper distributors with piles eight feet high on their carts pushed through, ringing bells to clear their path.

"Just joking on that magic." Lassiter turned and continued backward a few steps while others detoured around him. "I tipped a few of the local lads to get your belongings from ship to train."

Shaw's first reaction was to ask about the trustworthiness of these *lads* but he didn't want to sound like every other non-Indian he'd read comments from in the papers—or those he'd spoken with on ship, for that matter.

"Don't worry," Lassiter said with another wink, as if reading his thoughts. "They don't get paid until the luggage arrives in one piece." Then the man turned and was off again, speaking casually over one shoulder. "A quick rundown, Shaw. We operate one of the more modest hospitals in India, but quite vital to the Hyderabad area. Six doctors, plus our attendant staff. Somewhat off the beaten track but a good place to be most of the time."

"Most of the time?"

Lassiter waved one hand as if the thought were a fly buzzing his face, not even breaking stride to look back. Meanwhile Shaw struggled to keep up without bumping people or poking them with his scabbard, weaving around those who didn't swerve first.

Why had he been in such a hurry to disembark? The voyage by ship had been pleasant enough, relaxing, but most of the journey across he'd been anxious for it to be done, to get to the final destination. Now eagerness had transformed to unease. This world was so different, so busy and bustling, about as … well, foreign as things could get.

"No," he muttered, pushing the thought aside.

Comfort only led to complacency, and there was no progress when one was complacent. That was a state of mind for later years, seated by a fire to pen his memoirs. Wasn't change one of the reasons he'd come to India? To force himself *out* of complacency and the mundane. Too easy back home to rely on others for support. No. Better to embrace this discomfort, take the press of unfamiliar people, the physical closeness of those he didn't know, and the utter strangeness and unfamiliarity of his surroundings. It was a reality of this new life and he would need some time to get used to it.

Still, at the moment, it felt as though he trailed his father at the zoo, afraid to lose sight of the man … Not that his father had ever taken him to the zoo or anywhere else. A damp sweat broke out under the uniform, increasing that discomfort he'd resolved to embrace.

Lassiter slowed.

"Is it *always* like this?" Shaw gasped, forcing himself to catch up.

"Nah." Lassiter looked around. "You're lucky you arrived on a slow day." Another laugh and he turned to the route once more.

With a deep sigh Shaw pushed onward, wondering how much Lassiter was pulling his leg.

CHAPTER TWO

I<small>F THE SHIP'S DOCK WAS CROWDED THEN THE TRAIN STATION WAS</small> absolute madness. *More* people, pressed in even closer, some standing in one spot to await the train, others rushing back and forth performing tasks which were not immediately obvious. Smells of sweat and dust and metal rails baking in the sun. Lassiter led him through to where the front car would be. Fewer people lingered in this area and Shaw was able to breathe easy once again. The next space held a gap in the sea of people which would be for the dining car where no one would board. Past this gap were mobs of men, all Indian and certainly more than could fit inside the expected cars.

"So, new doctor and junior officer," Lassiter said, breaking in on his thoughts to continue their earlier conversation.

"I am."

"Well, you'll get medical experience here. Nothing groundbreaking or innovative you understand, but solid day-to-day medicine. Hope you didn't come looking for glory."

"Glory?" Shaw repeated, shaking his head. "No. I ..."

But *wasn't* that one of the reasons he had come to India? To make a mark for himself? To be noticed and set up in life? Shaw would serve Queen Victoria and do his part for England, but beyond that, what did it mean to him? Turning toward Lassiter he opened his mouth to speak, to explain all of this, but without knowing what he wanted to say closed it again.

"Never mind, Archie," Lassiter said. "You'll figure out why you're here ... or it will be figured out for you."

Two stocky youths arrived carrying Shaw's trunk and deposited it with other larger baggage to be loaded once the train arrived. They trotted back to Lassiter who placed a coin into the palm of each before they were off again, searching for other jobs to perform.

"Oh," Lassiter said, "when we get on the train do take off that helmet and sabre. It's a thirteen-hour ride and you might as well be comfortable."

"Right. Of course."

"We doctors don't wear them much," Lassiter continued. "Really only if McCready, our illustrious head doctor, decides we're going with the lads on patrol. Not even then if it can be avoided. Mostly they're decoration. As for your sidearm," he said looking at the holstered Tranter all officers were assigned with obvious distaste. "You can leave that in your trunk. No one expects a doctor to carry a gun."

Shaw had wondered as much while strapping the unfamiliar weapon on that morning, thinking about how he'd come to India to help and heal people, not shoot them. The weapon was not in fact even loaded, and he would be relieved to relegate it to the bottom of his trunk.

A steam whistle's blast in the distance interrupted their conversation and gave warning of the approaching train. Everyone milling about on the platform shifted stance in antici-pation, as if readying for the starter's pistol in some race. Fifteen minutes passed, punctuated every so often by the whistle, growing steadily more intense until the great metal beast arrived. The squeal of brakes and prolonged howl of releasing steam made all other noises mild in comparison.

Once disembarking passengers were out of the way those waiting pressed forward into the gap. Those cars further down packed to the doors in moments with the overflow of people scrambling to the rooftop. An insane way to ride. How many fell off when the train lurched back into movement? Surely their skills as doctors would be needed before they'd even left the station.

Shaw followed his companion into a much less crowded car. First class. The luxury of space was calming. Rows of upholstered seats sat two by two, facing one another, with a table between each pair for taking tea or playing cards.

The reason behind this abundance of space was immediately obvious: Only white people rode in first class, only Europeans. Never mind that native Indians were also British subjects.

Shaw's newfound calm turned to disquiet.

Lassiter took a seat so he would ride backwards and Shaw removed the helmet and sabre—happy for the action to occupy his hands. He took the seat across from Lassiter, storing the items underneath, then craned his neck to see at least ten empty places in the car while outside shadows cast by those riding above wavered against the ground, the sun lighting them from behind.

"Hmm," Lassiter said. "The idea of our Indian brethren treated differently bothers you, does it?"

Shaw nodded.

"Haven't you read Darwin?" Lassiter asked, crossing his legs and getting comfortable. "Survival of the fittest and all that. If the Indian people had been able to force us back into the ocean when we first came they would still rule their own land."

Whether Lassiter was serious or facetious it boiled down to the way people in England felt, those that gave India any thought at all. Social Darwinism. The duty of England to bring civilization to backward cultures.

"I have read Darwin," Shaw admitted. "Interesting thoughts in regards to animals and evolution. I've read on other interesting subjects, too, such as the Sepoy Mutiny."

Lassiter gestured one hand for Shaw to lower his voice. "Bite your tongue, man. That's about the greatest curse you could utter here."

Twenty years ago Indian troops began an uprising against the East India Company and their rule, a protest on the way native Indians were treated by the British. This insurrection started in Bengal and lasted a bloody, violent year but was ultimately unsuccessful ... Or mostly so. The East India Company was gone now, replaced by the Raj.

Shaw stayed quiet, staring back, not sure how much he could or should say, thinking he should be in India a full day before rocking the boat.

Lassiter shrugged. "Look, Shaw. Just keep in mind you're a minority when it comes to believing the Indian people are ... well, people."

With a grunt Shaw turned to watch the hustle and bustle outside. Lassiter relaxed, happy to allow him the time to stew over his thoughts.

As was the way for all trains, this one remained idle for some time before making that first jerk forward without warning, the metallic clank of slowly rolling wheels and one extended, mournful whistle blast accompanying the movement. Shaw watched the shadows of those above swaying with the movement, fully expecting a body to fall past the window. None did. Inch by inch the station was left behind as the train continued its gradual chugging toward full speed.

Once away from the station they soon rolled from Bombay into a countryside beautiful in its wildness, filled with banyan and baobab trees, with pink euphorbia flowers and other less easily identified flora. Nothing like back home. This was primal, less encroached on by man. Gorgeous and vibrant. A distinct beauty which helped to soothe his mind, at least for the time being.

He kept a curious, anticipating eye out for wild tigers as the train thundered on, buying into the penny dreadful stories of this country where those great cats hid behind every bush waiting for unfortunate victims to pounce on and devour.

Instead he saw pangolins, porcupines, and some variety of deer. Plenty of birds and smaller wildlife but no tigers.

Perhaps the train's noise chased them away.

Conversation continued between periods of watching this incredible tigerless scenery, helping the hours pass. As Lassiter mentioned, it would be thirteen hours before arriving at the closest station. In that time Shaw hoped to learn as much as possible about life at the outpost and what to expect.

"Why did you meet me at the ship?" he asked. "Surely a doctor has more important tasks."

"Oh, ours is not to reason why," Lassiter replied with his lopsided grin.

Shaw stared back, quizzical look on his face, until Lassiter sighed.

"You'll meet Doctor McCready soon enough."

"Our head doctor?"

Lassiter nodded. "I got sent to meet you as punishment for daring to be younger, and for reminding the good doctor through my mere existence that he is not."

"Ah."

"Oh, yes. Ah. And if he dislikes my comparative youth I wonder how he'll react to your actual one. Anyway, joke's on him. I'm happy to get away, even on my day off."

Lassiter barked out a laugh, half snort. Seeing he was alone in his merriment he shook his head, left hand burrowing deeper into his jacket pocket.

On their hike from ship to train Lassiter had kept that hand hidden inside his pocket the entire way, an act much more obvious now they were seated. At first Shaw thought the man's hand might be scarred or deformed, that he kept it secreted from some misguided shame, but Lassiter would remove it for two-handed tasks such as eating.

Some item of weight, and apparent value, rested in that pocket.

"Anyway," Lassiter said. "You're a doctor and you're well needed."

"Needed? Oh, to replace the other doctor?"

"Middlemarch."

"Right. He returned home?"

"In a sense. He took an unscheduled early retirement."

There was some obvious further meaning behind those words. Shaw waited.

"He's dead," Lassiter explained.

"Dead? Uncle ... The commander never mentioned that in his letter."

"No, he wouldn't have."

"I suppose Commander Armstrong must not have thought it relevant."

"Hah!" The reaction was too enthusiastic given the topic. Lassiter turned toward the window, lips pursed in contemplation. When he spoke again it was subdued, on the edge of inaudible. "Middlemarch was murdered."

"Murdered?"

Lassiter brought his gaze back to Shaw. "Oh, yes. Armstrong and McCready slapped a label of *accident* on it but we all know better."

"Murdered how? By who?"

"How? That part is easy. He fell off the cliff."

"Fell—?"

"Fell. Thrown. Pushed." Lassiter shrugged. "Jumped."

"Jumped?"

"Here's where it gets interesting. Suspicious. That cliff is a fifteen-minute stroll from the outpost. Now, I ask you, why would any man go out to the cliff at night by himself? Middle-march was no fool. Not the kind to go wandering about after dark, what with …"

Shaw raised an eyebrow in question.

"Not who," Lassiter continued. "What. *What* murdered him."

"I … don't understand."

Lassiter stared in Shaw's direction, through him, for a full minute before coming to some inner conclusion. He leaned forward, right arm resting on the table between them.

"Look, Shaw, don't go out at night. It isn't safe. If you have to go from one building to another do it quickly, and not alone if it can be helped."

"Why isn't it safe?"

"Something comes at night."

"Some*thing*? Is there …" he latched onto the most logical culprit his mind could conjure. "A tiger problem?"

"Tigers? Hah! No … but another predator to be sure." Lassiter leaned back in his seat. "Hmm, can't remember the last time I saw a tiger, actually."

"I—"

"Watch out for those 'uncle' slips, by the by," Lassiter warned. "Not all people you meet will be so accepting of that relationship. And I suspect Uncle Commander wouldn't be too pleased either."

Shaw made mental note to be more vigilant.

With that the conversation on ominous warnings was at an end and Lassiter returned his gaze to the window. "Won't be long before the train links up all of India, even the more remote parts."

"Does it stop at our outpost?"

"Nah, we still get to hoof it a ways once we get there. Well, not our own hoofs, but you understand."

"Why an outpost so far from the train?"

"Well, we have to protect the Queen's interests everywhere, now don't we?"

"Oh. Yes. I suppose we do."

Lassiter rolled his eyes and Shaw realized he'd missed the sarcasm. "No idea why, in all honesty, except the Prince of Hyderabad wants us there. He has his own army, but it's a huge province. Plus he is in love with western medicine."

"Ah, that makes sense."

"Does it? Hmm, maybe. Anyway, there are outposts all over India, and most predate the train system. As I said, just a matter of time until it all gets linked up. In the meantime we're here and there. Our outpost and hospital are the only one for miles, and a damned sight closer than a trip to Bombay or Calcutta to the sizable hospitals. Keeps us busy, though we seem a tad remote at times." At the mention of being remote his hand worked against whatever was secreted in that pocket. "Especially at night."

For all of Lassiter's strange characteristics, he was a likeable man and made for a pleasant and knowledgeable, albeit odd, traveling companion. They passed the next hour or more in conversation on outpost life, the people and setup, what could be expected. An Indian city named Bandagar with what Lassiter described as a "fair-sized population," was situated down the road from the outpost. Many of the citizens' day-to-day business consisted of supplying food and other necessities to the outpost. As that topic died down Shaw's mind came back around full circle and found something he wanted to know more about, in fact *needed* to know.

"This danger at night, Larry. What is it?"

Lassiter's head swung back with the speed of those tigers Shaw wished to see, as if he'd been jabbed with a knife rather than a question. He calmed, gave a nod. "Can't say I've ever seen it with my own eyes."

"Well, then—"

"This ..." Lassiter huffed out a dry, humorless snicker. "Look, this all sounds rather insane if you haven't lived there."

Shaw said, "I won't judge."

"Oh, yes?" Lassiter raised his eyebrows as if to say, *just wait.*

"I'll try not to."

"Very well, then." A deep breath and Lassiter ran one hand down his face, gathering his thoughts. "One night, about a year ago, Middlemarch saw this thing outside."

"Thing?"

"That's how he described it. A *thing.* This smoky grey shape drifting against the deeper black of the night. It was a dim shape which stayed to the shadows, indistinct until stepping closer to resolve itself into ..."

"Yes?" Shaw asked, leaning forward on the table between them. "Into what?"

"That's as much as I ever got from him. He would shake his head at this point, become agitated and say: *How do you describe the indescribable?*"

"Hmm." Shaw leaned back, embarrassed to have been pulled in, however briefly, by this Christmas Eve round-the-hearth ghost story.

"I told you how this would sound. Is this you not judging?"

"Sorry." Shaw gestured to continue.

"What Middlemarch *would* say was that once he saw this creature he couldn't take his eyes off it. He was paralyzed at the sight of it, while also horrified. He wanted to run but couldn't force himself to."

"Paralyzed? Then how did he—?"

"Escape? Pure luck. Middlemarch was inside the hospital, looking out one of the side doors, when he saw it passing by. It didn't see him though, and as soon as it shambled from view his mind was his own again. He didn't wait for it to return either, just took off running."

"Not sure that's lucky. He sounds safe enough inside."

"Hold on." Lassiter held up one finger. "As Middlemarch rushed away he had a realization. The whole time he'd been watching this thing he'd also been pushing against the door, trying to get out."

"Why would he do that?" Shaw was leaning forward again. "What stopped him?"

"Why?" Lassiter shrugged. "Your guess is as good as mine. What stopped him is where the luck comes in. That door is always getting stuck, and lucky for him it did. Anyway, not quite so paralyzed. After that he was never quite the same."

"Never the same how?"

"Middlemarch wouldn't look out windows after that, not when it was night anyway. And he never, ever, went outside at night. That's how I know he was murdered. He wouldn't have been on the compound alone, much less way at the cliff. Not without being forced there."

Lassiter fell silent while Shaw contemplated what he'd heard. A secondhand story of a nameless creature which only a dead man had seen, and that just the once. How much had changed from one telling to another? What had been added and embellished? He didn't doubt some danger lived in the wilderness—it was called wild for a reason—but this supernatural nonsense? No. There would be a logical, scientific explanation.

"The people of Bandagar have a name for it," Lassiter added. "Dhoosar Maut."

Shaw shook his head. The few words he knew in Hindi didn't cover either of those.

"Grey Death. That's as much as they will say on the subject, as if talking about it will draw this creature to them. That name stuck at the outpost but we all simply call it the Maut, when we talk about it at all. Mostly we follow the Indian example and don't."

"The Maut," Shaw repeated, turning the word over in mouth and mind.

An ominous name. A name more at home in those penny dreadfuls. Fanciful drivel to give one a shiver while sitting before a fire. "Is that everything?"

Lassiter drummed his fingers on the table before speaking again. "No. Not everything. Not quite."

He took a deep breath, letting it out in a slow, prolonged way. More finger drumming. For a moment it appeared the topic wouldn't continue, but then Lassiter gave a shaky laugh and waved the hand not in his pocket.

"Look, Shaw, I don't want you to think I'm some simple-minded man who believes every story he hears. Middlemarch was my friend, my *good* friend, and even I treated his story like the product of an exhausted mind. I looked for believable explanations for what he'd experienced, suggesting idea after idea. In the end he stopped talking about it."

Shaw nodded and that seemed enough acceptance for Lassiter to continue.

"There were a couple of ... well, gruesome discoveries which came later," Lassiter shuddered. "Armstrong promptly put these down to tiger attacks then just as promptly forgot about them completely. That's the official word, tiger attacks, even for what happened to Middlemarch. Any other explanations are considered nonsense and fairy tale. Only tiger attacks don't quite explain all the details."

"The gruesome discoveries?"

Lassiter shuddered again and shook his head. "Not just now, Shaw. Please."

He leaned to one side, head against the glass of the window, and closed his eyes, as if telling the story had exhausted him. Within a minute there were soft snores coming from the man so maybe it had.

Even in rest Lassiter kept one hand inside that pocket.

In the absence of someone to question Shaw turned the story over inside his mind. Two people removed from the original incident he found it difficult to find credibility in the circumstances. Certainly something deserved this fear, something dangerous, but believing in supernatural balderdash was a different matter.

Uncle Freddy's—No, no! *Commander Armstrong's*—assessment of tigers was the less fantastic, the more logical one. Whatever the actual facts, a definite danger existed and being cautious couldn't hurt.

When he awoke, Lassiter spoke as if he'd never told that fantastic tale, or anything at all about the death of Middlemarch. Shaw set the topic aside for the moment—though there were enough questions about these gruesome discoveries alone to last the remainder of their trip. They passed the journey in easy comradeship, Shaw already considering Lassiter his first true friend in India.

Conversation changed toward England and what Lassiter missed most about it—the food as it turned out. After quite some time reminiscing on a fish and chip shop in Mossley, Lassiter continued on to what could be expected of day-to-day life at the outpost.

There was little else to do on the train except talk, eat, nap, and watch the scenery go by. After so many hours travel the last of these somehow lost its charm. It was still majestic, but had become a commonplace beauty.

CHAPTER THREE

THE ENGINE HOWLED STEAM AND SQUEALED ITS BRAKES IN preparation for the next station. The sudden jerking motion brought Shaw back to the waking world, a bit surprised to find he'd been dozing. A vague dream already faded as he wiped sleep from his eyes.

Three smaller buildings and a platform came into view, with seven onboarding passengers waiting for the train to stop. The sun had set while they journeyed and only light from several lamps gave a jaundiced yellow illumination to the station.

Lassiter stared at this tableau with obvious apprehension.

"This is our station?"

Lassiter nodded, peering left and right. "There should be someone to give us a ride home. Come on."

The nervousness radiating from his friend was palpable, infecting Shaw even as they stepped off the train.

Would someone be there? Surely they wouldn't be expected to make that hike. Given Lassiter's despair toward the night it was doubtful he would consent to that.

Wanting some other focus Shaw scanned left and right, looking for his luggage being unloaded.

"Where would—" he began.

Off to the left lingered something so unexpected it pushed every other thought or consideration from his mind. A few steps past the edge of the station shuffled a full-grown elephant. Two native soldiers waited next to the animal, which had been saddled on top with a carriage. One soldier raised a hand in greeting which Lassiter returned.

"Huh."

"Problem?" Shaw asked, not taking his eyes from the incredible animal. For that brief moment he was a six-year-old boy wanting to run up and touch the baggy, wrinkled skin, the trunk, the ears.

"Far from it," Lassiter said. "When the British army came to this outpost Prince Kanwar made one of his elephants and a couple of drivers available for us. All part of making us welcome in Hyderabad. Mostly they stay down the road in Bandagar with family since we don't often have need for elephant rides. I suppose the commander thought we rated a special ride back rather than the usual horse and wagon. Curious. I wonder why that would be?"

Shaw struggled to get that six-year-old inside under control, half listening. "Have you ever ridden?"

"Once." Lassiter chuckled. "Word of advice? It's easier going up than down, like climbing a tree. Nice change of topic by the way, Doctor Shaw. Very seamless."

Once again Shaw ignored him, approaching the elephant. Expectant glee was plain on his face and he realized that inner six-year-old was nowhere close to being under control.

One of the drivers got the beast to kneel then climbed it, using certain places for hand- and footholds. He progressed in a slow manner though the man could have surely climbed it in seconds. All example for the Britishers without any implication the doctors couldn't do this on their own. It was appreciated. Without that example Shaw would have absolutely made himself look the fool on his first attempt. As it was he struggled to the top with a complete lack of grace, but no real incident. Somehow, while that was happening the two drivers had gotten his trunk up and into the carriage. A moment later Lassiter popped into the carriage, followed by the second soldier.

"Better sit, Shaw."

He nodded and settled on the floor of the carriage. Lassiter joined him but the two drivers remained upright and soon their mount had started lumbering toward the treeline of the surrounding forest. Shaw saw no trail but had to assume the drivers knew better about such tasks than an army doctor who'd been in the country less than one full day.

While the first driver guided the elephant the second set about closing the carriage with screen on all sides before they could reach the forest's edge. Once they passed from the train station's light, the gloom of the surrounding night closed in, wan moonlight coming through the trees to light the way.

"Safety in numbers," Lassiter muttered, looking over the edge of the carriage, though the murkiness below couldn't have allowed a view of the ground.

Noises from countless insects and nocturnal animals covered them like a thick blanket, as Shaw expected to likewise be covered in mosquitos. No more than a few got through the screened-in platform, and those were all slapped to death in short order. Did the poor elephant fare as well? And the humidity! Shaw had thought it humid on the train, and on the platform, but here among the trees it escalated to a new oppressive level, as if one should drink the air rather than breathe it.

The elephant, the drivers, or a combination of all three seemed to intuit where they were going. No hesitation on steps or rerouting because of mistake. Was the moonlight truly enough to navigate by? The beast continued at a steady pace while crickets filled the night with chirps. The heads of the drivers darted, scanning the darkness ahead. Occasionally they would lean together and whisper in their native tongue.

"Surely we are safe aboard this elephant," he said to Lassiter, still considering the possibility of tigers over this Maut. Seeing one in the wild would be magical, but meeting one at night was not the preferable way for it to happen.

"Safe," Lassiter said, attempting to look in all directions at once. "Perhaps."

Shaw left it at that. Fear is a personal concern, and just because it wasn't rational didn't mean it wasn't real.

"Shaw, I caution you to remain afraid any time you are out at night."

"Afraid?"

"Yes! Fear makes one wary, stops a person from taking stupid chances."

"Yes, well—"

"For now though." He took a deep breath and let it loose in a shuddering sigh. "You should enjoy the ride. I don't imagine this will happen too often."

There was truth to his friend's words, both about fear and pleasure.

"*That's* the outpost?"

The elephant had emerged from the line of trees and into a clearing. Lassiter relaxed, though his eyes stayed in constant motion. In all, the trip by elephant had taken just under an hour and Shaw was ready to get back on a surface which didn't sway and lumber with each step. It was a magical experience, but not a comfortable one.

Sprawling ahead was a wide settlement of buildings, some as high as three stories. The style of architecture was gorgeous, particularly around arches which were more decorated than other parts of buildings. Off to the left was a structure higher than all the rest, and more ornate.

"Afraid not," Lassiter answered. "A bit more than a few doctors and a couple regiments of army need. No, that is the city of Bandagar I was telling you about, one of the larger settlements in the province of Hyderabad."

"Ah."

"That building there"—Lassiter pointed toward the higher one Shaw had been appreciating—"is the local church."

"Church? I had assumed—"

Lassiter held up one hand. "A Hindu church."

"Oh! Of course."

"We have a more humble Christian chapel at the outpost for confessing our sins," Lassiter said, then dropped his voice to mutter, "If you're into that sort of thing."

"I would have expected the highest building to be the prince's palace."

Lassiter laughed. "The prince doesn't live here. No, he's in the actual city of Hyderabad, the other side of that train station."

"Oh, I see."

"Still, every city and town in Hyderabad province is like this. Kanwar is rich and takes care of his people. He also wants to make sure to stay rich *and* in power, so he is welcoming to us British army types."

"Is he afraid of other provinces attacking?"

Lassiter laughed again. "No, he just knows how to play the game and wants to be sure we don't take it all away."

"I ... don't understand."

Lassiter looked toward our drivers who gave no sign of listening though that undoubtedly meant little.

"The East India Company had a reputation of doing exactly that," Lassiter explained. "Under the Doctrine of Lapse—pretty name, no?—they could decide if any ruler wasn't fit. Then rule would be taken from the troublemaking prince and someone more cooperative put in his place. Usually a brother or cousin who couldn't hope to become ruler through the normal process."

"And now?"

"Under the Raj?" Lassiter shrugged.

A case of the more things change, the more they stay the same? Another lesson on life in India.

"The doctrine has been abolished," Lassiter continued, "but there are other ways. No one wants to be blown from a gun."

"Blown ...?"

"A method of execution. The person, some rebel or deserter most times, is strapped to a cannon and quite literally blown apart."

"Good lord!"

"Yes," Lassiter nodded, his smile fading. "Never seen it myself. Not our commander's style ... thankfully."

The Sepoy Mutiny was not so far in the past and could the country be far from the next one? Surely it was only a matter of time. These people would not tolerate the British on their land forever.

Shaw was embarrassed to find his own thoughts not much more enlightened. From all he'd read and heard he expected a range of huts and hovels for the Indian people to be living in. The reality was completely contrary and renewed his determination to experience rather than expect.

Lassiter changed subjects with a wave. "Our outpost is out the far side of Bandagar and up a short road."

The elephant continued its slow ponderous gait through the center of town, the way a horse and carriage might pass through the streets of London. It was surreal, to say the least, and emphasized he was not back home anymore.

"Our humble outpost has the six doctors and assorted staff I told you about earlier, plus two regiments of foot soldiers, a handful of those being natives to India. There are another fifty mounted soldiers and one heavy artillery, just in case."

"In case?"

"There are these enormous guns all over the country as I understand but who they're supposed to be pointed at I have no idea." Lassiter gave that grin of his. Now that they were back into the light of civilization his apprehensions had retreated.

"And the people of this city?" Shaw asked. "How many live here?"

"Who knows! A few thousand for sure. I hear a census is happening, but it hasn't made its way to this lonely backside of nowhere."

Nowhere? Yes, Shaw supposed this place was nowhere, at least in relation to other cities. There appeared no resource here that would be of interest to the army.

"But ... what does the outpost guard?"

"Guard?" Lassiter considered a moment, as if he hadn't considered the concept before. "British pride? The Queen's interests? Call it what you will."

Shaw grunted. Those were ideals he could understand. "But what are we guarding it from?"

"Well, someone has to keep India safe from the Indians." A tint of sarcasm colored the man's words, but not enough to indicate whether Lassiter's sympathies lay with the people or not.

"It *is* their country," Shaw said.

"And they're bloody welcome to it. Nothing here worthwhile other than the land itself, but planting another flag in a chunk of dirt doesn't make it worth keeping." He waved one hand. "Yes, yes. In Bombay, and Calcutta. Bengal. Even the main city of Hyderabad. Lots of resources there worth shipping back home."

The outpost eased into view, occupying a great deal of space and consisting of more buildings than expected. Each of the structures was of the same style as that in the city behind them, two stories high for the most part except one which was three and another that had only one level. This last was surely the stables. For a moment Shaw pictured a cavalry which all rode elephants like this one, but this was a long way from Hannibal's times.

It was odd that they would occupy so much space here with British troops when the prince had an army of his own. Survival of the fittest as Lassiter had said earlier?

"Your belongings will magically go from our elephant friend here to your room, much the way they went from ship to train."

Shaw glanced at the drivers who continued to pay no mind to the British. Undoubtedly they would be the ones performing this feat of magic.

"I have orders to convey you to the commander's office upon arrival."

Shaw nodded, wishing he could have a few minutes to freshen up, put on a clean shirt before meeting his commanding officer.

What else had Lassiter quoted? Oh, yes: *Ours is not to reason why …*

CHAPTER FOUR

"ENTER!"

Lassiter opened the office door and stepped inside, Shaw a pace behind. Inside, a man he'd last seen at ten or eleven years of age sat behind a desk. He came close to blurting an enthusiastic greeting to Uncle Freddy but noticed a second man in the room, occupying a chair to the right of the desk.

"Commander Armstrong," Lassiter said, his demeanor switching from relaxed to official. "The new man, Doctor Archibald Shaw."

"Commander," Shaw said, snapping off a salute.

"Doctor Shaw." Armstrong returned the salute without showing any overt sign of recognition, other than a slight twinkling amusement in his eyes. He gestured at the man occupying the other chair. "This is the head doctor, McCready. You'll be reporting to him."

McCready was older than his uncle by a decade, well into his sixties. Unusual for someone of that age to not be retired. A man still pursuing his life's calling? A surge of warmth and respect washed through Shaw toward this older man, despite what Lassiter had told him.

"Doctor—" Shaw began.

"He's too young, I tell you," McCready snapped, turning his back to Shaw. "I need experienced doctors. Ones who won't fold up or panic at the first emergency."

Shaw found himself struck dumb at being talked about as if he weren't in the room. He glanced at Lassiter, who betrayed no emotion other than a slight twitch at the corner of his mouth. Was he trying not to laugh?

"I appreciate your concern," Shaw said, refocusing on Doctor McCready, "but I assure you—"

"However," the head doctor interrupted, speaking to his uncle as if in regards to a dog who couldn't understand anyway, "you've given me no choice in the matter. Your privilege as commander."

McCready turned toward Shaw, finally acknowledging his existence while giving him a cursory looking over. "You'll take overnight shift in the ward tonight."

Shaw resigned himself to his fate. "Yes, sir."

So much for his hopes to unpack and get a refreshing night's sleep, maybe familiarize himself somewhat with the base.

"I say, isn't that excessive, McCready?" Armstrong cut in. "The man must be exhausted."

"I can take the shift," Lassiter offered, though he would have wanted a good night's sleep just as much.

McCready rounded on the commander, ignoring Lassiter. "You may run this outpost, Commander Armstrong, but I command the hospital. You can force a doctor on me, ask me to choose another to use as errand boy." Here he gestured at Lassiter. "But the running of that hospital is my duty ... Unless you want to replace me. Say the word and I'll pack and be ready for return to England."

The commander raised both hands. "Now, now, McCready. Simmer down."

McCready spun back. "As for you Lassiter, I suggest you get

some sleep yourself since you're scheduled for the shift after his."

"Certainly," Lassiter gave a somewhat exaggerated bow. "Your slightest wish is my command."

McCready narrowed his eyes while Lassiter stared back with that uneven grin, a hair on the safe side of insubordinate. After ten seconds of this standoff the older doctor grumbled some inaudible words and turned back in his seat.

"Better show Doctor Shaw to his room, Lassiter," the commander said. "Let him freshen up before his shift begins. With your permission of course, Doctor McCready."

The other man gave a single curt nod without deigning to look in their direction.

"Yes, sir," Lassiter said.

"Thank you, sir," Shaw added, not knowing what else to say.

They saluted and left, Shaw following Lassiter up the corridor, somewhat numb.

"Well, I was completely wrong," Lassiter said over one shoulder. "Old McCready took a real shine to you after all."

"These are your rooms. Not bad for army accommodations though a few steps short from Buckingham Palace."

Shaw stepped into the room he could expect to be a major part of his life for the foreseeable future. The main room held a single bed—comfortable and inviting at the moment—a bureau, a reading chair near the window with side table, and a desk with second chair. Through a door on the right would be a second room for washing up.

His trunk had already arrived and been placed at the foot of his bed.

"Thank you for getting me here. I suspect I would have been hopelessly lost otherwise."

Lassiter waved his right hand in his *don't mention it* gesture while Shaw's gaze dropped to the other hand.

"Look, can I ask?"

Lassiter glanced down, as if not quite knowing what Shaw wanted to ask about. For a moment he squinted at that other hand, somewhat confused. "No ... no ... I ..."

The signs of an addiction were evident and Shaw nodded in understanding, sympathy even. Inside that pocket would be some secret shame, such as an opium pipe ... No. Morphine was more the drug of choice where doctors were concerned. Yet that entire time on the train Lassiter hadn't given in to it, not that he had seen. Unless it was while Shaw had napped, but it hadn't been that deep a slumber.

Lassiter sighed. "It's not what you are thinking."

Shaw raised one eyebrow in question but stayed silent.

With one quick movement Lassiter closed the door and crossed to the empty desk. There he stopped, looking around as if wary of someone spying on them in Shaw's private rooms with the door closed. Satisfied he withdrew the hand from his pocket. A brief flash of some jet-black object, then it was obscured by Lassiter's turned body. When he stepped back again —not too far, mind you—the object remained on the desk.

Shaw approached and peered over his friend's shoulder. Lassiter had been correct, it was not at all what he'd suspected.

It was a black idol, less than a foot in height—between seven and eight inches—and depicting some horrendous monster. The creature was all tentacles and leathery wings perched atop a rectangular pedestal, which in turn was covered with indecipherable characters. The workmanship was exquisite, and instilled a sense of dread on first sight, as if looking on some relic which should have never been seen. Shaw found his eyes trying to focus elsewhere—anywhere—and it took firm, continuous resolve to remain on the idol.

"What in the nine rings of hell is *that*?" Shaw said.

Lassiter made no reply and Shaw leaned in closer.

"What is it made of?"

The material was a greenish-black stone with golden flecks, absorbing the light rather than reflecting it. No object like it existed in the British Museum, that was a dead certainty.

Shaw reached one hand to touch it, unsure he actually wanted to do such a thing. At a strangled cry from Lassiter— Had he muttered the word *mine*?—Shaw stopped. In deference to his friend he let the outstretched hand drop back to his side and merely gawked, hunkered forward with hands on knees.

The text around the block which this beast squatted upon was indecipherable, like some warped characters from the Cyrillic alphabet ... only it wasn't. In some untold way this idol conveyed the impression of an age greater than any known empire. British. Russian. Egyptian even. Maybe older than writing itself. Ancient.

"That is the most hideous figure I've ever seen," he said, voice low and, admittedly, reverent.

This carving commanded respect.

Fear.

Loathing.

"It is." Lassiter cleared his throat. "Horrible. And yet, I cannot seem to throw it away."

"Can't ...?" For a moment Shaw toyed with the idea of offering to do exactly that, but nodded instead. This wasn't an object to discard.

"As for your earlier question," Lassiter continued, one finger tracing the smooth shape of the idol. "I have no idea what it's made of. Some type of stone, I think, or perhaps bone? I've never seen any material like it."

"No, nor I." Shaw stepped away, allowing his eyes to drift from the idol. "Where did it come from?"

"Ah." Lassiter looked embarrassed, eyes on the idol rather than meeting Shaw's. "Yes, well ..."

"Larry?"

Lassiter spat out a laugh. "It was in the personal effects of Doctor Middlemarch. McCready compassionately gave me the job of packing my friend's stuff to ship home and ... and ..."

"You stole it?"

"No! No ... I ... Well, yes. I suppose I did at that."

Lassiter had no shame in his tone, no regrets. Just a sense of wonder at his own actions.

"I hadn't intended to, you see, didn't even know I'd kept it until later. I packed Middlemarch's belongings in his trunk, and alerted McCready I was done. That night I found the idol inside my jacket pocket." He tapped his left pocket, the idol's usual home. "It shocked me. Something that heavy but I hadn't even realized it was there. I went to return it to the trunk, and could swear I did, but once again found it in my pocket a day later. I keep intending to ship it back to Middlemarch's family, but somehow forget to do so."

"Hmm, I can't imagine anyone thanking you for *this* appearing on their doorstep."

"No."

It was hideous, yet undeniably fascinating.

"Where did Middlemarch get it?"

"No idea. I hadn't seen it in his room, not once. He could have had it a day or a year for all I know."

"What is it? I mean, this ... creature."

Lassiter shrugged. "Who knows? One of the local gods I would imagine, but who can tell which one. They have so many."

"A god of nightmares," Shaw said, stepping back from desk and idol.

This was no Hindu god, his intuition muttered. From his tone Lassiter didn't believe it either.

With one quick movement his friend grabbed the idol and returned it to its pocket, as if the exposure had worn him down.

"You'd best get a nap in if you're going on shift tonight. I'll make sure dinner is brought to the hospital for you."

Shaw agreed, realizing how exhausted he was, even though all he'd done on the train was nap, talk, and watch the scenery pass. Still, tonight he would start to earn his keep and wanted to be in best shape for it. Unpacking was a task for tomorrow. For now he would follow Lassiter's advice.

"Pleasant dreams, Archie."

With that Lassiter left the room, and Shaw found himself alone once again, for the first time since arriving in India.

CHAPTER FIVE

"No!"

Shaw awoke bolt upright, sure that he was lost.

Lost?

Not him personally. Not physically.

What then?

"My soul," he whispered into the shadows of the room.

The dream faded, like water seeping into the earth, which was a mercy. All that remained was a sense of being examined, judged, as he might watch some curious animal in a cage ... But the gap in his dream was greater than man and beast, more the distance between God and insect.

He wasn't the type to allow dreams to rule him, made of stray, uncontrolled thoughts as they were. But this one ...

No, it was gone now.

Gulping a glass of water from his nightstand, he stretched.

"Almost time anyway," he muttered, glancing at his pocket watch.

With a burst of energy and anticipation at the idea of his new position Shaw dressed and rushed out the door. Those couple fitful hours sleep would have to be enough to get through the night. Tomorrow morning would catch him up on his rest.

McCready's eyes glared in Shaw's mind as he followed the hallways from sleeping quarters to hospital wing, hoping he was headed in the right direction. The way the head doctor had looked at him, as if Shaw weren't worth his time or effort. Was it because the commander—and he congratulated himself on remembering not to even think of him as Uncle Freddy—had forced him onto the doctor's staff? Or was it as Lassiter had said, that McCready hated anyone younger than himself?

Whatever the reasons, he was determined to win the older doctor over and—

"You can turn up on time at least," McCready snarled as Shaw passed through the doors into the hospital's main office. "Better than your pal, Lassiter."

He thought to point out he'd only met that "pal" for the first time yesterday—or was it still today?—but decided it was unwise. *Don't rush into battles which can be avoided and will gain you nothing*, as Mother had said on more than one occasion.

"Yes, sir," Shaw said, wondering if doctors saluted each other. He snapped one off just in case, glancing around the room.

It was a fair-sized entry, meant for waiting patients to cool their heels. Ten chairs were arranged along the walls with one tiny desk on the far end for the doctor on duty.

"Leave that foolishness to the soldiers," McCready said, grabbing two clipboards from the desk and handing one over. "Come on."

Had Shaw imagined it? Had McCready's expression softened for the slightest moment?

"Try to keep up, *Doctor*."

Then again, maybe not.

McCready toured him around the hospital, starting at an office just off the entry where doctors could talk and keep current files. Both office and entry led into a set of six examination rooms, which afforded more privacy for the patients. From there patients could be led through one door to a quarantine area of ten segregated rooms, or through a second into the hospital ward. The ward held beds for fifty wounded, more than enough for current circumstances given all but six were empty.

Five of that night's patients had come from a bout of bad food—a common ailment for the outpost, particularly among recent arrivals—while the sixth was a soldier from the garrison near Hyderabad. This man had fallen off a wall and broken his back. Given that he couldn't move his legs he'd be going home after regaining some strength. What kind of life he'd return to with that injury was another question.

"This is the medicines closet." McCready tapped on a door in the ward with his knuckle. "The key is kept in the pocket of one doctor on duty, the spare in mine." He pulled two keys from a pocket and slapped one into Shaw's palm. "I have no sympathy for opium sots or morphine addicts. Any doctor with these or similar habits will find himself in Bombay awaiting the next ship home."

Shaw held up one hand. "Understood, sir. Not a problem."

With a grunt McCready continued along the hallway and waved the clipboard in his hand. "I expect meticulous inventory of our supplies to be kept at all times. If you use an item, mark it down. I will not abide finding we need more of some crucial supply in the middle of treating a man."

"Yes, sir."

Next came three rooms, side by side, with an operating table in each. Shaw stared at these, brain working. Operating on another human was an action he could do, and do well, but it wasn't an action he relished. Blood and death didn't make him squeamish, but the possibility of losing a patient did. Worse still, the idea that a patient *could* have been saved if he'd acted sooner or in a different manner.

"Problem, Shaw?"

He'd stared too long without saying anything.

"No, sir."

McCready's eyes narrowed and he spoke as if relinquishing an item of value which he would rather keep in his own pocket. "Aside from the boredom when nothing at all is happening, this is the worst part of the job." He knocked on one door for emphasis. "What happens inside there is difficult and bloody. On occasion it is disheartening, but we deal with it and move on as doctors must if they are to remain doctors."

"Yes, sir."

McCready's eyes narrowed again and Shaw cleared his throat, looking for the words which would sum up his convictions.

"I shall perform to the best of my ability inside those rooms, and deal with the disheartening side on my own time."

"Hmph." McCready crossed his arms, continuing to stare a hole into Shaw. "I also insist on the following of Lister's teachings here, washing hands and tools before and after treating wounds, fresh and clean bandages. Will there be any problem on this?"

Shaw had read Joseph Lister's theories on germs and treating wounds and operating rooms with a mixture of carbolic acid. It was ridiculed and ignored by many but his own experience was that these measures worked.

"No, sir. No problem."

"There best not be. This hospital has the lowest mortality rate in India and I will keep it that way."

With that McCready turned and stormed away without another glance.

"You are expected to remain on duty, *and* awake, the entire night, Shaw. Make your rounds on the hour to see if any of your charges need you."

"Yes sir, I can handle it."

"A mostly empty hospital with all patients asleep? I should hope so."

McCready tossed his clipboard onto the entry desk as he passed and stomped out of the hospital without so much as a good night or good luck. Just like that the tour was over. Shaw was alone again, only this time he was also in charge of an entire hospital all by himself for the first time in his career.

His hospital … until morning anyway.

With a deep breath and unsuppressed grin he began the first of many rounds, though they'd been through the ward minutes earlier. He wanted to familiarize himself, and would be the first to admit he was excited. At first he checked the patients every fifteen minutes, but it soon became obvious no change would come that quick and scant point.

Having no other tasks he started an inventory count of medicines and supplies, jotting numbers on the clipboard. It was routine process, predictable and more than a little on the tedious side, but he revelled in it. To have something utterly in his control was what was needed.

CHAPTER SIX

HYDERABAD, INDIA—APRIL 11TH, 1878

Dearest Mother,

You won't believe this but I rode an elephant. An elephant! It is well-nigh unbelievable and a marvelous introduction to life here. Not as comfortable a ride as horse and carriage but still magical.

Incredible that only one day has passed since leaving the HMS Agincourt. So much has happened, besides the aforementioned elephant. No, I haven't seen any tigers as of yet, but there is plenty of time for that.

Another doctor by the name of Lawrence Lassiter met me at the ship and has gone a great way to helping me become assimilated to the culture and processes here, though I have a long way to go on that front.

I saw Uncle Freddy last night on my arrival but was unable to pass on your greetings as the head doctor, McCready, was also in the room. Uncle appears well and healthy if a good bit older than the last time I saw him. As for Doctor McCready, I'm not sure what to think yet. He seems capable and efficient though completely lacking in basic personal interaction skills. Still, the former is more important I suppose.

Today I shall take time to scout around and accustom myself with these new surroundings. Making new friends has never been my strong suit but I shall try for now to at least make acquaintances among the people I'll be working with ...

"There you are. I thought you'd sleep all day."

Shaw looked up from his half-eaten breakfast—lunch for everyone else in the dining hall. Overnight shift was disorienting in relation to everyone else's schedules and habits.

Lassiter leaned against the table, his usual cheeky grin in place. "I've been waiting all day for you."

"Have you?" Shaw smiled back, rubbing some of the remaining bleary-eyed sleep from his face. "Here I thought you'd been in the hospital all morning."

Lassiter had arrived an hour early for shift and chased him off to bed which Shaw had agreed to with ease and gratitude after spending the previous hour trying to stay awake in the chair.

"Details." Lassiter waved it aside. "It falls to me to give you the guided tour of your new home."

He sat, pouring himself a cup of strong, black tea from the pot. "We'll take a walk, show you where to find everything and introduce you to some of the people. Most you'll meet as time goes by."

Shaw had been wondering on the best way to familiarize himself without being a nuisance, not wanting to be the obvious new arrival who asks the question that makes everyone roll their eyes.

"Another assignment from Commander Armstrong?"

Lassiter took a sip of his tea, which couldn't have been particularly hot anymore. He shook his head. "Not this time. Thought I would take pity and give you the attention I wish I'd had in my first days."

"Oh, thank you. That's very much appreciated."

Lassiter finished his tea in a few gulps and stood. "No time like the present."

"You don't want lunch?"

"Nah, had a late breakfast."

With that he was on his way, one hand in his pocket again. Shaw rushed to keep up, feeling as he had when trailing Lassiter from ship to train.

"You've seen enough inside the hospital itself, I'm assuming? Know all the details on that end?"

"I'm fine."

"If not you'll have enough chances to get fine. One eight-hour shift per day, six days a week—barring any emergencies when we can all be called in. One day off to rotate to a new shift time, but I'm afraid you're five days away from that."

He'd figured as much. No way McCready was about to grant a day off earlier than was necessary. Besides, after only one shift —and a good night's sleep—he didn't need one yet.

Lassiter pushed through the front doors and into the bright sunlight of a hot, Indian afternoon. They passed a group of Indian women headed toward the hospital. Shaw cocked a questioning glance at Lassiter.

"One big industry in Bandagar is laundry for the outpost. They come daily to take the hospital's dirty linens."

"Ah, I see."

That topic discarded Lassiter moved back to the tour. With a few dozen steps he came to the center of the outpost's circular compound, buildings around three-quarters of the area, a road leading out the other end—the one their elephant had taken last night. They could see the entire outpost by turning in a circle.

"Start with the familiar. That's the hospital building and our rooms, of course." Lassiter pointed at the one building Shaw knew well enough. It directly faced the road, middle of the semi-circle. "Total of three floors, top one for staff rooms, middle for administrative offices—McCready's and the commander's as well as file storage—and the main floor for the actual hospital … But you know most of that.

"To the right is where we just came from, our dining hall and supplies building, which doubles as church come Sundays. Also where the postmaster's office is. Any letters you send back home go there."

That building was larger than he'd realized, having made his way in a bleary-eyed stupor less than an hour ago. It was wide and, unlike the hospital, only two floors.

"Next is the armory," Lassiter said of a building on the right of the dining hall. "Well guarded, night and day, to prevent any ill-conceived hanky-panky."

Not that Shaw had any more fascination with these weapons than he did the sidearm now resting in his trunk. Still, it was an impressive building. Huge and undoubtedly holding all sorts of items for bringing bodily harm.

"Followed by the storage house, also guarded, though God knows why. I suspect the two guards are meant to keep each other awake through the night. Anyway, that building is for all of those items which don't have another obvious home. In most cases where items go to be forgotten when they can't just be thrown away. Unless said item is so fascinating it's waiting to be shipped back to London for display or storage in the museum." Lassiter shrugged. "The next building is for visitors."

A narrow building of eight to ten rooms, the size and shape of a more sizable house.

"Visitors?" Shaw asked. "Do many people come here?"

Lassiter waggled his hand back and forth in a so-so gesture. "Some come from other parts of India, political people or higher-ups in military. Don't go expecting to see Queen Victoria. Mostly it's for wives who come to visit their husbands with hopes of taking an heir back home with them. Those who can afford the extravagance of that sort of trip anyway. It gives some privacy for said heir creation."

Here Lassiter waggled his eyebrows and Shaw chuckled, inappropriate gesture or not.

"You a married man, Shaw?"

"Not me."

Lassiter chuckled. "Why complicate life, right?"

Shaw was about to ask about Lassiter's own marital status when the man continued on, directing him toward the buildings on the hospital's other side.

"Furthest left you'll find the stables, made obvious by all those horses being led in and out. Also hard to mistake it for anything else when you get close enough." At this Lassiter tapped his nose and Shaw wrinkled his own in agreement. "Actually, it's kept quite clean, which the soldiers appreciate I'm sure. That last building closest to the stables is their barracks."

It was only beaten in size by the hospital. Two floors, both wider and deeper in dimensions than any other building. The barracks were closer to the hospital than the stables, leaving a noticeable gap, wide enough for another building, between the two.

"Inside is a recreation area. Darts, card tables, library and reading area. We're welcome to join the lads whenever we want."

"Good mornin', Doctor."

One soldier in a group of six passing by greeted Lassiter who waved back.

"Lads! Come meet the new doc."

They stopped and came closer, the front man who'd greeted them more enthusiastic about it than the rest.

"This is Doctor Shaw," Lassiter said. "Shaw, these are some of the stalwart heroes you'll be treating for cuts and scrapes."

"Good morning," Shaw said.

"Now this one," Lassiter said, pointing at the lead man, a tall burly youth with shocking red hair, "you'll see more often, and I would wager in spectacular fashion."

The men behind laughed, not unkindly. Rather like those in on a story.

"Aw, Doctor Lassiter, it was just that one time." The man's Irish lilt came through heavy in the words as he self-consciously smoothed his moustache, which all soldiers seemed to have in some varying degree.

"Oh yes, I remember it clearly." Lassiter turned toward Shaw. "Corporal Walsh here fell down the stairs of his barracks one morning in full kit. Bounced himself out of consciousness and into a short hospital stay."

The man flushed a red to rival his hair but wore a sheepish grin.

"Comin' for the darts tournament tonight?" Walsh asked.

Lassiter shook his head, pushing the left hand deeper into his pocket. An action Shaw was sure only he had noticed. "Not tonight, I'm afraid."

"How about yerself, Doctor Shaw?"

Shaw was touched at being included already. "I'd like that, but I'm on night shift at the hospital."

"Well, you may end up seeing Walsh anyway," one soldier spat out, seeing a target and taking aim for it.

Walsh, back to his fellow soldiers, rolled his eyes, but smiled. As they continued on their way toward the barracks the men laughed and Walsh joined in. One clapped him on the back.

"Good lads there," Lassiter said, watching them go. He sighed. "Come on, I'll introduce you to your fellow doctors."

Shaw followed his guide back toward the hospital and down the hallway. They passed through the double doors and made their way to the office where two men conferred by the desk.

"Lassiter? Thought you'd be in your room," one man, tall and bespectacled, said.

The other, shorter and squat, chuckled.

"Showing the new doctor around," Lassiter responded. "You two are of course the highlight of this tour, right after that fragrant pile around back of the stables. Anyway, Shaw, this witty gentleman is Doctor Adamson." He pointed at the man who had spoken, then gestured at the other. "And his ever-present counterpart is Doctor White. *Gentlemen.*" And his tone emphasized the irony he apparently felt. "This is Doctor Archibald Shaw."

The other two shook hands then made small talk for several minutes, mostly asking about news from back home and his ship's journey. Conversation started to come back to medical procedures and Lassiter hustled him out, back toward the tour.

"Capable doctors," Lassiter said as they left. "Both exceptionally skilled in the operating room ... though don't tell them I said so, don't want them getting swelled heads. Sadly they lack any ability to have normal conversation. When not attempting humorous observations they lapse into medical talk for lack of any other interests. Before you say anything, yes, that topic does hold some fascination, but who wants to talk about it all of the time?"

Shaw wondered how different he was in that respect. He'd made his way through medical school and excelled in certain areas, spent hours with his fellow students in debates about individual ideas and what they were going to do to set the medical world on its ear. Outside of medicine did he have much of interest to say?

Moderation in all things. Another aphorism of his mother's.

"What did they mean about expecting you to be in your room?"

"Ah." Lassiter waved his right hand again. "Just spending off hours by myself lately."

Shaw glanced from the side of one eye at his friend, who looked elsewhere. His left hand worked at the idol in his pocket.

Reassuring himself it was still there? Receiving calm from its touch?

"Haven't been too sociable since Middlemarch's death, I suppose."

Lassiter fell silent, lost in momentary thought. It was obvious the man missed his friend, as obvious as the fact the two were closer than he'd let on. And yet, in the middle of his grief, he'd come to meet Shaw, made him feel welcome, and escorted him back here.

Shaw placed one hand on Lassiter's shoulder, hoping to convey all he didn't know how to say. Luckily Lassiter was never at a loss for words. He spun back toward Shaw, giving a quick nod to show the support was appreciated before forging on.

"See what I mean, though? That's their attempt at wit. It shows how any topic outside of medicine leaves them floundering for creativity. 'Thought you'd be in your room?' Really!"

"True. There are so many better topics they could comment on."

"Wha—?"

"Ah well, missed opportunities." Shaw grinned and changed the subject. "You said there were six doctors here. Counting Doctor McCready that only makes five."

Lassiter let out his braying laugh, what Shaw was already coming to consider the true him, and followed the conversation. For some reason banter with his new friend, a skill Shaw never had much luck with in the past, came easy and naturally.

"Ah, yes, Shaw. Nothing wrong with your math skills," Lassiter smiled. "The last is Doctor Neufeld."

"A German?"

The surprise showed in his tone. It would be unusual for a man to join the British service who was not of their heritage, or from one of the colonies.

"Well," Lassiter said, "they practice medicine in Germany

too, I suppose, but in this case it's just the name. This man is as English as the Queen."

"Empress."

Lassiter stopped, brow furrowed. "Huh?"

"We're in India," Shaw said, trying for a sly grin. "Victoria is Queen of England, but Empress of India."

Lassiter's mouth dropped open a moment before breaking into a smile of his own.

"Well said, Shaw. We'll make a native of you yet."

Shaw's smile faltered at the mention of natives. It was reminder that the true natives here were not treated as equals. Like riding on the roof of the train while the British were seated inside.

"At any rate," Lassiter continued, not seeing or more likely ignoring Shaw's reaction, "Neufeld is another fine doctor, but also a bit of an artist to boot. Doesn't seem fair one person having so much talent."

"Artist?"

"Yep. Painting and charcoal sketches. Likes to capture the flora and fauna on his off hours, has pictures all over the walls of his room and an easel set up near the window. Not my idea of an enjoyable pastime but to each his own. At least the man can hold a conversation."

CHAPTER SEVEN

BANDAGAR, INDIA—APRIL 13TH, 1878

Good morning Mother,

I suppose I shall write for several days in each of these letters since the post only goes out every two weeks, unless I want to hike an hour into Hyderabad. Now that the aid of daylight is here I can see there is an actual path leading between here and there, quite well cleared too. Still, I'm not sure on the advisability of wandering around in the wild by myself.

A couple of extended sleeps have me back to normal again. I have completed my second overnight shift now and say I much prefer sleeping at night to working through it. Still, it's a satisfying way to learn the ropes as it were, more calm and quiet though no less exhausting. Perhaps that is why McCready put me on that shift to start, less damage to be done that way. I don't blame him for being cautious, I just wish he wasn't so prickly about it.

Relationships with my fellow doctors continues to evolve. Lassiter gave the guided tour yesterday and I met Doctors White and Adamson. Unsure what to think of them yet. They rather remind me of the bullies back at boarding school, and you know how well I got along with them ...

"Your pal Lassiter is an odd one," Adamson said at breakfast the next day.

Adamson and White had joined his table without invitation or preamble and began as if they'd all been in mid-conversation. White nodded with emphasis, chewing his food while Shaw stared back with one eyebrow raised in question. The night shift had been lengthy and tiring, the change in sleep schedule and struggle to keep awake continuing to take their toll. He wanted nothing more than a day's sleep after eating a quick breakfast.

"Oh, you know," Adamson said, rolling his eyes. "Locked in his room when he isn't on shift. One hand always in his pocket guarding who knows what."

White again nodded.

Shaw was amused that they didn't know about Lassiter's idol. Had they been aware of it while in Middlemarch's possession? Perhaps *he* hadn't carried it around.

White turned attention toward Adamson. "Tell him what happened when you tried to put your hand in his pocket."

"He grabbed my wrist," Adamson answered without shifting focus from Shaw. "Twisted it, then took a handful of my coat and pushed me hard enough to stumble."

"And what reaction did you expect when sticking your hand in another man's pocket?"

Adamson snorted, rolling his eyes again. "Come on, Shaw, you have to see how erratic and ridiculous his actions are."

White stopped chewing and snapped his fingers with sudden inspiration, a sudden thought appearing to come. "Hey, you traveled on the train with him all those hours. You must have an idea what he keeps in that pocket."

Both men leaned forward as if awaiting the greatest secret in all of history. Shaw wanted to be accepted by his fellow doctors, to become friends, and was more than happy to join them while eating, but talking about someone who wasn't there went against his nature. He shrugged, continuing to eat.

"Oh, come on," Adamson said, slapping one hand against the table. "You must know something. He was in your room."

White returned to nodding.

"He was, yes."

The two leaned forward again.

"Well, the amount of attention you two are putting to investigating Lassiter's private business is impressive." Shaw chased a mouthful of breakfast with some lukewarm tea. "But as you said, Lassiter is my friend. I don't know about you but I don't gossip about friends."

Both leaned back, Adamson making a harrumphing noise.

White looked at his food, picking at one fried egg with his fork. "Just trying to make conversation."

"Word of advice, Shaw," Adamson jumped in. "If you buddy up to the strange ones everyone will assume you're strange, too."

"Yes," he said, standing though his meal was not quite finished. These two had managed to chase his appetite away. "We are indeed judged by the company we keep."

White smiled, as if happy they were all agreeing. On Adamson's face was a recognition of what had truly been meant. When Shaw turned to leave without so much as a *good day*, Adamson's expression had shifted to annoyance.

"Hey," White said a moment later. "Was he talking about us?"

A bridge had been burned there, or at the least singed. Better diplomacy could have been exercised but he always had low tolerance for childishness, especially when tired. Shaw was pleased as he walked away, true to his own beliefs. A working relationship would still be possible with those two, though *they* wouldn't ever be pals.

He should have headed straight to his rooms, needing sleep

as he did. Instead Shaw found himself back at the doors to the hospital itself. It had been just under an hour since Lassiter had relieved him.

"Forget something?" Lassiter asked, poking his head out of the examination room to see who'd come in.

"No, I ..." Shaw started, then recognized he had no real reason to be here. He supposed it had to do with showing support to a friend, though he had no intention of telling him about White and Adamson's questions.

"Never mind. Come on back here."

Shaw followed through to the back where an unfamiliar man stood.

"Shaw, have you met Doctor Neufeld? Neufeld, this is the new man, Doctor Archibald Shaw. Prefers to be called Archie."

The other man rolled his eyes. "The way I prefer to be called Kenny, no doubt."

Lassiter gave an innocent shrug as Neufeld extended a hand to Shaw. The two shook.

Shaw hadn't met Doctor Neufeld yet. It was Lassiter who came each morning to relieve him while Neufeld, who'd been sharing the morning shift with Lassiter, came an hour later. An idea of McCready's which allowed one group to overlap with the next for a short period and gave better control and handover of the hospital. This happened on all but overnight shift since that was one doctor by himself.

Shaw glanced around the examination room, an unspoken question on his face.

"I am acting as patient for the moment," Neufeld said.

Shaw turned to Lassiter then back to Neufeld, unsure if this was some joke he wasn't understanding.

"Doctor Neufeld has been suffering from nightmares," Lassiter said, returning to a more serious doctorlike demeanor.

The other man nodded. "Sporadic nightmares. Suddenly they

come and keep me awake for a period of time, then just as suddenly they will be gone."

"And you believe the cause is physical?" Shaw asked.

Neufeld threw his hands up in a half surrender. "Hoping would be closer. I have no idea."

"Unfortunately, neither do I," Lassiter agreed. "I've given our friend here a physical examination and found no symptoms out of the ordinary other than signs of some understandable exhaustion."

Considering the problem Shaw looked from one man to the next. "Weather changes?"

Neufeld shook his head. "It's always some degree of hot or another, except during the rainy season when it's hot and wet."

That was about what he'd expected. Shaw was curious what these monsoons he'd heard about would be like. Being some-what elevated at this outpost it was hopeful they would be unaffected.

"Diet?" he asked.

Neufeld gave a small grimace. "No real change there. I eat what everyone eats and have since coming to India eight years ago."

"Any circumstances weighing on your mind?"

"Except my inability to sleep? Not particularly."

"Are these nightmares a recent experience?"

"Somewhat." Neufeld shook his head. "They've been off and on for the past year."

"A year?" Lassiter asked, then became thoughtful, one finger tapping against his lower lip.

"Is that significant?" Neufeld asked.

Shaw saw Lassiter glance at the other doctor, thoughts churning inside his head. What else had he mentioned being about a year? Oh yes, when Middlemarch supposedly first saw this Maut creature.

"Hmm, no." Lassiter looked away. "Nothing specific."

Neufeld retrieved his clipboard from the table with a sigh. "A few nights' insomnia won't affect my ability to perform, at least."

"Just your paintings," Lassiter said.

Neufeld's eyes darted to the side, as if some evidence of what Lassiter mentioned was in the room, then shook his head.

"I thank you both for your concern." He started to leave then turned back. "Nice to meet you, Shaw. I think we're on evening shift together next week."

"Oh, that's good to hear."

He thought of White and Adamson. There would be a time when he would share shift with each of them, and with luck sensitivities would be smoothed over by then, but he doubted it. Something about those two. White was more the follower and that sort had potential to be better once away from the bad influence. Only time would tell.

"Keep all this talk of bad dreams to yourselves, please," Neufeld added. "I can imagine McCready's reaction."

They both agreed as the doctor headed back toward the hospital and the few patients in beds. Lassiter remained at least half in thought. His left hand worked against the idol in his pocket, like a man rubbing a rabbit's foot for luck, or protection.

"His paintings?"

Lassiter roused. "Hmm? Oh, yes. Neufeld confided that his sketches and paintings depart from the usual flora and fauna during his nightmare phases. They become decidedly more macabre."

CHAPTER EIGHT

BANDAGAR, INDIA — JUNE 9TH, 1878

Dearest Mother,

Has it truly been a week since I've added my thoughts in this current letter? (Looking back I see this is indeed true). I suppose it's a testament to the fact that life here has settled into an orderly, predictable routine. A fact which I certainly appreciate. Hard to believe that I am headed into my second month here.

The hospital runs like clockwork. Doctor McCready has performed his job as administrator without reproach, even if he does treat us youthful doctors like shameful, illegitimate relations at times ... Well, perhaps some reproach on that.

Our shifts have become busier ... much busier actually, with short bouts of quiet in between the hectic periods. Feast or famine. Having six patients in the ward that first night was an anomaly, one of the lulls. Every battalion or outpost for miles around ships us their wounded for treatment. Broken bones, concussions, accidental bullet wounds, any injury more severe than a sprain which a field doctor doesn't have the resources to treat came to us.

The week after my first the hospital started accumulating patients on a steady basis until the ward was full and spilling over into quaran-

tine rooms for lack of space. Top this off with a daily influx of patients from groups around Hyderabad province—though these men would usually go back the same day—and it wasn't unusual to be on our feet from start of shift to end, even on the overnight.

I prefer events this way, learning more from too much to do than too little.

During those infrequent quiet periods McCready has taken to sending me on patrols with the soldiers, as Lassiter had warned. My punishment for daring to be young. It appears this is reserved entirely for me but at least it gives an opportunity to wear my helmet and sabre. Mostly these marches are to keep the lads busy and out of trouble, which I suppose applies to myself as well. As near I've been able to tell there is no danger to protect Hyderabad or Bandagar against ...

/

On that first patrol—in Shaw's second week when the hospital ward was not quite so busy—they hiked past the cliff where Middlemarch had fallen to his death. There was no doubt this was the place. Each of the soldiers muttered about it while alternating glances between the cliff and himself, as if it were a place of particular danger for doctors.

"Y'know the story already then?" Corporal Walsh said, sidling up beside him.

"Yes, Doctor Lassiter told me, though this is the first I've seen of it." They were quiet a few more strides before he added, "Awfully far from the outpost."

Walsh nodded. It was no great insight and had without doubt been discussed at length already. This cliff was a fifteen-minute stroll from the outpost, and could be reached in a five-minute sprint, but why would Middlemarch have headed here at all? *Had* someone chased him? Could it have been suicide?

There were no answers to be had here, that much was certain, and Middlemarch was beyond interrogation. This would just be one of those mysteries destined to be talked about, made into legend in time.

Later patrols took him in other directions, giving an idea of what lay around the immediate vicinity of the outpost. Being assigned to patrols was infrequent enough that it was more a break in routine than the intended punishment, and a decent way to get friendly with the men. Most days activity in the hospital kept him busy and away from patrols.

"I no longer question why we're here," Shaw confided in Lassiter one morning while on shift together. "At first I couldn't see the need for one full doctor, much less six. But now, after these last five weeks ..."

Lassiter lowered the sandwich he'd just taken a substantial bite from and chewed. Shaw's own lunch sat on the desk, waiting for his attention, a sure sign business was slowing when doctors on duty could stop for lunch at all, much less together. If McCready noticed he'd be in for another hot march.

Lassiter swallowed. "So you've grasped we're a bit of a focal point?"

"I have, but I still wonder why we're not in the main city of Hyderabad. Surely that would be more sensible?"

Lassiter shrugged. "Prince Kanwar is an influential man, and he wants us here."

Shaw snorted a reply, remembering what Lassiter had told him on that first night. The East India Company had done their best to engineer influential Indians out of the equation, ensuring those who would do their bidding be left in power. Matters under the Raj were not likely *that* much more enlightened.

"Scoff if you will," Lassiter said, taking another bite. "There's enough reason, but that man does have influence. I have no idea how it happened. Seems like an oversight somewhere."

After two months Shaw was still not sure if his friend believed half of the drivel he spouted, and if so which half. Most of what was said was certainly intended to shock or amuse. Lassiter looked thoughtful, an idea occurring to him, and Shaw braced for it. Lassiter's "spontaneous" ideas had a habit of being extensively pre-considered.

"Perhaps Prince Kanwar has heard the sun never sets on the British Empire and wants to be part of that."

"Why would any Indian want us here?"

"Why, Shaw, you sound like one of those reformer fellows, preaching equality."

Shaw snorted another reply. Lassiter knew his politics and beliefs: People are people, and deserve to be treated as such. Social Darwinism was just a thin veil to conceal the underlying racism.

"We're all British subjects." It was a thought he'd voiced more than once.

"True," Lassiter agreed. "It's just that some are more British than others."

Shaw opened his mouth with a retort when Lassiter waved the entire argument aside.

"In any case the prince *does* want us here. He is enthralled by western medicine and ways, believing India needs to be a marriage of the two." He gave Shaw a sidelong glance with his best mischievous grin. "Besides, if we *weren't* here you wouldn't be able to go treat the people in Bandagar." He made an exaggerated sign of thinking. "Hmm, maybe *that's* the prince's motivation in having us here."

Shaw shrugged and made his way over to his own sandwich, having little other response. It was true, he'd been heading down the road to Bandagar on his days off to help where he could and Lassiter knew it. His helping treat the Indian people was not against any regulation, but it *was* looked on as an oddity. Many in the army thought of them as lower class and Indian soldiers were treated as less than those from back home.

Bandagar's sole doctor was overwhelmed with the amount of day-to-day problems. Animal bites, broken bones, concussions, and infections, but also the long-term effects of severe malnourishment—aftermath of an almost two-year drought and crop failure. Before the drought there'd been four doctors, able to keep equal with demands. Two had died during those bad times and the third just up and left. Now Doctor Patel worked fourteen-hour days in an effort to stay somewhat even with the demand.

Every visit to Bandagar Shaw saw people wandering through the city, their minds gone. Not the same people over and over either. No, insanity was prevalent among the citizens there, and a higher percentage of the population afflicted than there should be. Could that be traced back to the malnourishment and stress of the past two years? Possible. The area had missed the worst of current illnesses such as cholera and diphtheria so any insanity was not apparently caused by disease.

At times these insane people would be brought in to see Doctor Patel, guided by family, blank vacant expressions and mouth working at words without volume. Sometimes they would be in a higher state of agitation, trying to wander off and thrashing to be free if restrained. Whatever the cause Shaw saw no way to cure these poor souls.

"You see yourself as some saviour to the Indian people."

Shaw rolled his eyes, knowing the argument would take this familiar route, and also knowing it was not how he saw himself at all. There were people in need of help which he could give, and he wasn't about to ignore that. He helped where he could, sharing ideas—and when he could, supplies—with Doctor Patel.

Lassiter rose to his feet, lunch finished. Some fresh piece of this debate was coming, clear from the slight twist to one corner of his mouth.

"Ask yourself this, Shaw. This equality you believe in, does it work if the Indian people *need* a white man to ride to the rescue?"

Lassiter didn't wait for a response, grabbing his clipboard and leaving for rounds. Shaw didn't have one anyway and the words bounced around inside his head minutes after Lassiter had left the room.

CHAPTER NINE

Bandagar, India — June 11th, 1878
Dearest Mother,
There are times when Lawrence Lassiter infuriates me. Between his insistence that there is some sort of monster in the surrounding wilderness — an unseen bogeyman to blame all unexplained events on — to his attitude toward the Indian people. It irks me. Though, if I am being honest, what is most irksome is that in everything he says there is some small element which makes me consider his words ...

"What have you done this time, Walsh?"

The young corporal sat in the examination room on the table wearing a sheepish expression.

Two other soldiers at the outpost shared the name Walsh, none of them related. Only this one had been into the hospital twice since Shaw arrived—three times now. The man had a deserved reputation of being slightly accident prone, but had yet to cause permanent damage, either to himself or someone else. Not yet.

"Ah, doc, would you believe I tripped goin' down a hill and landed badly on my rifle?"

"I would believe this, yes."

Walsh gave his *Aw, shucks* grin and that lack of guile was enough to make Shaw smile. Walking disaster Walsh might be but he also had a winning personality that made him completely likeable. Shaw treated all patients equally, but he liked chatting with this boy more than most.

Boy? Seven years at most separated them. Were they not at such dissimilar stations in life they could have been friends.

"Well, let's see it, Walsh."

The soldier raised his tunic and showed a ragged furrow from upper ribs to waistline, along the right-hand side. Bleeding had already slowed.

"Hmm, long but not deep. No stitches this time."

Walsh breathed a sigh of relief.

"I would think you'd be used to stitches by now."

"Well, I suppose. Doesn't mean I look forward to 'em though."

"Hmm, fair enough," Shaw said, getting to work on cleaning the wound.

"I got to thank you for not makin' a big deal out of this, doc."

"Well, I could tell you to be more careful, but I suspect you already know that."

"Yes, sir. Mum gave the same advice all the time when I was a lad. She gave up eventually."

Shaw finished applying a bandage and inspected his work. "Well, try your best."

"Always do."

"If you have much pain, or if the wound becomes inflamed, come back and see me."

"Yup. Will do." Walsh got to his feet, securing his tunic. Once done he made no motion to leave.

"Something else, Corporal?"

"I—Well, some of the lads say you go to Bandagar and help treat 'em."

The use of the word *them* made Shaw grit his teeth. Us and them, Briton and Indian, classes and castes, the same ugly problem always rearing its head.

"I do."

Walsh tipped him a grin and a nod, as if unable to find the words he wanted and hoped this would convey his true attitude. Shaw smiled back at him. Could be he wasn't the only one seeing the native Indians as people.

He accompanied the soldier back to the entry.

"Well, thanks, doc. See you soon."

"Not too soon, I hope. Unless you're just stopping in to say a greeting without any broken bones."

"Aw, I ain't broken a bone in years."

The words were said with such pride that it pulled a chuckle from Shaw.

Walsh marched out the door, passing Lassiter who was on his way in. "Sir," he said.

"Walsh," Lassiter greeted, then crossed over to the desk.

"Shaw, you are a true man of the people. Between the soldiers and the Bandagarians you have quite the appreciation."

He accepted the compliment, taking it at face value though unsure it was meant as such.

"We're all British subjects," Shaw said for the hundredth time, and as Lassiter opened his mouth to reply he added. "Yes, yes … Some are just more British than others."

Lassiter shrugged, but looked more thoughtful than usual. He waved a hand—the one not in his pocket—pushing the subject aside. A shift of feet and he stared out the window at the setting sun.

"What are you doing here anyway?" Shaw asked. "Neufeld is on shift next."

"Nope." Lassiter shook his head without turning around. "He's sick."

Shaw made a noise of sympathy. Neufeld had once again been afflicted with thrashing nightmares and a brain fever during the night.

"Sensitive artist types," Lassiter said with a sniff. "At any rate, I ... needed to get out and about. Too much time on my own."

No comment on that point. Shaw was just happy to see Lassiter again, to be honest. His friend had been spending too much free time in his room this past week, taking meals there and assigned to overnight shifts by himself. Undoubtedly he spent his time seated in the dimness and staring at that ugly idol of his, as Shaw had caught him doing one afternoon about a month ago. Since then Lassiter kept his door latched.

"It's back," Lassiter said, not turning from the view outside.

No need to ask what the *It* was. Dhoosar Maut. The Grey Death. Since Shaw's arrival the sightings had been sporadic, always from a distance, always just a glimpse. Someone in a group thought they saw some shape among the trees, but no one else would see it. Of course that would be attributed to the Maut, along with all other vaguely glimpsed movement from the corner of one's eye. Then all sightings would stop for a while.

The officers, McCready and the commander in particular, ridiculed belief in this thing, giving it no credence whatsoever. Even so, no nighttime patrols were ordered and it was common knowledge all personnel were expected to travel in pairs or more after nightfall.

Tigers, any officer would say.

For his part Shaw didn't doubt some danger lurked out there, he just refused to believe it was any supernatural monster ... but he wasn't so sure it was a tiger either. Would a tiger be frightened off by a second man being there, or keep itself from being seen so consistently?

In the past month all sightings had dwindled to zero. Even the imagination of the more superstitious men had calmed down.

"One of the soldiers saw it after dinner, moving among the trees."

"Hmm."

Lassiter turned from the window. "Does your doctor friend in Bandagar have any thoughts on it?"

Shaw shrugged. "To be honest I haven't talked with Doctor Patel about it."

Lassiter shook his head, looking as if the answer was expected. "No, of course not."

It was unusual to not hear the man cracking a joke or making light of a situation. Not since their ride on the train had he slipped into this serious, introspective point of view. It was, quite frankly, eerie.

"It seems the people in Bandagar are not affected by it," Lassiter said. "There are no reports of missing people or strange happenings."

"Would we hear if one Indian went missing?"

Lassiter thought and shook his head again.

One missing native would mean nothing to the British army even if they did hear about it.

"Maybe that's why the prince wants us here," Shaw said.

Lassiter turned toward him, head cocked to one side, hand coming from his pocket for once.

"For protection."

"Hah! Barking up the wrong tree there. Though, you could be on the right path. What if Prince Kanwar just thinks this Dhoosar Maut would be happier with a bunch of Britishers?"

"Doctor Shaw! Doctor Shaw!"

One of the Bandagar Indians who helped around hospital rushed in. When he saw Lassiter the man stopped and looked toward the floor. The other doctor's hand had already slipped back into his pocket, protecting that ever-present treasure.

"What is it, Balvinder?" Shaw asked.

"A man was hurt in the courtyard, unloading supplies."

"Can he move?" Shaw grabbed for his doctor's bag.

"Yes."

"Well, bring him in then."

"Doctor Shaw, he's … an Indian man, and one from outside of Bandagar. I don't know him. He and his son were here, helping unload, when he was hurt."

"Oh, I see. Of course."

He should have seen. The man would have already been brought in otherwise. Yes, treating Indians in their own town was one thing, but bringing a non-soldier into the army hospital would not be looked on with the same favor. Still, could he just—

"Well, don't leave him lying in the dirt," Lassiter said. "Bring him in."

Balvinder glanced up, first at Lassiter then to Shaw.

"What?" Lassiter added. "Haven't you heard? We're all British subjects."

Balvinder gave a quick bow and left the room while Shaw stared at his friend, searching for some sign of irony or derision, a joke only Lassiter himself would find amusing.

"Don't blow it out of proportion, Archie."

Shaw continued to stare and Lassiter rolled his eyes.

"Look, maybe after hearing you say it for the thousandth time …" He gave his dismissive hand wave and turned toward the door.

The change in outlook couldn't be that quick or complete, but it was a step and Shaw was proud of his friend for it. He would most likely always think Indian people needed to be governed, but it was possible Lassiter was starting to see them as people.

"McCready won't like this," Shaw said.

"Probably not." Lassiter could have left right then and been free of the situation. He had the opening and the time before their patient was brought in, but he didn't move, or look like he considered it. Instead he snorted a laugh. "McCready doesn't like much of anything."

When the wounded man was carried in, through the entry and into the examination room, he was speaking in his native tongue, much too fast to follow. Eyes rolled inside his head as the man attempted to concentrate. He was dressed in what had once been a kurta but could now only generously be called rags, much below the usual quality of even beggars in Bandagar. A boy, the son Balvinder had mentioned, waited near the door, expressionless and evaluating.

The poor man had turned away at the wrong moment and taken a heavy bag of rice across the neck and shoulders. It had driven him to the ground, burying him underneath it. For a minute he had lain still and even now remained dazed and unsure of where he was. His speed of speech was slowing, eyes were focusing, but wide, like an animal realizing it was surrounded by predators.

"Nothing to worry about," Shaw told the man, while Lassiter peered into his eyes.

The man made no sign he understood and retreated from Lassiter's attentions. Shaw glanced at Balvinder, who provided translation, but once again the man made no change to the way he looked at the two doctors.

"Well ... No concussion, it would appear," Lassiter muttered.

Shaw reached for the man's shoulder and was surprised as he leapt to his feet, staggering back and baring his teeth. Wild and ferocious.

"And no apparent broken bones," Lassiter added.

Throughout it all the man's son stood at the door without reaction. No outward sentiment of worry on the boy's face, no hopeful expectation. The way someone might look at a glass of water.

"Seems he only had the wind knocked from him," Shaw said.

"Yes," Lassiter agreed. "Back on his feet already. A good sign."

Balvinder nodded, ready to show the patient back out.

"Hold on," Shaw said, passing through the door to the shared office.

Inside the desk drawer were several of the candies which he would take with him on visits to Bandagar, for the children there. He offered it to the son who looked back as if not understanding what it was.

"It's candy," Shaw said. "You eat it." He made a gesture of eating and understood it was a poor game of charades. "Balvinder, could you translate, please?"

Balvinder did and the expression on the boy didn't change one twitch, but he reached out and took the offered treat, making no move to put it into his mouth but holding it in one loose fist.

"Huh," Lassiter said, crossing the room. "Never saw a kid not ready to eat candy." He skirted a side table in the cramped area and caught his coat on one metal edge, tearing the pocket with a loud rip. The idol didn't spill out, but it was definitely on display for all to see.

The patient's eyes went wild and huge once again. He breathed one word in a low, reverent whisper. "Kali."

From the door, the boy echoed his father and shuddered. His first reaction of any sort.

All sets of eyes were on the idol, upright inside the pocket as if glaring back at the room of people. Lassiter slapped both hands against the flap of pocket, holding it back into place. He looked up, finding all attention in his direction.

"Excuse me," he murmured, rushing in a straight line past the boy and exiting from the room.

The father's wild eyes followed.

The two doctors caught hell from McCready for treating a civilian at an army hospital. Lassiter, with a more-than-usual lack of tact and an even greater amount of agitation, pointed out the patient had been hurt while working to unload food for the outpost, and that the real reason McCready didn't like it was that the man wasn't white.

Their upbraiding ended there, with a tight-lipped warning that they were not to treat non-army personnel at the hospital again without express permission. Shaw agreed, as did Lassiter, but not without boring a hole into McCready with his scowl.

"What was that about?" Shaw asked as they left the head doctor's office.

Lassiter grumbled. He'd been in a foul mood since the previous day when the idol had come close to spilling from his pocket. He'd returned for his shift in a fresh coat but kept to himself for the evening and hadn't spoken more than a few words.

Shaw opened his mouth to speak again when his friend came to a sudden halt, interrupting his righteous stalk through the hallways. Lassiter rounded and glared back at the closed office door. "Officious, pompous ass."

Lassiter hadn't said anything incorrect, but these were also obvious observations, ones Shaw had been experiencing since his arrival and which Lassiter had been enduring even longer.

"We saved a man's life!" Lassiter continued. At the sign of Shaw's one raised eyebrow he exhaled. "Well, as far as McCready knows we did."

Closer to the facts.

Lassiter seethed. "All he cares about is appearances and following the rules."

"That's his entire function here."

"Is it? Strange. I thought he was here to perform medicine and save lives, no matter who the patient might be."

Lassiter was warming to this newfound outlook.

"We won't change the world overnight," Shaw said.

"Hmph! Change the world. Still going with the saviour role, I see."

It was said without judgement or barb, but they were words Shaw had been mulling over since Lassiter brought it up the other day.

"Perhaps, but it's better than that attitude."

He pointed toward McCready's office and his friend smiled, for the first time since before last night's activities.

"I find your logic unassailable," Lassiter said with a sigh that released his gloomy expression. "Now, what do you say to some breakfast?"

CHAPTER TEN

BANDAGAR, INDIA — JULY 2ND, 1878
Ah, my dearest Mother,
There are times in life when, looking back, it all seems to have passed in a blur. That usually comes, in my experience, from days consisting of predictable routine with nothing particularly worth remembering. Other times it's from such profound and emotional occurrences that a man's mind tries its best to shy from the very memory ...

One evening, a few weeks after treating the man and his son, Shaw found himself returning to the outpost later than usual. He'd spent that entire Saturday, his day off, in Bandagar with Doctor Patel, helping where he could. Afterwards he was pulled into conversation with the doctor, speaking on current ideas in medicine, as doctors everywhere end up doing. Shaw was not so unalike White and Adamson in that respect.

At that time of year the sun set close to 7:00 PM and his watch told him the hour was close. Shaw set off at a brisk pace, one nervous eye on the disappearing horizon.

The passage from Bandagar to outpost was short, less than a ten-minute walk, and in reality a person could see one from the other with ease when the sun was up. Yet that no-man's-land between the two was viewed as the most dangerous once dark had fallen, as dangerous as being in the surrounding trees themselves. Even for himself, Shaw didn't dawdle when it came to being outside at night.

But why?

Why rush and panic for some phenomenon he'd never seen, never experienced? He hadn't even seen the handiwork, as Lassiter called it, of this supposed creature. No, nothing had changed his mind on the existence of this creature since he'd first heard of it on the train from Bombay.

So, why the rush?

Shaw slowed to a stroll at just about the halfway point between city and outpost. His eyes darted side to side, as he continued on at his more usual pace while congratulating himself on choosing science over superstition. Science always triumphed over the unseen dangers man feared while still living in caves … and yet, had circumstances changed so much? Science would also state, with empirical evidence, that *tigers* could be roaming at the edge of this very darkness, a fear for which his Neanderthal ancestors had every right to be cautious.

Yes, that was enough to speed him forward again, but for a more level-headed reason than some fantastic bogeyman.

In moments he'd passed into the lit courtyard of the outpost and slowed again, wondering on the subject of fear. Surely the fear of unknown and unseen was worse than that of knowing what was actually there. It's a primal fear, a part of man's inner psyche left over from those caveman days when every unfamiliar noise was a potential danger prepared to eat them. The topic tickled his mind and he began formulating a potential article for medical journals back home.

Preoccupied in this way he continued toward the hospital and his room, working through his ideas and wondering how best to research it. This article might not get written but it was an interesting—

His subconscious nudged at him, had been doing so for the past minute.

Something was off.

The night was silent. No crickets chirped, no birds flapping about finishing their day or bats chittering, beginning their night. Even the air was still.

Shaw twisted, looking around, wondering if a storm was coming ... but, no. That didn't feel right.

So, what was it?

Unknown.

Sounds of recreation came from the barracks, the soldiers engaging in some game or other. Perhaps another darts tournament. For a moment he considered joining them, seeking the comfort of other people, but all he wanted was the comfort of his own chair.

Yes, best to just get inside.

"Steady on, Shaw," he scolded himself, continuing his journey toward the hospital.

Ahead, between his goal and the dining hall, one patch of black shifted independent of the rest. Shaw slowed, wondering who was brave enough to wander between buildings after dark.

"Who's there?" he called.

No answer.

The shadow came forward, resolving into a manlike shape, though the gait was slow, the movement ponderous.

He slowed, squinting into the gloom, trying to pick out some detail as the shape came closer to the edge of illumination, closer.

He stopped.

"Who is there?" he repeated.

Even as he asked Shaw knew this was no member of the outpost.

One half-step backward on his part as this obscure shape continued forward.

On the edge of dark and light, still between the two buildings, it stopped.

Waiting.

Staring.

The article on fear's concept disappeared from his mind as the real thing forced its way into his brain. More than fear.

Terror.

His soul was filled with a sudden unreasoning, irrational desire to flee. A *need* to flee. Yet, he did not. Could not.

This shape in the blackness shuffled a step closer into the electric lights, revealing its features. Revulsion covered Shaw like a hot, filthy blanket.

He couldn't look away.

A monster! Its skin grey and leathery, like the flesh of some long-dead corpse. Stooped and clawed, right arm longer than the left, inches from dragging against the earth. It had entirely black eyes, like two pieces of midnight, and a slack, open mouth.

The Dhoosar Maut. Lassiter's Grey Death. The name suited but still came nowhere near to truly describing it.

How do you describe the indescribable?

Fear and nausea slammed into him, grabbing him, while an overwhelming sense of hopelessness pressed down, like being under a giant's thumb. More than the promise of death seethed in this creature's shape. A death of the body was one thing, but this spoke of a death of mind and spirit and all he'd ever held dear.

His right foot stepped forward without consent.

Then his left.

"No." Shaw managed a ragged whisper. "No! Please!"

Who was he pleading to anyway? Not this monster, that was certain. It would have no mercy. To a god who allowed such a horror to exist? No. He'd always chosen science over religion.

Right foot. Left.

This creature was not of science, not of God. It was ... other.

Right foot again.

The Maut made no step to advance, calling Shaw across the courtyard toward it instead. Shaw's mind retreated to gibber in one corner, knowing full well when he reached the shadows that would be the end.

Madness waited.

Twelve feet left. Eleven. Ten. Shaw approached that dim corner between hospital and dining hall. Body and mind turned traitor, he was helpless to stop the advance.

"Evening, Doc."

Walsh's round face filled his world, stepping between Shaw and his view of the Maut.

"Where ya goin'?"

"Going?"

The spell was broken and Shaw took a step back. Fear remained but not the irrational fear that had been pushed into him, rather a panic of what would happen if he should ever look on it again.

"Walsh," he said, like a drowning man clinging to a life preserver. "Walsh."

"Yes, sir." The soldier cocked his head to one side, smile sliding away. "Somethin' wrong?"

Walsh started to turn, back the way Shaw had been traveling.

"No, Walsh. Don't!"

Too late. The soldier already looked toward the edge of darkness. Shaw tensed to tackle the man and prevent him going to his death.

"What is it, doc? You see somethin'?"

"I …"

With caution Shaw peered around his unwitting rescuer, sure that it would be a case of only he being able to see the Maut. Laying eyes on it again the trance and horror would return and make him rush forward to his end.

But it was gone.

Gone.

"I … No. No, nothing."

Walsh turned back and levelled a serious gaze on Shaw. "Shouldn't be outside alone, doc."

Shaw nodded, numbly, and fell into step beside the youthful man, heading toward the barracks with him.

"Coming to play darts?" Walsh asked.

Shaw looked at the barracks and shook his head, took a step back and corrected course back toward the hospital.

"Hey, doc, you feeling well?"

Even if he'd had the presence of mind to respond Shaw wouldn't have known what to say. Instead he continued on toward the hospital, speed increasing, sensing Walsh's worried eyes on him the entire way. With a shudder he entered the building then picked up speed, racing through the corridors and up stairs until reaching his room. Once inside he locked the door —an action he hadn't taken before—closed the curtains, then collapsed into a ball on his bed.

He wept, much like a baby would.

At some point sleep came but wasn't the mercy it should have been. Shaw found himself engulfed in dreams of black despair. Knowledge that all was not right in the world, that his belief in a logical, comprehensible reality was utterly wrong.

Some dreadful abhorrence waited, just outside the edge of light and when that last light was gone he would be devoured.

They all would.

CHAPTER ELEVEN

Exhausted and miserable, muscles aching, Shaw awoke feeling as though he'd run through the night. He lay there, cautiously probing at his mind and found it weary but his own. What's more that mind had been busy sifting information while the body slept and had come to one disturbing conclusion: The madness infecting those in Bandagar, it had been caused by the Maut. *That* was what happened on the edge of dark and light where it lurked. The Maut devoured mind and soul.

Shaw was on his feet, pacing.

But how does that fit into what Lassiter said about gruesome discoveries?

It didn't seem to.

Had he been mistaken? Attributed some other attack to the Maut? Lassiter had been wrong about the Indian people, they *did* show signs of encountering this … this …

Supernatural monster?

"No," he hissed through clenched teeth. "No!"

Just because it wasn't evident at the moment didn't mean there wasn't a more logical, more natural explanation. One existed, of that he was certain. All was explainable with the necessary data.

That was a matter for later. For now, whatever the nature of this Maut, something must be done!

He stormed from the room, unaware of either time of day or the fact he still wore yesterday's clothes, rumpled and disheveled from a fitful sleep. Ignoring all greetings or acknowledgments from hospital staff and cleaning women he sped through the halls until coming to Uncle Freddy's office.

Shaw knocked, remembering that one trifling piece of expectation.

"Come in."

A pleased expression creased the commander's face as Shaw burst through the door. Then the other man saw the state Shaw was in.

"What is it, man? What's happened?"

A foot inside the door Shaw started rambling his story. Commander Armstrong came and guided him toward a chair, closing the door as they went. He told his uncle everything, including the theory that this beast was devouring minds in Bandagar. Toward the end his words had escalated to raving shrieks.

While his mind might once again be his own, that did not mean it was in proper order.

"There, there, Shaw." The commander patted one shoulder.

At some point during his narration the commander had poured him a brandy which remained untouched, sloshing as he gestured.

"You've had a shock to be sure."

A shock? Yes! Yes, Uncle Freddy was right of course. An awful shock. His belief in the rational world had taken a hit and he still struggled to put his thoughts back into their proper boxes.

Shaw downed the brandy in a shot, coughing as it burned his throat.

"You must realize that what you are spouting is nonsense though," the commander said, voice calm and soothing, as if speaking to a panicked child who'd had a nightmare. "Preposterous."

"But—"

"A monster that lives in the wilderness around us? Which drives men mad by looking at it? Does that sound rational?"

Rational. That word again. "I—"

"The men have their stories of this Dhoosar Maut, but they are simple men. Soldiers. Their focus is on fighting, and without a clear target to fight they create one. It's what they know."

A simple explanation, a sensible one.

"The natives have their own ideas, primitive and superstitious as they are, ways to explain what goes bump in the night."

"Yes, but—"

"Now you saw something, that is certain. No man would suggest different."

Yes. Yes! Of course he had!

"But you are a man of medicine, a man of science. Return to that world. Leave this one of fantastic explanations to those less educated."

"But I—"

"You will find, in time, that what you saw was quite knowable. A tiger, most likely. A terrifying encounter for any man, but a logical one. The soldiers' talk of monsters has infected your thoughts, colored your perceptions."

Shaw's eyes locked with the commander's and he found himself nodding, though not knowing why. He knew the truth, knew what he'd seen and experienced.

"Good, Shaw. Good. Now forget all of this nonsense. The men need you, as do I, to be a level-headed doctor."

More nodding on Shaw's part.

Once again he was guided, this time to his feet and back toward the exit. The commander rested one hand on the knob, glancing back—wary of Shaw raving once again. But the shouts had gone out of him, along with any desire to discuss this further. Uncle Freddy did not, would not, could not, believe what Shaw had told him.

With a muttered "Goodbye," Shaw drifted through the hallways, from one space to another until back at the door of his own living quarters. Rather than return to the isolation of his room and more fitful, delirious sleep, he went to Lassiter's door.

His friend would listen.

Shaw knocked.

Inside came a quick, furtive sound of movement.

Then nothing.

Another knock, emphatic.

Then a third.

Sound from the other side as Lassiter approached to the door. Hesitation, a shuffling of feet, a debate on opening it.

"Larry, please."

A crack appeared as the door pulled inward, just wide enough for an eye to peer through the opening.

"Shaw?"

A hesitation, then the door opened wider and Lassiter slouched before him, wearing only his dressing gown, cinched loosely and exposing too much. His condition was pale and exhausted.

"Are you well?" they both said.

Miracles are often unimpressive, everyday occurrences that just happen at the right moment. This was one of those miracles and elicited a smile from each, though both were devoid of real humor. Lassiter stepped aside, an invitation which Shaw accepted with gratitude.

Inside the room was an aura of oppression, of a blackness reminiscent of his encounter with the Maut, but surely that was only his own thought process combined with the room's lack of cleanliness. Lassiter had allowed it to slide toward hovel status. Curtains drawn to keep the light out, bed sheets half on the floor, twisted and untucked. Barely picked at food—several meals worth—sat on his side table, and there on the desk, like a malevolent demon, was that squat, ugly idol.

Shaw couldn't look on it. Not now.

"What's happened?" Lassiter asked.

Again a rambling, babbling recount of the tale. His friend listened, eyes darting to the idol then back to focus on Shaw. By the time Shaw was done he had Lassiter's full attention.

The man looked afraid.

"You were lucky," Lassiter muttered, wiping one hand down a sweaty face. He crossed to the desk, retrieved his idol and slid it into the pocket of his dressing gown.

"I beg your pardon, Shaw. I haven't been sleeping well lately. Ever since we treated that man in the hospital, but it's gotten worse this past week."

Shaw nodded, sensing it needed some response, but in truth barely heard his friend's words. He launched into his idea that the insane people in Bandagar had been driven so by the Dhoosar Maut, but explained his inability to reconcile this result with the ones Lassiter had hinted at. His mind whirled, searching for information and struggling for some way to work this all into his concept of the world.

"Remember? You spoke of gruesome discoveries on the train ride. This creature's handiwork. When you told me about what happened to Middlemarch."

Lassiter waited, the hand inside his dressing gown seemingly providing him with comfort and patience until Shaw finally stopped to inhale.

"Hold that breath, Shaw." Lassiter raised one hand and brought the ramblings to a halt. "Good."

He crossed the room and poured water from a pitcher into two glasses.

"I don't have any more to add to the story of what Middlemarch witnessed." He crossed back and offered Shaw one of the glasses. "But those gruesome discoveries ...?" He returned the left hand to his pocket again. "How sure are you about this theory on the insane Indians?"

Shaw took a deep breath, ready to continue his rant, but Lassiter held up one hand again.

"And, what do you propose be done about it?"

That stopped him.

Yes, he was sure about the connection between those insane men and his own experience. It felt true, even without any necessary tangible evidence. They were connected, with absolute certainty. But what *could* be done about it? What could anyone do?

"I don't doubt you've hit on some new point," Lassiter said, collapsing into his other chair, leaning on one arm heavily. "As you pointed out, we wouldn't notice an Indian disappearing. Hell, unless the entire city of Bandagar went missing at once I doubt we'd notice. One or two of the regular men who come here for deliveries could be replaced without any remark from us."

"More than one or two. I've noticed a dozen, wandering and mindless."

Lassiter considered. "If you've seen a dozen I'll wager it's more."

He was right. What they thought they saw and what was reality would be differing. Some of those afflicted would have wandered off to die, while others would be hidden in their homes, cared for by families.

"Those gruesome discoveries?" Shaw persisted.

Lassiter shuddered, the way he had the night of their train voyage. "There were two occurrences," he said, taking a deep breath. His own water glass held in one hand, ignored or forgotten. "Both happened within a month of each other. Both, funny enough, being somewhat recent recruits that had arrived here. The first was found at the edge of the outpost and we weren't even sure what we'd found at first." He got to his feet, pacing. "Yes. If a person is drawn in, entranced as you explained, that would explain why he would go without a fight. Insidious! How could anyone fight such a monster?"

"The body?" Shaw asked, trying to steer him back toward the conversation.

Lassiter looked at him as if he'd just arrived. It was interesting how the more manic and animated Lassiter became the more calm Shaw felt, as if he were drawing the calm out of Lassiter. More likely it was his doctor's instincts kicking in, trying to keep a patient from panicking.

"Right. Yes," Lassiter said. "Well, we found poor Private Barnes at the edge of the outpost, a few feet beyond where dark and light come together. His skull was there, and a few other bones with bits of flesh and gristle still attached, about what a cook might throw into a soup pot. His rifle lay there, unfired. Now I ask you, if it were a tiger would his rifle be unfired?"

Shaw leaned forward, full attention on the story, trying to absorb every detail.

"Further into the trees we found a red puddle, blood of course, but other parts of his body as well. He'd been ... well, torn apart is about the best description, flesh stripped from bones. The sight was enough to turn me vegetarian for a month, like one of our Hindu brethren."

Lassiter shuddered again and downed his water in a few gulps.

"Private Yates was a bit different. Poor guy had only been here a week when he went missing."

"Missing?"

"Yes," Lassiter nodded, crossing the room to refill his glass.

He waved the pitcher toward Shaw, who shook his head. "One soldier had come around the corner in time to see Yates walk into the trees. Again his rifle lay on the ground, abandoned. This soldier rushed over but by the time he crossed the compound Yates was gone. Wisely he did not go in after him but went and got some friends. Six of them went looking, but Yates had disappeared."

"Did the soldier see anything, when Yates entered the trees?"

"A quick movement in the darkness, much like what you'd seen but less close up."

"Where was Yates found?"

"Very good, Shaw. Yes, he was indeed found, on the far side of Bandagar."

"Torn apart?"

"Yes, but not as much as Barnes." Lassiter took a drink. "A couple of Indians who work here brought us to Yates, speaking to us in rapid English, then to each other in even faster Hindi. Still, it wasn't so quick that two words weren't picked out."

"What words?" Shaw was sure he already knew.

"Dhoosar Maut."

"Dhoosar Maut," Shaw repeated, turning it over in his mind.

"It seemed as if it had been interrupted with Yates."

Shaw narrowed his eyes, considering. No. The fate of Barnes and Yates didn't fit in line with what he'd experienced, more physical than what he'd known awaited him.

They both sat quiet for a minute.

"Commander Armstrong knows about this?" Shaw asked.

"Of course."

"Why didn't he believe me?"

"He did."

Shaw shook his head.

"Oh, yes. As much as he will allow himself to at any rate. Armstrong saw the end result of both attacks. He was the one who ordered no one outside alone after nightfall."

"Then why—?"

"He's a man of action, a man of physical means. He's likely never found much in life which couldn't be resolved by fist or gun, or at the least a show of intimidation. Now he's faced with some evil that doesn't fit into his concept of the world. He doesn't know how to react. Worse, he doesn't know how to resolve this and keep his men safe, while at the same time he can't exactly go outside for help without looking like a superstitious fool."

Uncle Freddy's words about soldiers and superstitions and the natural, scientific world repeated inside his mind. Had the man been trying more to convince himself? Shaw opened his mouth with some retort on how to resolve this, on how to fix the situation. No words came.

How did one destroy a creature which could affect the mind?

There must be some way. There had to be.

Some vital piece of information was missing, a step between the entrancement of the Maut and the tearing apart of those soldiers. What link was missing that joined those two?

Lassiter leaned to one side in his chair, once again running a palm down his sweat slicked face. He exhibited the signs of complete exhaustion and Shaw was far enough outside of his own head now to see his friend was suffering.

"Do you want me to get you something to help you sleep?"

"Sleep?" Lassiter's eyes widened then he shook his head. "No. No, when I close my eyes, I see …"

But he only shook his head again.

"Dreams? Like Neufeld?"

Lassiter thought about this for a moment before shaking his head a third time. "No. His are nightmares, horrible scenes and circumstances. Mine feel more like some great onlooker, some judge … watching me. I … I sometimes hear …" He emitted a shaky laugh and turned toward Shaw. "Forget it. Just nightmares. Exhaustion makes them into more."

CHAPTER TWELVE

BANDAGAR, INDIA — JULY 23RD, 1878
... There are worse things in life than those occurrences which happen to ourselves ...

"Where's Lassiter?" Doctor McCready demanded as he swept into the hospital wing, stethoscope in one hand.

Shaw stood from his seat at the entrance room desk, where he'd been filling in some of the never-ending forms they'd been tasked with.

The early morning shift had started ten minutes ago, with Lassiter and McCready scheduled to relieve him. Neither had arrived. Not uncommon for McCready to be late, occupied as he was with administrative tasks and other extra duties. It was the head doctor's prerogative to arrive when able, and if he wasn't sharing duty with another doctor then the one being relieved just had to make do as long as it took.

Lassiter being late was slightly more unusual, though not by much. Since their talk in his room a couple of weeks back he'd become even more absorbed by his idol, to the point of losing track of time. Shaw worried for his friend. Once McCready took over he would head for the rooms and rouse Lassiter from his stupor. It was time to confront him on this ... Past time to be honest. It was affecting his work and becoming more noticeable.

"Running a bit late, I suspect."

"Hmph," McCready grumbled. "Fine. You can stick around until Lassiter is good enough to show up."

"Oh, of course."

So much for the plan to go rouse his friend. Shaw would have to hope he came around on his own. Surely Lassiter would stroll through those doors at any moment.

Enough urgency existed in the hospital to occupy Shaw's time without making excuses to go in search of Lassiter. Some malady had sped through the outpost like a raging fire two days previous, filling the hospital's beds with patients. Many of the soldiers had been forced to seek their help with painful cramps, fever, and vomiting. Some spoiled food? The water? Whatever the case, Shaw, McCready, Neufeld, and Lassiter had missed out on the effects so far. More than half of the soldiers, including Commander Armstrong, and much of the other staff, looked as if they'd been danced on by the prince's elephant.

Had Lassiter succumbed to whatever this was? A definite possibility when dealing with an unknown cause.

An hour into his unscheduled double shift Shaw had finished the immediate forms needing attention and started the next rounds of the ward. One soldier, particularly affected, groaned, forehead covered in a sheen of sweat. An unspoken plea haunted the man's wide eyes. Shaw brought him a glass of water, allowing a few sips.

"Not what you signed up for, hmm?"

The private shook his head. "Thought the worst would be someone shooting me."

The man groaned again and closed his eyes.

Another hour passed and their charges were under control, though no more comfortable. His thoughts returned to Lassiter. McCready didn't show any concern past looking toward the entry doors occasionally, then at his watch.

Shaw couldn't very well ask to look for his friend either. With the commander affected McCready had been pulling double duty taking care of command decisions along with his own medical duties. The man was obviously exhausted.

It was the first time Shaw experienced any degree of sympathy toward the man. Though McCready would say something soon enough to destroy the newfound accord.

Shouts came from the outer hallway, drawing both doctors to the entry. Three soldiers burst through the double doors just as Shaw and McCready arrived, a fourth person dangled between the two in back.

"Doctor!" the lead soldier shouted again.

McCready slapped one hand against the desk. "Gentlemen, may I remind you this is a hospital. If your friend is sick bring him through to the examination room."

"Not our friend," the lead soldier said, stepping aside. "One of yours."

Lassiter.

McCready let out a hiss of surprise while Shaw stepped back as if he'd been punched. Another second passed before Shaw's professional side took over.

"Come with me."

The two soldiers carrying Lassiter brought him through to the examination room and placed him on the table. Shaw rushed to his friend's side.

"What happened?" McCready demanded.

"No idea, sir," the lead soldier said. "We found him outside."

"Outside?" Shaw asked.

"Yes, sir."

His mind spun to that too-vivid memory of the Maut and for

a moment he was back there, reexperiencing that pull on his sanity.

"No," he whispered, forcing the thought aside.

Lassiter's skin was cool. How long had he been out there? It was unlike him to be outside, but conceivable that Lassiter had forced himself to go get some breakfast or some air. Had he been stricken with this illness?

Was this the Maut's terror?

"Come on," he whispered, searching for pulse at Lassiter's neck, and again at the wrist.

Nothing.

He listened for a heartbeat and received similar results.

"No!" Shaw whispered. "Please, no."

McCready stood next to him while the examination continued. Shaw clung to the hope that if he found some affliction, some wound, it could be properly treated and bring Lassiter around. His mind babbled nonsense at him. He was a better doctor than that and knew the reality. He just refused to accept it.

"He's gone, Shaw."

Shaw's hands started at the lower extremities, working up each leg. Checking the torso for wounds, for some sign of what had happened.

"Shaw," McCready repeated.

"I heard you."

He continued, finding no signs of trauma. At the neck he loosened Lassiter's coat and sucked in a surprised breath. A purple ring of bruising surrounded the throat.

"Strangulation?" Shaw said.

This was not the Maut's work. This was a person.

This was murder.

McCready stepped forward, examining this wound, eyes narrowing. His jaw set into an angry clench, and a single muttered curse escaped his mouth before he was rounding on the soldiers who'd brought Lassiter in.

"Outside you say? Where?"

The older doctor's hands were tight fists, as if ready to strike the closest target.

"Between the barracks and hospital, sir. Towards the back."

"Near the edge?"

The two soldiers in back nodded, looking for all the world like they wished they could be anywhere else. The last, their unspoken leader, stood between them and McCready.

"In the shadows," this man explained, then added as inspiration hit him, "It would have been completely dark there last night."

McCready stared at the body a moment, chewing on his lower lip. He turned and headed for the doors. "Come with me," he said to the soldiers. "Shaw, you wait here."

Shaw barely heard the order, barely saw the other doctor leave, barely registered that McCready had been alarmed by something more than one of his doctors dead before him.

"Aw, Larry," Shaw whispered, placing one palm flat against his friend's chest.

———

Commander Armstrong burst through the doors and into the examination room. As usual he was dressed in uniform but his face was pale, unshaven and his eyes watery. The jacket hung askew on his shoulders, as if thrown on too quickly to ensure the right button had met the matching hole. He was far from having recovered from this sickness, but one of his staff dead—murdered—was an incident which would pull him out of bed, no matter how sick. McCready was a pace behind him. The two hovered over Lassiter's body, staring down.

"Don't you have patients?" McCready snapped.

Shaw took a step back, agreed numbly, and headed for the door, stopping before he truly left. The head doctor turned toward his uncle, speaking in low tones which carried just enough so every few words was audible.

"… them … strangled … return …"

McCready pulled back the collar and Armstrong nodded to words the older doctor murmured, looking even more pale.

Risking another tongue-lashing Shaw stepped closer, quietly, until he could overhear.

"—broken years ago," Armstrong said.

"Broken or not, there is someone left doing the work."

"No. Impossible! For my money it's a couple of lone savages who still follow the way of Thuggee."

Thuggee?

McCready exhaled, his disgust plain. "Why strangle Lassiter?"

"These people need no reason. Their goddess demands sacrifice, and they do all for Kali."

"Kali?" Shaw blurted, regretting it as the two turned.

McCready shot one eyebrow up in a *Didn't I tell you to do rounds?* expression. He opened his mouth to speak—some vicious comment—when Armstrong jumped in, one shaky hand raised.

"There's no unhearing it, McCready."

The commander beckoned Shaw forward and he went, not making eye contact with McCready. The older doctor would have harsh words for him later when they were alone again. But, damn it, this was his friend lying dead on the table.

"What do you know about the Cult of Kali?" Armstrong asked.

Shaw looked down at Lassiter's body, the purple bruise of strangulation. He could almost hear his hee-haw laugh.

"Shaw?" Armstrong said softly.

"I … Only what details I remember from boys' adventure

stories," he said. "A murderous cult, killing for their goddess, Kali."

Though hadn't he heard her name more recently? He paid no attention to superstitious nonsense or religion and couldn't place exactly where, not at the moment.

"Be glad you know little of it," McCready grumbled.

Armstrong took a deep breath, a sign Shaw remembered from childhood that a story was about to come. The man leaned against the examination table, more ready for bed than official duties.

"The cult was a brutal thing, performing widespread murder across India for five hundred years. That is until the British army broke them up in the '70s."

It was said with distinct pride, in the manner some would say "The sun never sets on the British empire." A quote Lassiter had said more than once.

"These lunatics believed that in the ritual murder of others they were serving Kali, goddess of death and destruction. Feeding her the souls of those murdered."

Armstrong shrugged, acknowledging he had no real knowledge on the finer points of the cult's beliefs.

"They murdered by strangulation," McCready added.

"Forbidden to shed blood, for some reason which would only make sense to them."

"But if the cult was broken—" Shaw said.

Armstrong waved a hand reminiscent of Lassiter's habit of dismissing inconvenient facts. It made Shaw's heart hurt to see it. "You know what fanatics are like. This is one or two hold-outs who have been lucky to avoid notice until now."

McCready looked at the commander, mouth open to speak, then glanced at Shaw and closed it again.

"Hmm, they'll be hidden somewhere nearby," Armstrong reasoned. "We'll send out patrols to search. They will be found, don't you worry about that."

"And you'll be going with those patrols, Shaw," McCready said. "That's later though. For now you can pack Lassiter's belongings to ship home."

Shaw opened his mouth to object, but instead found himself agreeing. It was the least he could do for this man who had shown him such kindness and friendship.

"Now, Shaw," McCready said.

"Yes, sir."

He didn't bother pointing out that the head doctor would be alone in a hospital full of patients. Let him discover that on his own. Shaw wandered out of the door.

Thuggees.

Kali.

How did they fit in with Lassiter?

He knocked on the door, knowing full well no one was inside to hear it. Somewhere inside was a crazy glimmer of hope that this had all been a mistake, a fever dream, or a hundred other such explanations he knew to be utter nonsense. His friend would never answer the door again.

Lassiter was gone.

Still, a knock was proper. Respectful.

Each door in this residential part of the hospital had a lock on it, which were seldom used. Either you trusted your fellow doctors or you didn't, and if you didn't it would be difficult living there ... Or at least trust them enough to know they wouldn't enter your rooms without permission. Even Adamson —who would slip his hand inside a man's pocket—wouldn't have broken that unspoken rule of privacy.

"May I come in, Larry?" he whispered, then spun his head left and right to make sure no one else was listening.

No answer. He would take that as an affirmative.

He also wondered if he was losing his mind.

No, the doctor within responded matter-of-factly, *you are merely in shock at what has happened. McCready sending you to take care of Lassiter's belongings is an insensitive gesture of power on his part and wholly inappropriate. This is your way of coping.*

It got him through the door.

The room inside was still the slovenly mess it had been last time he'd seen it. After opening the curtains he glanced around, struggling for a place to start in an overwhelming job. Finally he settled on removing the bed sheets for laundry. It started the string of tasks at least.

With the sheets removed and deposited in the hallway Shaw returned to the bed, pulling Larry's steamer trunk from its spot at the foot. It was mostly empty, like his own, except for a blanket which had likely not been used since coming to India.

Where to start in filling it?

He decided on the bureau, ferrying clothes from drawer to trunk, ensuring each article was folded neatly and placed with care for whoever would be on the receiving end. Who would that be? A mother or father who hadn't seen their son in years? Not a wife, Lassiter would have mentioned her at least in passing. Shaw realized how little he knew of his friend's background beyond his being a doctor, and that just served to emphasize the grief.

Items off a shelf came next, mementos and knickknacks. Books, mostly medical related, but one by Dickens which came as a pleasant surprise. *A Christmas Carol*—Shaw's personal favorite. Running one finger along the spine he wished with his entire soul he could speak with Lassiter about it. Had his friend enjoyed it? Had he read others by Dickens? With a deep sadness Shaw slipped it into the trunk. Doctors' paraphernalia such as a stethoscope came next, most of which would be returned to the hospital.

It took less than an hour to pack Lassiter's entire life, making the task all the sadder. So little to show for so many years served in India.

After closing and latching the trunk Shaw headed toward the door, stood in the frame about to leave when he grasped what was missing.

"The ugly idol."

He slipped back into the room determined to do a more thorough search, looking under the bed which he'd already glanced under, and slipping his hands to the bottom of the trunk to explore under that blanket. It wasn't there, of course. Lassiter carried it everywhere with him. If it was anywhere it would be in the pocket of his jacket.

Only, it wasn't.

Shaw had examined his body for wounds, and even given that he had not been looking for the idol, it would have still registered in his subconscious as being there.

It was gone.

Larry hadn't thrown it away, that much was certain. Lost then? Again, no. That idol was not an object Lassiter would have misplaced.

What was left?

Only one option.

Stolen.

Had Lassiter been killed for it?

CHAPTER THIRTEEN

"OUR TIME FOR MOURNING IS BRIEF," COMMANDER ARMSTRONG said at the head of all those assembled. He looked better than he had earlier in the day while standing over Lassiter's body. The uniform rested more in place, face shaved though covered in a sheen of sweat. "We have a murderer to catch, and catch him we shall."

The day had barely reached noon.

News of Lassiter's death had flown through the outpost and those not incapacitated from the illness stood at attention on the outpost's circular compound. Some of those partially recovered had forced themselves from bed to join the hunt.

No mention was made of Thuggees or Kali. No details on the murder. They searched for a stranger who had murdered Doctor Lassiter and that was enough.

"Bandagar is the most likely place for this ... villain, to be hiding."

Shaw would go to Bandagar with the men, helping in the investigation. McCready decided it would be best and Shaw agreed. He had a rapport with the people and would be able to keep it from becoming too heavy-handed, hopefully. Privates

Chattha and Sandhu, two Indian men who'd joined the British army, were also part of the search. Neither was native to Bandagar, but both were more native than all these British wandering about demanding answers.

Travelers passing through looking for work were not uncommon in Bandagar, but after a prolonged day of questioning it was found there were no real strangers. Most were family members who had returned from other parts of India and could be vouched for, though in the absence of better suspects these people were questioned well past the point of allaying suspicions.

A dead end.

Time wasted.

Day two found them split into several smaller groups and sent out to investigate the surrounding area. The strategy for these marches was to head in one direction for half of the day, searching for signs of someone holed up along the way, then, after lunch, turn around and come back by another route.

Shaw wondered if his uncle honestly expected any progress to come from this process.

If it was indeed the Thuggees—and the commander and McCready appeared to recognize the handiwork of the cult— then they must be long gone from the area by now.

"Doctor Shaw?" a voice said. "Yer comin' with us?"

He turned to see Corporal Walsh with some other soldiers, all smart and alert in their red jackets and white helmets, rifles slung over their shoulders. Smells of sweat and gunpowder accompanied them like a perfume. Shaw wore the familiar blue doctor's jacket which differentiated him from other soldiers, but he'd strapped on his revolver before leaving the room. An item which had remained at the bottom of his trunk since that first day he'd arrived. It felt conspicuous and unnatural, as if he were beating a drum and screaming for attention.

No one noticed.

"I guess they thought you might need a doctor along, Walsh."

The other soldiers all chuckled, more to break the tension of the day than anything else. The joke had been instinctive rather than heartfelt and Walsh knew it, giving a subdued grin. Just like that Shaw had been somewhat accepted into the group, if not as a friend—because officers and enlisted men did not buddy up—then as an ally, or at worst an oddity.

Lieutenant Shaw? Oh, he's all right, for an officer.

Off to one side Privates Chattha and Sandhu waited, not quite part of the group, not quite a group of their own. The other soldiers didn't exclude them so much as not going out of their way to include them.

"Good morning," Shaw said to the two Indian soldiers.

Chattha and Sandhu returned his greeting without coming closer to join. It was something Shaw wished he knew how to get around, but today was not the day for it.

Ever the Saviour of India, hmm, Shaw? Lassiter's voice echoed, and he agreed with a sad nod.

A captain came at a brisk pace, map in hands. "Fall in, lads."

The soldiers lined up for the march. Only Shaw and the captain wore sidearms while each soldier carried a rifle, straps over their right shoulders. None looked like they relished the idea of a walk on such a blistering hot day—and every day in India was blistering hot from experience. At the same time, each had a look of grim determination to get the job done and find this culprit. This wasn't an aimless march for the sake of marching.

"Thank you for joining us, Doctor," the captain said.

It was always *Doctor* from the army officers, not his military rank, even though the doctors served in the army as much as any regular soldier. The rank of doctor was more important than the rank of lieutenant, or so Shaw believed.

Their squad left the outpost in neat formation, double line of twelve soldiers with the captain leading. The accompanying doctor was not expected to march in line like the rest, but was not to be at the front. Not much point in bringing a doctor if they were the first to fall victim to danger. Likewise they were not last in line as that was more vulnerable to potential ambush, though it seemed less likely in the daylight.

Once outside the outpost a suitable distance the soldiers were allowed to take a more relaxed formation and chat among themselves as they went. Common practice on marches, as long as the men kept their wits about them and didn't become too rambunctious.

"Don't you worry, doc," Walsh said, ambling up beside him. "We'll find Doctor Lassiter's killer."

Shaw gave a nod, not trusting himself to speak and hoping Walsh wouldn't go too far on this topic.

"I heard he'd been strangled," a private beside Walsh said. "Right out there in the street."

Walsh gave the man an elbow. The private made a face, realizing he'd spoken a touch too freely.

"Musta had powerful hands," another soldier further up said, on the edge of audible.

Yes. The hands of a madman.

Shaw had asked his civilian friends, cautiously, about the Thuggees and their goddess while searching Bandagar yesterday. What he'd discovered was the stuff of nightmares.

Thuggees worshipped Kali, goddess of death and destruction, from the 1300s to less than twenty years ago—far too recent to say they were smashed for all time in his own humble opinion. These people performed their silent murders on the roads and highways around India, killing mostly native men while avoiding the murder of women and Europeans.

Lassiter's murder was a contradiction then, incongruous.

Children of those murdered would be adopted into the cult, raised to believe as all Thuggees did, that in the ritual murder of others they were performing a sacred service. Without these murders Kali, goddess of death and destruction whom they fearfully worshipped, would return to destroy all mankind.

That such preposterous rot should exist in modern, enlightened times was ridiculous. Irrational thinking was what happened when a people were suppressed within their own country. Shaw shook his head, though whether in disbelief or a reminder to keep his mouth shut he wasn't sure.

The sun beat down, the air stifling and humid. Ahead the men continued their conversation in hushed tones, looking back at times to see if he'd overheard. Shaw played dumb, listening without giving sign. The topic must have been well worn by now. Nothing of much interest happened around the base, and the murder of a doctor and officer was considerable news. These were the rehashed thoughts on a subject more than a day old.

Walsh had hung back to keep pace beside him and gave a sympathetic shrug. "Sorry."

"It's fine, Walsh," Shaw said, not wanting to talk about it and hoping the other man would let the subject drop.

"You'd think we would have noticed someone strange hangin' about the outpost," Walsh continued, changing topic slightly.

Shaw opened his mouth, ready to stop the conversation before it got started when the words struck him and he did remember someone unusual. That man and his boy who'd come into the hospital a couple of weeks back. They'd both reacted to the sight of Lassiter's idol, and wasn't that where he'd heard the mention of Kali? Surely they hadn't treated Lassiter's own murderer and made this whole situation possible.

"Doc?"

Shaw started, realizing Walsh had been talking. "Sorry, what did you say?"

"Just asked if the heat was gettin' to you. These walks ain't easy."

Shaw waved the concern aside. "I'm quite all right, Walsh. Lost in thought I suppose."

Walsh nodded, returning his attention to their day's purpose. "Davies suggested a trail he'd seen on an earlier march. That's where we're headed. A few yards off the usual path but a possibility."

"And we have to investigate every possibility," Shaw said.

They followed the road to the trail Walsh had mentioned, then that trail until it became a rough path. This path went on for some time before branching off onto two narrow, single-file paths which barely qualified as animal runs.

"Right path first," the captain said.

It went on for ten or fifteen minutes before coming to an end in a sheer rock wall. Peering up saw it continue for at least thirty feet.

"Not going any further from here," one soldier offered.

The captain looked around, finding nothing to contradict the soldier's comment, and led them back to the spot where the two paths had branched off.

"Quick break," the captain called. "Five minutes then we try the other path."

The soldiers relaxed, drinking from their canteens, seeking some shade. All the usual actions soldiers have been doing since soldiering began. All too soon the five minutes was done.

"Right." The captain got to his feet, securing his own water. "Let's get moving."

With some low groans the soldiers lined up again.

"Come on, lads," the captain said, starting down the path.

One by one the soldiers followed their captain, with Shaw toward the back, two soldiers taking position behind him.

"Wouldn't want to get caught out here at night," one soldier said.

At that mention a few of the less experienced soldiers looked around, as if night would fall right then and there, though the day had not even reached noon. They each gripped the straps of their rifles tighter, eyes furtive. Shaw remembered the night he'd seen the Maut with vivid recall and did his best to keep the uncertainty from his own eyes.

Another fifteen-minute hike following this path and the group marched into a wide clearing surrounded by bush and scrub.

"Another dead end," the captain said with an annoyed shrug, turning in a circle as the others joined him.

Each soldier did the same, as if needing personal confirmation that this was indeed a dead end.

A waste of time. Lassiter's murderer was not here and Shaw could only hope one of the other groups had had better luck.

"Sir, look at this," Walsh said, heading across the clearing.

The captain followed and examined some bushes where Walsh had come to a stop. "I don't see anything, corporal."

"Couple'a broken branches. See? Someone's passed through here recently."

"Or some*thing*," another private muttered.

The captain heard, glared, and then nodded his acceptance of the clue. He grabbed at the bush and gave a tug, rewarded with it coming away in his hands, unattached to the ground at all.

"Huh! Suspicious enough I'd say." The captain threw the bush aside to view a newly exposed path. "Volunteer?"

Walsh stepped forward. Without a word he unslung his rifle and entered the path, the others falling into step behind him.

The path turned out to continue on, winding through trees and bushes, into rocky, hilly terrain. On either side came massive boulders with an upward slant to the path. Progress became more of an effort, each step a danger with rocks under foot threatening to twist an ankle.

"There's no way anyone came through here," the private who'd mentioned being out here at night said.

Ahead Walsh stopped and gestured for the rest to come

forward. The squad moved closer together to take in this new discovery.

"A cave?" one soldier said.

"That's bloody ominous, innit?" another replied.

A hundred feet or so from them an opening lay against the side of a sheer rock wall, as if it had been painted there by some skilled artist. The path they'd followed continued around to the right. Dead leaves and browning, sunblasted grass occupied the space between.

"Well, then," the captain said, as if he'd expected to find this exact cave. "Exactly the suspicious sort of place we need to look into."

The men tensed, ready for orders, each staring at the cave as if it were a cobra waiting to strike.

For Shaw's part he was thinking how cave air was cooler than outside air. How soon before the captain decreed it safe for a non-soldier to enter?

"Right, men—" the captain began.

A shout came from ahead. One man raced out of the cave opening, hurtling toward the soldiers through the high grass like a runaway horse cart. Eyes wild. Right arm flailing while the left remained hidden behind his back. He was a native of India as far as Shaw could tell, dressed in traditional white kurta, scraggly beard broken only by the man's grimace.

"Ready, men," the captain warned, all business again.

The squad snapped to attention, rifles levelled. The first row kneeled while the second positioned behind, allowing a clear shot for each man. But was this the one they hunted, or some hermit unhappy at being disturbed? Either could explain the wildness of his expression and agitated state. Shaw moved to stand behind the captain, squinting at this approaching man.

"Stop!" the captain barked, drawing his own sidearm. He repeated the warning in Hindi. *"Ruken!"*

The man didn't stop, or even slow his approach. Instead he

drew the concealed arm from behind his back, holding a length of wire. A garotte, ready to strangle.

"Halt right there! *Ruken!*" the captain repeated, arm out and palm vertical. "Last warning."

The man was now no more than ten feet away.

"Chattha," the captain said.

Private Chattha fired without hesitation. The bullet caught the approaching man high in his chest and knocked him backward into the dust where he lay unmoving, garotte still grasped in one tight fist.

No one lowered their rifles other than Chattha who reloaded, quick and precise.

"That our murderer then?" Walsh asked.

The captain shrugged. "It would seem so."

Not the man he and Lassiter had treated.

"Well," another soldier said. "I guess that's—"

Another yell, another rapidly approaching native, this one dressed in a much more ragged kurta, streaked with dirt. This man's face was more familiar to Shaw.

"No," he whispered.

But it was. The patient Lassiter and he had treated back at the hospital. He was wild-eyed and raving but there was no mistaking him.

"Sandhu. Fire," the captain ordered.

This time the second of the Indian soldiers took the approaching madman down—was the captain testing them for loyalty? Sandhu lowered his rifle and spat in the direction of the dead man.

"Personal dislike?" Shaw asked, though his attention was focused on the man he'd set back on the road to murder.

"These Thuggees are a blot on our country and a mockery to my faith."

"Hold on!" The captain spun around. "No one said a word about Thuggees. Those were wiped out years ago."

Private Sandhu gave a slight bow of his head in acknowledgment to his captain, but that agreement didn't come anywhere near his eyes. A deep anger smoldered there, and in Private Chattha's as well. This was personal, a reaction which had come from generations of terror inflicted on the Indian people by this cult. Sandhu busied himself reloading his rifle.

The captain ordered the squad forward but before most had taken their first step another hurtled from the cave, a second man on his heels.

"Walsh. Martin," the captain ordered.

"On the right," Walsh said, picking his man.

Both soldiers fired, taking their targets in the torso. Martin's spun before falling.

Four dead men littered the ground, yet another two sprinted from the cave before the squad could advance.

"It seems like a distraction," Shaw muttered.

The captain glanced at him then back at the approaching men, giving one quick nod, whether of respect, surprise, or simple agreement Shaw couldn't guess. The captain picked two soldiers to fire while the previous ones reloaded.

"You four," the captain said, selecting those who had not yet shot. "Follow that path and see if there's a back door."

"Yes, sir."

The four started down the path as three more deranged men came hurtling from the cave as fast as anyone could. The speed of lunacy.

"Rotate through men," the captain said, drawing his revolver. "Keep the order while others reload. You four, keep moving, quickly."

Three soldiers fired while the chosen group rushed along the path to the right, rifles pointed upward to avoid shooting a friend in the back. They disappeared up the rocky trail as the remaining eight soldiers inched forward, meeting the lunatics who came in earnest now. Shaw stood near the captain, powerless and wishing for the safety of the outpost. Eight men, plus the captain, before an endless storm of Thuggees with their mad eyes and silent attacks. So much for Commander Armstrong's assertion that this was one lone holdout.

Wave after wave of fanatic opposition barrelled toward them at their highest speed. The soldiers fired their rifles then fell back to reload while the next group took their turn. The captain too had fired his Tranter, emptying it.

"Doctor," the captain shouted. "Your revolver."

He unclipped the holster but went no further. "I ..."

"Give it to me, man."

Relieved he was not being asked to shoot Shaw whipped the gun out and gave it over to the captain. The man tossed his empty back.

"Reload that."

Shaw did, fumbling with the bullets then performing a second exchange for his own now empty pistol.

The soldiers gave ground. One step. Two. Three.

The Thuggees were terrifying, and much too close.

Firing and reloading were no longer an option, though the captain still managed one last shot from his revolver while drawing his sabre. The soldiers, more experienced than the cultists, levelled their bayonets to dispatch the enemy. They had superior weapons and experience, but the Thuggees had strength, numbers, and a complete lack of concern for personal safety.

The madmen were on them.

To Shaw's right Walsh went down under three of the silent men, one with hands closing around the soldier's neck.

"No!"

Shaw rushed forward, kicking one man across the face like a football. The lunatic rolled away, lying in the dust, dazed and scrambling to recover. The other two didn't acknowledge the attack and continued about their business. Grabbing Walsh's dropped rifle Shaw swung it like a club, the stock taking the first Thuggee across the temple and dropping him like a cow at slaughter. The final man jumped to his feet and rushed him, as if thought and action were one. Shaw lifted the rifle, hoping to intimidate the man but knew it to be a useless effort. The madman would impale himself on the bayonet first.

No. Shaw shook his head. He couldn't take a life, not this way.

"I'm a doctor," he said, hating the feeble sound of begging to his voice.

A shot rang out and his would-be assailant fell.

The captain, holding two lunatics off with his sabre, had shot his final bullet into the man threatening Shaw. Walsh forced his feet under him and grabbed his rifle, ready to defend though obviously groggy.

Beyond the battle came a cry. Three of their four comrades who'd headed around back emerged from the cave opening, rushing toward the battle. Each fired as they came closer then reloaded, fired then reloaded, taking down the cultists caught between two superior forces.

And still the madmen refused to surrender.

The soldiers on this side rallied and pushed them back, the rifles toward the cave entrance firing, one after another after another. In the end the soldiers had the superior weapons. Garrottes and fists against rifles and bayonets had little hope, even when fueled by madness. Still, the madmen had had the numbers, had been on the verge of overwhelming the soldiers and there were bruised throats to show for it. What if they'd stayed in one group rather than sending those four men around back? Or if the cultists had simply waited for them to enter the cave before attacking, where it would have been more cramped and rifles less effective.

What if *their* group had been caught in a pinch attack instead?

A shudder rippled through Shaw at the thought.

It was a mercy they couldn't know the answers to what-ifs.

The men, wide-eyed and breathing heavy, rounded up those surviving Thuggees who had only been wounded, or had fallen to a bayonet and still struggled to rise and continue the fight. These were tied, hands behind backs and one to another in a chain.

The man Shaw had kicked away from Walsh was added to the group before he could get full senses back, while the one he'd hit with the rifle butt remained immobile in the dirt. Shaw knelt beside this man, feeling for a pulse, then listening for a heartbeat, finding neither. The man's eyes were open but unseeing, the side of his head a patch of purplish-black bruising.

Had he hit him *that* hard?

"Thanks, doc," Walsh said from just behind. "They really had me there."

Shaw nodded, not looking around. Walsh said nothing more on the subject, leaving him to his thoughts.

This man was dead. Not unusual given all that had happened, but *he* had killed this madman. Yes, it was only a difference of time, for the survivors would surely be executed, but he was a healer, not a soldier. His calling was to restore life, not take it.

"There *was* another entrance, Captain," a soldier said. One of those four who'd gone around the back. "Or an exit I suppose. Don't know how many got out before we arrived."

"Any left inside?"

"Some," the man said. "Murphy's in there guarding the few we caught. Bunch of tunnels branching off the main one that'll need searching. We rushed through to catch them in that pinch."

"Well done. Tell Murphy to bring his prisoners and add them to the rest," the captain said, once again in control of the situation. He turned to the soldiers, rifles unslung and ready to shoot any prisoner who decided to renew their attack. "Two of you men continue guarding that lot. The rest of you check out that cave."

The group of fanatics stood, bound one to another and casting glares of malice at the soldiers. Ropes held them back more than the threat of shooting. Some needed the attention of a doctor, but bared their teeth at Shaw when he approached to offer aid.

"Leave them for now," the captain advised.

Instead Shaw wandered after the soldiers headed for the cave, looking for some distraction from his own thoughts, a place to be of help.

"Let the men enter first, please, Doctor," the captain said.

Shaw neither looked back nor spoke, but followed the others into the cave. Last in line.

Inside, torches flickered every ten feet, increasing visibility while their oily, black smoke detracted from it. Better than the alternative of utter blackness. The air inside was immediately cooler, with a steady breeze drifting in through the front opening and traveling toward the back. Somewhere ahead water dripped with slow steady rhythm, the scent of wet stone drifting to the entry.

The soldiers followed the passage toward the first of those branching off, rifles at the ready. Shaw followed, no real aim in mind other than to escape the heat and distract his mind from what he'd done. As they neared the offshoot he found his attention grabbed by a roof-to-floor drawing on the opposite wall. Colorful with its yellow, white, black, and red, the drawing depicted Kali with her multiple arms and judging expression. The skill of this artist was competent, but no better than any primitive drawing. Another similar depiction followed, then another, pulling Shaw deeper into the cave. The artist's skill improved while each picture evolved further. Kali's arms became less defined, more the tentacles of some monstrous octopus, her head going from feminine to bulbous, eyes flat and dead. Staring.

He grabbed a torch, following the pictographs further.

All color had been dropped in favor of deepest black, with some chalk white for highlight and depth. The details of this new version could give a grown man chills in the bleak flickering light.

Kali stared back.

The coolness of the cave no longer felt comforting. It was damp now, chilling. It clung to the clothing and worked its way through to lay against the skin.

Shaw shivered, but continued.

On his next step his foot kicked against some object, sending it clattering across the passage. He followed the trajectory as it came up against the opposite wall inside deeper shadows. For a moment he hesitated, then went to the item, picked it up.

Lassiter's ugly idol.

"But ... why would this be left behind?" he muttered.

They'd killed Lassiter for it, hadn't they? Some ghastly treasure to them. So why leave it behind when they'd fled? Had one of them dropped it?

No. This wasn't an object one left behind, or lost.

It weighed more than any object its size should, and was unpleasantly warm to the touch, like the barely throbbing heart of someone close to death. It matched these final hideous pictures on the cave walls, filling him with revulsion ... and yet ... there was some strangeness. Something fascinating he needed to examine more later.

When he was alone.

"Doc?"

"Hmm?" The familiar voice and approaching footsteps brought his attention back around. He slipped the strange find into one pocket. "Yes, Walsh?"

"You all right?"

"Me? Yes, fine."

"Sorry, you were standin' so still I thought you'd had some kinda attack."

He clapped one hand against the corporal's shoulder. "I'm fine, Walsh."

The soldier accepted that and pointed toward a branch he'd come from. "Found an altar or somethin' down that one."

"An altar? You mean, for … sacrifice?"

"Nah." Walsh shook his head. "Too small, unless they were sacrificin' animals. More like somethin' for display."

"A display?"

For an idol, maybe?

Walsh shrugged. "Whatever was there, it's gone now."

"Taken by the ones who got away?"

"I guess." Walsh looked over his shoulder. "Place gives me the creepy-crawlies."

"I was thinking much the same thing."

It wasn't simply all they'd been through. An oppressive attitude permeated this cave, a sensation of being observed, scrutinized. As if—

A shout from behind them.

"Got another one!"

A soldier emerged from a cave branch prodding a child ahead of him.

"Good job, Davies," Walsh said.

It was the boy from the hospital. The lunatic's son. He gave no struggle, walking with eyes straight ahead and betraying no emotion, resigned to his capture.

Walsh fell into step behind this procession, leaving Shaw to once again bring up the rear, following until they all passed into the sunlight and warmth of the day. Out here it all seemed less oppressive, except for the dead bodies of cultists everywhere.

The boy was secured to the train of nine surviving lunatics, still staring straight ahead. The other prisoners clenched their hands and glared at the soldiers, making no secret of what they would do if freed.

"But ... he's just a boy," Shaw muttered, then demanding of the captain, "What will happen to him?"

"To who ...?" The man turned and looked as if only now realizing any difference existed between this boy and the others. He didn't show any particular concerned. "Same will happen to the others I imagine."

"Execution? He's just a child!"

"Child or not, there's no denying he was with these madmen."

Shaw pressed his lips together, searching for a better argument.

"Sorry, Doctor, but this boy's fate is in Commander Armstrong's hands."

"The commander. Of course."

Yes. He would speak with his uncle as soon as they returned. The commander would see the difference between this boy and those lunatic animals.

Thoughts rolling, argument prepared, Shaw fell into step with the group as the hike back to the outpost began. One hand rested inside his pocket, against the idol, finger tracing the indecipherable wording.

Yes, that was what it was.

Words.

CHAPTER FOURTEEN

"He's just a boy," Shaw said, pleaded, repeating the same argument he'd used with the captain.

"And one of those bloody lunatics," McCready added. "Just another murderer."

Armstrong looked up from his desk, eyes going from one to the other then back again, as if watching tennis.

"He may have become one in time," Shaw agreed, "but he's only, what, ten years old? Eleven?"

"Old enough to kill."

Armstrong drummed his fingers against the desktop and Shaw focused on him.

"Surely you can't agree with executing a *child*."

Armstrong glanced to McCready, who stared back, arms crossed, his argument made.

The commander cleared his throat. "Both McCready and I have more experience with these lunatics than you do, Shaw. We've seen children indoctrinated into the cult before and I tell you, I doubt this boy can be rehabilitated."

Shaw goggled at his uncle, speechless, the life of this child slipping away from him.

"However," Armstrong continued, "since you feel so strongly about it, what do you suggest? Find a family in Bandagar to take the boy in?"

McCready huffed out a bitter laugh. "Oh, I'm sure they'd be happy for the extra mouth to feed, if you could find one to take in a Thuggee cultist."

Armstrong glared at the use of the word *Thuggee.* McCready gave no acknowledgment but made no further comment.

No, a local family might not be best. An impulsive idea entered Shaw's mind and was out of his mouth before he could truly consider it. "I will take him in."

McCready made a disgusted noise and Armstrong raised one hand to silence the man.

"You will, will you?" The commander narrowed a gaze on Shaw, considering, tapping one finger against his desktop. "Are you sure on that? It would mean he is *your* responsibility, Shaw. Anything he does is likewise your fault."

His fault. His responsibility. Shaw nodded, accepting the terms his uncle laid before him with complete enthusiasm, would have agreed to anything at that moment to save this boy. It was the right course of action, he was sure of it. Just as he was sure no one without an uncle as commander would have been allowed such an option. In the distance, he could once again hear Lassiter calling him the saviour of the Indian people, though it was soft and without judgement.

"Very well, I will release this boy to your care. He will be staying in *your* rooms," Armstrong continued. "Under your supervision."

"Well," McCready grumbled. "At least the first person he murders will be you, Shaw."

Armstrong once again waved him to silence while still staring at Shaw. "Make whatever arrangements you need to. You can free him in the morning."

Shaw opened his mouth to thank his uncle, to tell him he needn't worry about this, that he'd made the right decision.

"Dismissed," the commander said.

Shaw closed his mouth. With a nod of thanks he headed out the office door and along the hallway, heading toward the cells and his new charge. There would be much they needed to talk about before tomorrow.

"A moment, Shaw," McCready called.

With an inward sigh he turned back toward the head doctor, ready for further lecture on the nature of this boy. Or perhaps this would be a general tongue-lashing, reprimand, or a segue into some outlandish order.

"You saved a man's life," McCready said. "At the cave."

Shaw was taken aback that this part of the story had already made its way to his superior, and undoubtedly the commander as well. So, this was what the reprimand would concern, the life he'd taken. That was fine. He'd done his own upbraiding on the march back from the cave. Part of saving this boy was about doing what was right, but another was making up for that life he'd taken, balancing the scales inside his own soul.

"It's a difficult action," McCready said, "for a doctor to take a life."

Shaw agreed, lips pressed into a tight line, not trusting himself to speak.

"There are times when we must remove a limb for a patient to survive," McCready said. "Think of this death as the removal of some greater disease."

Without waiting for comment from Shaw or to see if his words had effect, the older doctor returned to the commander's office, leaving a bewildered and uncertain Shaw behind.

Had McCready just tried to be supportive?

"You'll be my assistant," Shaw said, standing just inside the door.

The boy gazed back, face blank.

"If you want to be, of course." Though Shaw knew full well the other option for this boy was not a tolerable one.

No reaction. No change to that expression.

The only furniture in this cell was a bed, which the child sat on, and a wooden chair. Shaw crossed the room and pulled the chair closer, taking a seat. He leaned forward to be on level with the boy's eyes, but not so close to be threatening.

The boy spoke English, or at least understood it. Yes, at the hospital he'd reacted as if following the conversation, hadn't he? Or was that imagination, caused by Shaw's own desires? Would the boy have to be taught a language along with everything else? Shaw wished now he'd taken the time to learn more Hindi.

"Do you ... understand?"

Still no reaction.

The boy was unflinching, back as straight as a beam. The eyes were emotionless, yet drilled into Shaw.

Shaw leaned back again, wondering on options. Private Sandhu or Chattha could translate for him—

"Why?"

Lost in thought, Shaw had almost missed the word. It hadn't been whispered, or deferent in any way, as some of the Indian people were with him. One short reply, as much statement as question.

"Why?" Shaw said, scrambling to understand. "Why what? Why will you be my assistant?"

The boy looked toward the window. Outside construction of a scaffold had begun for the upcoming executions. That structure held a definite message. A show of force. A show of control. Elsewhere in this makeshift prison the nine Thuggees howled and screamed in anticipation of their deaths. Defiant and mad to the end.

"Ah, you mean why will you not be out there with them?"
The boy nodded. Once.

"We do not execute children."

The boy's eyes betrayed neither belief nor disbelief. There would never be a discussion over the debate he'd had with Armstrong and McCready. Some words are better kept hidden.

When it was clear no more would be coming Shaw cleared his throat, looking for the next topic. At least he had confirmation the boy understood him. It was a step in the right direction, but what was the next one?

He was making this up as he went. There were no examples from his childhood on how best a man could speak to a child and provide comfort. Lord knows he hadn't had anything of the sort as a child. He'd spent more time at boarding schools than home with his family, and when he did return home for holidays it was as an unfortunate burden. Oh, not to his mother. No, she was always happy to see him, but a boy wants attention from his father, too.

"Very well, let's start with your name."

The boy stared at him.

"What is your name?" Shaw rephrased, thinking the original might have been unclear.

No response. Just a continuing focus with those emotionless eyes, not a twitch to a muscle.

"Ah, well, I'll go first then. My name is Doctor Archibald Shaw. You can call me Shaw, like everyone else seems to, or Doctor if that's more comfortable for you. Not many people other than my mother use my given name."

Though he could hear Lassiter calling him *Archie* and would happily be called that to his dying day if it would bring his friend back.

At the mention of a mother the boy's eyes shifted right and back again. A memory? A regret? Had this boy's parents been murdered? Had he been forced to watch?

"No? Well, no point rushing it, I suppose," Shaw said in his most amiable voice, getting to his feet. It seemed that they'd reached the extent of their interactions for now. Trust took time. "In any case, you'll be staying with me. I'll need time to get an extra bed set up so I'm afraid you'll have one night in here."

But he was talking to himself. The boy had drawn back, horror clear in his expression. Glancing down to see what had been so alarming Shaw found the idol there, it's head poking out the top of his pocket. He'd forgotten it was there and reached for it, but the boy made a gurgling noise and retreated further. Shaw dropped the hand back to his side.

"Bad," the boy said, wide eyes still on the idol.

Given that the word was uttered in English, Shaw took it as warning for himself. Shaw wanted to tell him it was just an ugly idol, that it couldn't harm him, but the look on the boy's face stopped his words. It was the most emotion the boy had shown and it was pure terror.

"Very well," Shaw said, one hand out in a calming gesture. "I won't touch it."

With a jiggle of his jacket the idol lay flat inside the pocket. He buttoned the flap, vaguely wondering how it had come to be standing upright anyway.

No. Unimportant.

Right now Shaw had a valuable opportunity to gain this boy's trust, to show him that his concerns and fears were taken seriously. What this boy must have gone through! Raised by lunatics, forced to witness untold horrors, his head filled with superstitions. It was a travesty.

The boy made another gurgling noise and Shaw refocused on him, realizing his mind had been allowed to wander. That look of panic remained on the boy's face and Shaw followed that gaze back to his own hand. It was halfway inside his pocket once again.

Shaw withdrew his hand, as if finding a cobra there. He had no memory of unfastening his pocket.

"How in the world ...?"

Thoughts of Lassiter returned, sequestered in his room, coming out disheveled. The idol had consumed his every waking hour at the end. Had it been more than his own personal mania? An outside influence?

Preposterous.

And yet, his hand drifted back toward the pocket, unbidden. He sealed the flap then removed his jacket, rolling it into a tight ball to deposit by the door. There!

Memories of his finger tracing those letters as they returned from the cave played through his mind, bringing a desire to pick the idol up. Shaw kept his attention, denying that pull.

He sat again, looking the boy in his wide eyes.

"I'll ... get rid of it ..."

Yes, that would be the wise action to take. This thing needed to be disposed of ... but his friend had been murdered for it—of that he was certain—and to just destroy it, or drop it down some well would be to make Lassiter's death that much more meaningless. Shipping it back to Lassiter's family, or Middlemarch's, would be no favor to them.

No. This was all rationalization for keeping it himself. He saw it. Once more he focused on the boy, placing one hand over his heart, though unsure the gesture held the same meaning here in India.

"I promise you, I will dispose of this idol."

The tone to Shaw's words, or perhaps just his expression, got through and the boy relaxed again. His eyes went from Shaw to the bundled idol and back again. Shaw's words, or the promise he'd made, galvanized his own mind as well and pushed that influence from him.

And, he knew exactly where to put it.

"I'll do it right now." Shaw hopped back to his feet. "I'll be back shortly with food and clothing."

"Singh."

Halfway to the door Shaw turned back, not sure he'd heard correctly. Was he being asked to sing? He didn't have much of a voice for carrying a tune.

Once again the boy sat on his bunk, composure returned, as if he'd never retreated.

"Doctor," he said, pointing one finger toward Shaw. Then he placed that same hand against his chest while looking Shaw in the eyes, as if speaking to a child. "Singh."

"Oh! Of course." Shaw smiled, embarrassed that under-standing hadn't come sooner. "I'm pleased to meet you, Singh."

Should he shake the boy's hand? No, he had a better gesture of friendship and trust. Scooping his balled up jacket under one arm, Shaw prepared to leave.

That nagging question still itched at Shaw's brain. Why would they have left this idol behind? Singh might have some insight, but now was not the time to ask.

Time enough for that later.

After leaving Singh, Shaw headed straight across the compound for the storage house, his idol bundled inside of the jacket.

No! Not his *idol. The* idol.

He gritted his teeth and forced his attention elsewhere.

The half-completed gallows filled the open space between stables and barracks, four legs and platform already erected. This construction signified the opposite of all he stood for. And yet, he too had resorted to violence and killing when the time had come.

McCready's words returned to him: *Think of this as the removal of some greater disease.*

There was some truth, some logic, woven into the older doctor's words, but they held a jaded view which Shaw wasn't comfortable with. They were too resigned to the fact, giving carte blanche to kill again if circumstances permitted. He didn't want to ever be that cavalier with the idea.

Yet one certainty rattled inside his mind: Saving Walsh's life by the killing of one deranged lunatic was a choice he would repeat without hesitation. That bothered him, but maybe as long as it did so he wouldn't look into the mirror and see McCready staring back.

The thoughts went round and round inside his head, like that snake eating its own tail.

At the door he nodded to the man on guard who snapped off a smart salute. A new man here, confirmed by the gesture. No one saluted doctors and Shaw preferred it that way.

"An item for the museum."

"Yes, sir," the guard said, all attention to his crucial duty.

Anything going into storage was permitted, and any officer could deposit an item without difficulty. Retrieval of that same item would need the commander's written authorization.

Inside Shaw headed toward the back, where crates of items found in exploration of the area were held. These were awaiting the next shipping day to England. Oddities and curiosities mostly, destined for display or storage in the British Museum. One crate sat open, ready for his deposit.

Should this idol go to the museum though?

Wouldn't it be better on the bottom of the ocean?

Enough! It was an ugly idol and no more. He'd allowed the stress of the day and Lassiter's sad obsession to color his own impressions. It was all silliness.

Ridiculous to dispose of something for a trick of the imagination.

Was he that weak of mind?

"I am not."

Shaw focused on the crate, bundle held in both hands. The museum had enough treasures already. More than they could display. It wouldn't be right to relegate such an item to storage.

"I should keep it."

But he'd made a promise to Singh.

Singh doesn't need to know.

"Doctor?"

Yes, he could keep it in his steamer trunk.

"Doctor," the voice repeated, closer.

He turned to see the guard, the new man. "Yes?"

"Is everything well? You've been in here a long time."

"I have?"

"Yes, sir. Almost an hour now."

An hour? How was that possible? He'd just entered, hadn't he?

"Are you going to place it in the crate, sir?"

Shaw looked at the idol, still wrapped in his coat, still held in his tight hands, and wanted to say no.

"I made a promise," he said instead.

"Uh, yes, sir."

Before Shaw could think about it he dropped the entire bundle, coat *and* idol, into the crate and slammed the lid closed. With a shaky smile to the soldier he turned and headed for the door, wanting to put distance between himself and that *thing*.

Outside he forced a tuneless whistle and recrossed the compound, headed toward his rooms, pushing thoughts of ugly idols and crazed cults from his mind. A new mission filled his mind: To bring clothing and food for Singh, and set up a second bed in his room.

With each step he chided himself for allowing imagination to run rampant in regards to that idol.

Ridiculous!

And now he would need to request a replacement jacket as well.

CHAPTER FIFTEEN

Bandagar, India — July 28th, 1878

Dearest Mother,

How bleak it all must sound in reading this. I considered destroying this letter and beginning again, but prefer the unedited version. It is just more honest.

In any case it is, I'll admit, a bleak time for me. The knowledge that I have a child's welfare in my hands encourages me to get out of bed each morning.

Lassiter's death has hit me hard, as did the knowledge that such evil as the Thuggee cult could exist in this day and age.

Uncle Freddy won't admit publicly that our nine prisoners were Thuggee cultists, but that didn't stop the word from spreading. The soldiers who'd been at that cave had been warned by their captain against repeating unfounded theories and with that threat hanging over their heads it took a full twelve hours for the first whispered rumour to make its way back to me in the hospital. From there it spread like grassfire …

Four days later, when time came for the hangings, most at the outpost were in attendance, as well as at least a hundred from Bandagar. This mixed crowd of soldier and civilian packed the compound, spilling onto the road leading back to town. Those at the outpost were there to see justice. The people of Bandagar—much like Privates Chattha and Sandhu who themselves were positioned near the gallows—had come to see a blight on their society stamped out.

A public execution was no place for a child, especially not one who knew all of those being put to death. Shaw kept Singh in the hospital that afternoon, busy with an extended list of tasks, or so he thought. When time came, he found the boy at a window two down from his own, making no effort to conceal himself, arms at his side. Shaw debated for a full minute, propriety warring with instinct.

Yes, this wasn't any event a child should *have* to see, but it was conceivable this was something Singh *needed* to see. "I think you would have a better view from over here."

Singh made his way across the room, taking place beside Shaw without comment or hesitation. They waited together, unspeaking. Shaw wondered if there were any words which could be said in this matter. He didn't excel at small talk and Singh didn't seem to appreciate it anyway.

At least they were a sufficient distance from the gallows. That would save Singh from the more gruesome details, and increased Shaw's confidence in his decision. A set of field glasses perched on the window ledge, left there for some unknown reason at least a month ago. He felt no need to pick them up and hoped Singh wouldn't show an interest either. The entire spectacle was grim enough without getting a closer view of it.

People milled about, reminding Shaw of the crowd at the train station the day he'd arrived. Only here people of both Indian and European background stood together, united against a common enemy.

It would start soon.

An elephant's trumpet blast rose above the din of those assembled, interrupting conversations and pulling all attention to the road. Necks craned and people rose on toes for better view.

"What ...?"

Lumbering up the road leading through Bandagar came four elephants, covered carriages on top swaying with each step. The animals were decorated in colorful symbols, with a cap over their foreheads, gleaming gold in the sunlight.

Another trumpet blast.

Now Shaw did bring those field glasses up, pulled in by the spectacle and his own curiosity. "Prince Kanwar. It must be."

Unable to proceed further the massive animals came to a stop and kneeled, discharging several people, each less ornate than the elephant which had brought them, except one man. He dressed in the silkiest of robes, beads and jewels woven into the fabric. His headdress held a magnificent, jeweled feather at the center.

The Prince of Hyderabad province made his way along the road, crowd at the edge parting with respectful bows before him and his entourage, Prince Kanwar smiling as he passed. From the outpost end others parted for the commander to make his way through, McCready following in his wake.

The chatter of the crowd renewed as both groups came together. Armstrong stood before the man, welcoming him but showing no deference, no humility. It was clear in the commander's mind that the two were equals, and if not that the scales tipped in the commander's favor. Kanwar meanwhile composed himself with regal attitude, not haughty but aware he was royalty.

Once again the crowd allowed these most important of men passage through to the gallows, Armstrong leading Prince Kanwar to the best seats in the house, as it were.

Had he known the prince was coming? Did a prince announce his intentions toward someone like Armstrong? Shaw shook his head, aware these were questions he would unlikely ever have answers for.

Another hush fell across the crowd as the nine condemned prisoners were brought out. No ropes secured them today, but iron chains in an X confining their hands to feet. Each one was further confined by a length of chain securing them to each other.

There could be no possible escape.

A gamut of emotions covered the faces of those outside. Anger. Relief. Curiosity. Fear. Disgust. Plain on every face save those of the nine prisoners.

Ah, those nine.

They should have been afraid, angry, defiant while waiting their moment to climb the stairs to their deaths. *Should* have been. Instead they stood with what could only be described as enthusiasm, looking into the crowd and grinning like a cricket player ready for the match.

As each one's turn came they were released from the chains and guided up the stairs to the noose, still grinning. At his time the sixth cultist broke free, soldiers advancing to prevent his escape. They needn't have bothered. The man hurtled up the stairs to the gallows and pushed the hangman aside. He grabbed the noose and slipped it over his own head then, without any hesitation, dropped into the hole to his death. A death all the worse for the fact that he not only welcomed it but relished it.

More tribute to their goddess?

Insanity.

How did one punish those willing … *wanting* to die for their cause? These nine weren't warnings, they were martyrs.

The crowd fell silent after that, and Shaw was glad for the fact they were no closer. Three more executions followed, then a tight-lipped prince made his way back toward the elephants. He left without a glance back.

Singh was the opposite of the cultists, and the spectators as well. He betrayed no emotion either good or bad. And when all was done he returned without comment to the tasks of changing beds.

Shaw wanted to call after the boy, to ask if he was well, if he needed anything. Once again the ghost of his father who'd barely been a father reared his head. In the end he watched Singh walk away for fear of driving him away instead. He had to hope in time that Singh would choose to confide in him. It was still early in their relationship.

The outpost had never seen the like of those executions, and it unnerved everyone. The commander in particular.

Later that day, with many slaps of an open palm against his desk, he declared the cult broken for all time, as others had done a couple of decades earlier. He then glared around at the assembled officers, daring anyone to contradict him.

"If any soldier so much as breathes the word *Thuggee*," Armstrong said through clenched teeth, "the commanding officer of that man will be held accountable, as much as the man himself."

Shaw wondered what the commander would do if McCready should mention the word. For that matter, what would happen to McCready if one of the doctors uttered the dreaded word *Thuggee?*

"An aberration!" Armstrong continued, rising to pace while delivering his message. "Undoubtedly caused by the switch from East India Company to the Raj."

McCready jumped in. "Those circumstances caused a vacuum of sorts, drawing in these lunatics."

"So, you see." Armstrong turned toward the room, gaze passing from face to face. "These were not true Thuggees."

A contradiction then. If these were not true Thuggees then how could the cult be broken, once again, for all time?

"Yes, sir," all agreed, knowing their part in the pantomime.

Armstrong looked relieved, as if acknowledgments made it all true.

Much as Shaw wished he could believe the words, they had the appearance of so much wishful thinking. He'd been at those caves, survived those fanatics throwing themselves at the soldiers in endless sacrifice, examined those drawings on the cave walls, and watched their faces as they went to the gallows.

They would be back.

———

"These ... Thuggees," Walsh began.

Shaw raised an eyebrow, more of a warning to be cautious than anything else.

Walsh sat across from him in the examination room. No prying ears, not at the moment at least. "Don't worry, doc. I know who I can and can't talk to."

It was the greatest compliment Shaw had received in recent memory and it slipped him into a more pleased state, even after all of the death and mayhem of the past week. Shaw couldn't forget the actions at that cave, relived them each time he closed his eyes.

So did Walsh, it seemed.

"I see 'em when I sleep," he said. "I ... Doc, have we seen the last of 'em?"

"The commander says we have. That they were an aberration, an anachronism."

Walsh held no change to his expression, holding that gaze until Shaw looked away.

"No, Walsh. I don't think we have."

It was a risk to speak so plainly to a non-officer—would have been a risk to speak to officers this way—but he knew Walsh better than most. They'd formed a connection at that cave. He'd come in under the pretense of headaches but what he needed was to talk. Now the young corporal sagged, as if hearing confirmation of what he'd dreaded.

"They frighten me, doc. That somethin' like that can exist. They're not some other soldiers believin' what they're told. These men, they're completely outta their minds."

Shaw nodded.

"They came at us in waves but if they'd attacked all at once we woulda been finished."

Shaw nodded again.

"So why didn't they?"

It was a fair question, and one he'd turned over again and again in his own mind. Was it just so that others in the group could escape out the back door? A greater sacrifice than what was gained.

And why leave that idol?

The idol.

His idol.

Shaw pushed the thought away, firmly.

"I don't know," he admitted.

Walsh let out a sigh. Shaw's words had comforted the man, but what could he say to put anyone's mind at ease when his own was a whirlwind of doubts?

"I think they are done for now," Shaw said. "They will need time to grow again."

Walsh looked understandably uncertain. In a populous country like India where the native people were treated second best there would always be those who could be drawn into a cult like that.

"The commander says the cult is broken for all time," Shaw

said, "but I don't believe it, and I doubt he does either. It's what he has to say."

"So, what do we do?"

"Do? What can we do? Wait and see?"

Walsh rolled his eyes and got to his feet, not liking the answer any more than Shaw. "I guess. I just wish we could do somethin', you know?"

"I do."

They stood silent a moment, each lost in thought before Walsh cleared his throat.

"So, uh … I wanted to thank you for savin' me at the cave. They were all over me, like I was drownin' and …" He shuddered. "Anyway, I know that's not easy for you, what you did."

Shaw didn't like being reminded that he'd taken a life, but from Walsh he could accept it. "If you need to talk about this again, come back and see me."

It was a thinly veiled excuse to have someone to speak with himself. A friendship between the corporal and himself might be impossible, but inside the walls of an examination room they could at least compare thoughts and support.

"I'll do that, doc."

CHAPTER SIXTEEN

Shaw woke that night, confused and disoriented. Moonlight came through a window to his right, illuminating the area.

But ... this wasn't his room.

He wasn't even in a bed.

"Where ...?"

Before him squatted a wide wooden box, a crate, the lid lifted away from its bottom. His hands were inside, rummaging, brushing against rough fabric a moment before he forced them to pull back.

The crate where he'd discarded the idol.

"What the hell?"

He slammed the lid then glared at his shaking hands, as if they'd taken on a life of their own. Very much how it seemed at the moment.

"Sleepwalking," he muttered, backing from the crate.

He'd never done that before, not even as a child. Why here? Why now?

Had it been that conversation with Walsh? Discussion of Thuggees had brought this idol forward in his thoughts. It had been on his mind as he went to sleep and here he was.

Yes. That tracked as logical.

He left the building.

"All done, sir?"

Shaw looked at the guard—same one from several nights back when he'd dropped the idol here—and gave him a quick nod, wishing he could ask about how he'd gotten in there without sounding like a madman.

He mumbled some thanks and turned toward the hospital and his room.

"See you tomorrow night then, Doctor?"

Shaw gave him a quick wave then took two more steps before coming to a stop and returning.

"Tomorrow night?"

"Sorry, sir. None of my business. I just mean since you come every night."

Shaw looked toward the storage house, eyes on the door as if it had grown teeth.

"Every night?"

"Yes, sir. Well, since that first night you came to drop something off."

"Every … I …" A cold chill broke out all over his body. A week's worth of sleepwalking? He took a deep breath. "I don't suppose you know when this all is set to ship?"

"Yes, sir," the guard said, face splitting into a smile. Happy to know some news an officer didn't. "Day after tomorrow."

"Day after tomorrow. Right." Shaw rubbed at the back of his neck. "Good."

Ignoring the guard's quizzical expression he turned and headed toward his room, wondering on ways to keep himself from sleepwalking tomorrow night.

Shadows. Drifting. Menacing. Calling.

Demanding.

The idol called. A stern headmaster with dwindling patience.

He must go to it, must get into the shadows and trace his fingers around those carved letters.

"Doctor?"

Yes, those letters were *almost* decipherable. Almost. He knew the intent behind them, the desire. Could almost pronounce those words.

Almost. Almost.

"Doctor."

Almost ...

"Doctor!"

The world rocked.

No.

He was being shaken.

"Wha ...?"

"Doctor, wake up."

Wake? But ... No. The idol commanded. He must—

Wetness, sudden and unexpected, impacted his face and Shaw's eyes shot open.

Light. Blurry and blinding.

"Wha ...?"

His voice came out faint, mouth and throat dry.

Shaw licked his lips, taking moisture from the water trickling down his face.

"Nightmares," a voice said, as if from the far end of a hall-way, but coming closer.

Singh's voice.

One of Shaw's hands rested on the doorknob of their room and he turned back. The boy stood to his right, feet bare and eyes narrowed, an empty glass in one hand.

"Where do you go, Doctor?"

It was the longest string of words Singh had said yet and Shaw should have been delighted. He barely noticed.

"I ... I'm ..."

... going to see the idol before it is shipped back to England.

"I ..."

... was sleepwalking. Again.

Further to his right, in a space between their two beds, sat the chair he'd started his vigil in, where he'd had every intention of staying awake through the night. Tea on the side table, no steam rising from it. His book lay on the floor, discarded and forgotten.

"Singh?"

A knowing expression crept to the boy's face, a look that said *he* knew where Shaw was heading.

Shaw turned back toward the door, his hand still resting on the knob. A memory of it rattling under his hand as he'd tried to leave broke through the fog of his brain. He pulled on the knob again, the door refusing to open.

"What ...?" he repeated.

The deadbolt, installed on each door but rarely used. It was slid into place.

"You ... locked the door?"

No answer from Singh, yet Shaw could sense the one quick nod.

He ran one hand down his face, wiping the mixture of water and sweat away.

"Thank you," Shaw said, unable to make eye contact. "What time is it?"

"Three."

"Three," Shaw repeated and stepped away from the door, crossing to his chair and dropping heavily into it.

"Same time," Singh said, and when Shaw cocked his head to one side he added, "Every night."

Did everyone know of this sleepwalking but him?

"Thank you," he repeated, forcing himself to look into the boy's face.

No judgement there, only acceptance. Singh crossed to the

night table and refilled the glass he held, bringing it back to Shaw.

"Chess, Doctor?" He gestured toward the board, waiting on their shared desk.

It was new. Shaw had introduced him to the game just the day before. In the few days since Singh had been released to his custody, since they'd watched the Thuggees executed, Shaw had struggled with how best to do right by Singh. He'd provided food, clothing, and shelter, and the next obvious step was education.

Knowing nothing about raising an orphan boy he continued to make it up as they went. Chess was a respectable place to start, a way for them to connect, and Singh had taken to the logic and strategy as if playing for years.

"Yes, why not?"

Singh brought the board to the side table and pulled their second chair closer. Sipping at his water Shaw realized how dry his mouth had been. They set up pieces and soon both were drawn in by the game, a welcome distraction. With each passing minute as they got closer to the dawn, the fogginess of sleep-walking receded, as did the fear from his dream.

Some sort of brain fever? Like that which seized Neufeld from time to time?

The first rays of light seeped in around the shutters, burning away the remnants of the previous night. What was left was an embarrassed shame, his face red for it. How much power he'd given to that ... that ... thing.

That damned idol.

Preposterous.

His own mind had him sleepwalking!

Shaw crossed to the shutters and threw them open, letting the healing rays of sunshine fill the room.

Yes. Completely absurd.

Did the cavemen also think their nighttime fears ridiculous once the sun had risen?

"What do we do today, Doctor?"

Shaw smiled, appreciating the longer strings of words Singh was using. A sure sign of their increasing comfort together. There was hope he was doing a competent job of this after all.

"Today?" Shaw said. "Well, breakfast first. Then ... Then I want to watch those crates being loaded."

Singh gave one nod, as if this were the most logical action a person could want to do.

Preposterous nonsense or not, once that damned thing was on its way he could stop fixating on it.

"After that, since I don't need to be in the hospital until later, we can continue with your lessons."

Another nod.

Yes, he could do a credible job of education at least.

Little did he know that Singh would be educating him at the same time.

Shaw was pleased to find that not only did Singh have the desire to learn, but already had basic understanding of the alphabet, and of math, catching on to each fresh concept with ease. A hunger burned inside the boy and he approached each new lesson with a need to understand. Singh had obviously received education earlier in his life, before being inducted—abducted?—into the cult, though he had scant memory of those pre-cult days.

A greater shock was discovering that Singh was only eight years of age, rather than the ten or eleven Shaw had estimated. The boy was tall for his age, with solid muscles already forming. When he reached adulthood Singh would be quite the imposing figure.

That size was one reason the cultists had taken him, recruited as a Thuggee, but the greater reason was his education. They'd wanted him to read the script on that ugly idol—halfway to England by now. When Singh couldn't he'd been relegated to the bottom of the cult's ladder, needing to prove his worth.

"I still don't understand why they would have left it behind," Shaw said, coming back around to that one fact which still made no sense. "Especially after killing Lassiter to get it."

Singh gave it some serious thought, looking up from the writing he'd been practicing to sift through whatever knowledge he had on the subject. He shook his head. "I do not know, Doctor."

He'd started speaking in longer sentences, though still only when necessary and just enough to get his point across. Singh didn't speak for no reason.

"No," Shaw said. "No, of course not. I apologize for bringing it up. I don't wish to make you relive those days."

No reaction. Singh didn't even shrug.

"I'm sure it was nothing more than we'd caught them by surprise. Why else would they leave their only treasure behind?"

Singh cocked his head to one side. "That was not their only treasure."

Shaw turned toward the boy, a prickling racing along his spine.

"Or, their greatest one," Singh added.

"A—Another idol?"

There couldn't be two like that!

Singh shook his head.

"What then?"

"A book."

"A book?"

An idol. A book.

"Oh!" Shaw snapped his fingers. "That altar held this book!"

Singh had no response.

No, Singh wouldn't know. He'd been too low in the cult to be trusted with such information, or to be so honored as to touch the treasures.

"A book of what though?" Shaw said, more to himself.

"Evil."

He looked at the boy and suppressed another shiver. An evil book?

Ridiculous, and yet these cultists evidently believed it.

Thoughts came to Shaw one after another and he spoke to himself, getting up to pace.

"So these cultists who escaped took the book with them, a greater treasure, forgetting the idol. Hmm, maybe. Maybe. Then the rest were left to sacrifice themselves so their leaders could escape."

"No."

Shaw stopped pacing and raised one eyebrow in question, a gesture which had taken several occurrences before Singh caught the meaning.

"They sacrificed themselves for the book to escape."

Shaw gave an incredulous glance. Singh spoke of this book as if it were alive. Certainly it was of some misguided importance to the cult but … For a moment Shaw tried to imagine giving his life for any object—a bible, if he were more religious?—and found it outside his ability to conceive.

Still, this *was* a group of lunatics. Was it so hard to attribute yet another mad notion to them? No. Not so hard.

"Doctor?"

He looked to find Singh staring. The boy tried to lift one eyebrow in impression and managed to only raise both. Shaw laughed aloud, forgetting thoughts of cults and murders, idols and books, relegating all of that to the past. The edge of a smile creased Singh's mouth and Shaw counted it on par with being knighted by Queen Victoria.

"What say we go find something a bit more fun?" Shaw said,

closing the book on sentence structure they'd been working on before the conversation diverted.

CHAPTER SEVENTEEN

Bandagar, India — January 15th, 1879

Dearest Mother,

*Singh continues to impress me in all that he does. From the speed
with which he comprehends and absorbs each new subject I teach him,
to his sheer desire, his hunger, to learn. Around the hospital he is the
greatest of help, accompanying me on all of my shifts.*

*I worry that I teach him too much about our own culture and not
enough about his own. Should I be doing more to find blood relations of
his? I have made enquiries, of course, but all have come back negative
so far. From what Singh has told me, at least from what he remembers,
he was an orphan before the cult came along. One thing Bombay has is
an abundance of street orphans.*

*At least here Singh is well liked by others such as Doctor Neufeld,
who plays chess with him now that I no longer provide a challenge, and
Lassiter's replacement, Doctor Barrowman. Even McCready grudgingly admits Singh is a help around the hospital ...*

"Shaw, will you get your house boy to clean up the examination rooms?" Adamson said, making a notation on his clipboard as he entered the hospital's entry room.

Shaw looked up from his own paperwork, annoyance clear on his face. Adamson knew better. "Singh is *not* a house boy!"

They'd had this conversation before, and it was obvious Adamson was only trying to irk him, as obvious as the fact that it worked. Since Lassiter's death a year ago Adamson and White's attention had transferred to Shaw, all of their witty observations revolving around his and Singh's relationship. *House boy* was one of their milder topics. This week's hospital rotation schedule had Shaw on duty with Adamson, an assignment he dreaded.

Singh studied at the desk next to Shaw, reviewing a thick book on modern British history. Currently he was into the section on India's colonization and would shake his head every page or so. It was the most emotional reaction he'd had to any of the study books.

Adamson shifted focus from his clipboard, an act of concerned confusion. "But what *should* I call him? Surely you don't think of him as your son?"

This last was said as if he'd proposed the greatest scandal. More than a year of his attentions and Adamson still only understood half of what would truly bother Shaw. That idea was not one of them. Still, the man kept trying.

And Shaw kept pushing back.

"You could call him Singh."

"Oh, right. Of course." Adamson turned toward the boy. "Singh, go clean up the examination rooms."

Singh made no change, continuing to read. Adamson looked at Shaw and shrugged.

"Would be nice if your house boy ..." He raised a hand to fend off the oncoming rebuke. "If *Singh* actually understood English."

"Oh, he understands. Could be he's waiting for you to say please."

Adamson's eyes narrowed and the teasing grin disappeared. Shaw's grew at the hit he'd scored. A combination of a doctor saying please to anyone beneath his station and the idea of using manners with one of the Indian people was loathsome to someone like Adamson.

"I don't know why the boy is even here, Shaw," he snapped.

"Why? Because I am teaching him while things are slow in the ward."

Adamson made a noise of disgust at the idea of his teaching one of *them*. Shaw ignored it.

"And because Singh is a great help around the hospital," he continued. "You know as well as I do that he reorganized the supply closet better than even McCready had."

Adamson's eyes twitched left, in the general direction of the closet, as if he could see it through solid walls. No one could criticize Singh's organizational skills and they both knew it. Even McCready had grudgingly acknowledged the better system in place which arranged items by type but had an area for quick retrieval of those items most commonly used.

"Well, perhaps you could ask *Singh* to be that *great help* and clean up the examination rooms then."

With that Adamson spun on his heel and left, no doubt believing his point had been made.

Shaw looked to Singh who still had not reacted. One of his quirks was that he would not speak to everyone. People like Adamson he would give an impression that he didn't understand English as well as he did. White got slightly better results, but only when he was without his counterpart. Singh wasn't rude or confrontational, but it was his way of refusing to be treated as a slave. It made Shaw hesitate to pass on any task which had originated with Adamson.

"Shall I clean those rooms now, Doctor?" Singh asked without interrupting his reading.

Shaw laughed. "Yes, please. If you don't mind."

The boy placed a paper to mark his place then was on his way.

Shaw had to wonder just how much Singh was getting from the book. Back in England this textbook would be accepted facts to memorize and regurgitate. Here the stories and ideas of this current section were a way of life, a history of his people ... and a sadly one-sided account which would not be factual from any Indian's perspective. Not for the first time Shaw wondered on the education he was providing for the boy. Was it for Singh's benefit or his own?

Saviour of India.

"Oh, be quiet, Larry."

One benefit to their lessons, and one Shaw hadn't thought to expect, was that his own education continued as much as Singh's. The more he taught Singh about the European world he came from, the more Singh taught him about Indian life. It was inevitable, he supposed, and certainly the way it should be, but there were details about his own culture of which Singh knew nothing, and Shaw wasn't able to help with that. This included one topic he hadn't even considered but should have.

One Sunday Shaw walked to Bandagar without Singh to deliver some supplies and returned quicker than expected. It was unusual for him to not stay and chat with Doctor Patel but the man finally had a new doctor to train and was quite excited given that it was his own son coming back from school.

He started to cut across the compound, intent on reaching the hospital doors. Singh had been reading about the revolt in the United States and Shaw was curious on his opinion. Movement between hospital and barracks grabbed his attention as he neared the destination. There, seated on crates and leaning forward in conversation were Privates Chattha and Sandhu, with Singh before them, arms crossed. The boy nodded slowly, a reaction Shaw knew meant he was thinking about some piece of information, absorbing it.

Singh had never shown great interest in his countrymen before but Shaw didn't think anything odd of the scene until Private Sandhu noticed his approach and nudged Chattha. As he neared, the two soldiers got to their feet and said some parting words to Singh, Sandhu patting the boy on one shoulder, each man greeting Shaw but not slowing on their way past. He watched their retreating backs until they'd rounded the corner. When he turned again Singh was staring toward the ground, a look of deep consideration on his face.

"What was that about?" Shaw asked.

Singh shrugged, brows furrowed. His mind was far away.

It worried Shaw.

In the past year Singh had opened up to talk with him about many matters. He still didn't talk without reason, and was given to waves of deep introspection, but Shaw would have said they'd become close, or were starting to. At the least *he* had grown close to Singh and was afraid of losing him. His mind jumped to the possibility the two privates had been pointing out how Singh and Shaw were not the same. Would they have suggested that Singh be better off among his own people? For that matter, would they be correct?

He wasn't Singh's father, no matter what Adamson may say in his jibes. If Singh wanted to go he had no right to keep him from doing so.

Singh started past and Shaw fell into step beside him, neither of them rushing.

"Confusing thoughts," Singh finally said.

Shaw kept quiet. Early on he'd recognized the best way to get Singh talking was to give him space to do so. Too much chatter from others and he was content to allow that other person to fill the space with their own words.

"Complicated thoughts," he added.

"I ... don't understand."

"Neither do I."

Singh glanced at him and the look of confusion and concern on Shaw's face. He came to a stop.

"I asked them about religion."

"Oh!" Shaw said, his mouth dropping open. "Oh, I see."

Only he didn't, not really. Religion had never played a huge part in Shaw's own life, not past attending church as a child with his parents or at school, fulfilling expectations. Medicine and science were his religions. He was neither atheist nor believer. It was simply something he never gave much thought.

The soldiers distancing themselves as he approached was understandable now. The British army did not encourage local religions, thinking they were all cut from the same cloth as the Thuggees. As far as Singh's confusion went, well, what religion made sense if a person wasn't born into it?

"They were telling you of Hindu beliefs?" Shaw tried to sound as if he knew some information about this topic.

"Partly. Gurbachan is Sikh."

"Gurbachan?"

Seeing Shaw's one raised eyebrow Singh took pity. "Gurbachan Chattha and Sahil Sandhu."

"Ah, I had no idea of their first names."

Did he recall *any* of the soldier's given names other than Corporal Walsh? Not offhand at least, and how many knew his first name to be Archibald?

"So, Private Chattha is Sikh, and Sandhu is ...?"

"Hindu."

"Right. And the confusion comes from ...?"

"Gurbachan tells me we are all equal in God's eyes."

Shaw nodded. "I like that."

"Yes," Singh said, considering it a moment. "Sahil, though, tells me we all have an inner divine light."

Shaw mulled that over as they continued toward their rooms. "Those don't seem contradictory."

Singh was quiet for several paces and Shaw allowed him peace to process the ideas.

"They are not," he said.

"Then the problem comes from ...?"

More paces in silence before Singh came to a stop.

"Kali is a Hindu goddess, and many in the cult were Hindu. How is this possible?"

Thoughts of the Crusades came to Shaw's mind. How much murder had been done in the name of God? Would those on the receiving end see any difference between God and Kali?

Thankfully Singh's question was more rhetorical and the boy turned without waiting for an answer.

"Gurbachan also tells me Singh is a Sikh name, but Sahil says not necessarily."

Like falling dominoes this was getting away from Shaw, beyond his area of knowledge. Even discussing the religion he himself had been born into would have been difficult, given his lack of devout beliefs.

Singh needed an expert, but just because Shaw couldn't answer the questions didn't mean he couldn't find those who could. Later that day Shaw went in search of the two privates. As he broached the subject their eyes shifted, Chattha taking a step back as if Shaw were trying to draw them into a trap.

"Look," Shaw said, "I need someone to help Singh find his own answers."

The two soldiers relaxed. Sandhu rubbed at his chin.

"Can you help him?" Shaw asked.

Chattha shook his head, a moment later Sandhu joining him.

"We're soldiers," Chattha explained. "Not holy men."

"Singh is asking questions which are difficult to answer," Sandhu added. "Perceptive questions."

Singh had a tendency to ask questions which made adults stop and think.

"I ... I don't know what to do. How do I help him?"

The two soldiers considered their responses then continued hesitantly.

"There are holy men in Bandagar," Sandhu said. "We could introduce Singh."

Chattha nodded.

"Umm ... Both Sikh and Hindu?" Shaw asked.

The soldiers looked at each other and shrugged. They were friends in the army, being more similar to each other than the soldiers around them. Shaw wondered if their divergent beliefs would have prevented that friendship outside.

"To both," Chattha agreed.

And that easily Singh was introduced to two religions, accepting both but belonging to neither. He would go to Bandagar once a week and spend part of the day with one holy man, and the rest with the other. He embraced yoga and meditation. Many times Shaw would come into their rooms only to find him in a deep trancelike state, or in a posture which would have been impossible for himself. He wanted to ask about it, to show interest, but it seemed too personal to intrude on without invitation.

Chattha confided in Shaw one day that Singh's studies were helping to calm his spirit and bring focus, to resist the evils of the world.

The concept was fascinating, but outside of Shaw's ability to grasp. He was just happy seeing Singh immersed in his own culture.

Bandagar, India—July 31st, 1879
  Dearest Mother,

The tigers have reappeared in the area, close to one year exactly after Lassiter's death. It seems I must measure everything, both good and bad, in regards to that event.

A routine patrol returned to the outpost yesterday, exhibiting a sense of excited wonder mixed with mortal terror. They'd seen a tiger, been stalked by it in fact. If not for their numbers and constant vigilance the beast would have undoubtedly attacked.

Wild tigers! It is like magic. Something I've been dreaming of since arriving in the country. They are every bit the danger as any other creature out there, but these at least are part of the natural order.

CHAPTER EIGHTEEN

Bandagar, India — March 2nd, 1885

My dearest Mother,

Life has taken a perverse satisfaction in causing me anguish and misery, as if some malevolent force focused its attention solely on my torture. Setting my existence over a burning flame.

I have decided to continue with this correspondence even though you are no longer on the other end to receive these letters. I'll simply keep these in my trunk rather than post them since Father would have as little interest in my ramblings now as he did in my childhood.

Nevertheless, we all must carry on in the face of adversity ... I believe that is another of your truisms. I shall try to live up to your example.

With each year Singh has grown in height and no longer resembles that child who'd been in danger of execution. Already he has passed my own five foot nine and shows no sign of stopping. Wide of shoulder and heavily muscled underneath his robes, at the age of fifteen he is perched on the edge of manhood, looking older than his years as he always has.

Adamson never calls him house boy these days, not in my presence and certainly not in Singh's, though he and White undoubtedly say worse when neither of us are around.

It would seem the assertion of Commander Armstrong—as I always think of him these days—that the Thuggees are gone is a correct one. At the least gone from around Bandagar. It has been six years since Lassiter's murder and our lives have returned to a normal routine ... Not that past events have been forgotten. Unfamiliar Indians passing through the area are unfairly scrutinized and untrusted while here. None show signs of anything more sinister than a desire to feed their families.

Evidence of Thuggee handiwork is still out there though.

We receive papers from parts of India: Bombay. Calcutta. Madras. Rajputana. Punjab. Occasionally there will be a story which jumps out. A prominent man strangled in the streets of Mysore. Several people struck with insanity near Bengal. One man, a professor of language, disappeared in the night at Madras.

Pointing these out to the commander meets the same response each time ...

<hr />

"It's a wild country, Shaw," Armstrong said. "People die all the time. These reports mean little."

McCready fixed a glare on Shaw. "Don't you have enough to do without spreading rumours? That doctor in Bandagar could use your help I'm sure."

Being allowed to help Doctor Patel and bring supplies was the commander's attempt to mollify him, as was his being allowed to raise Singh without interference. Shaw accepted both, though it didn't stop him from raising concerns when he saw them.

The newspapers themselves didn't help, being a week old at best and far too late to be of any value. Still, it angered him to know these killers were still active with nothing to be done about it.

Shortly before the tigers moved on from the area Neufeld's nightmares returned.

His paintings had been getting somber, more brooding, going from wildflowers and nature scenery to animals at night, and finally ending on scenes of death. These were sparked, we all thought, by the tiger mauling. The entire outpost had seen the end result of that and it was enough to give anyone nightmares.

A squad staggered into the outpost, guns at the ready and carrying one soldier who'd been attacked while on patrol. Furrows of ragged claw marks scored his back with deep puncture wounds of teeth in one arm which he would never regain proper use of. All in that patrol were panicked, looking around for the next attack. Several walked backwards, guarding the way they'd come.

"It still stalks us," Sandhu said as the doctors took their comrade away to the hospital.

Another soldier to be sent home.

That would be the last sighting of a tiger, at least for the year 1885.

Later, the unfortunate soldier treated and sedated, Neufeld returned to his room to paint. It was a calming influence and often helped him sleep, but not that night. Next morning found Neufeld's door ajar, the doctor still at his easel.

"I say, Neufeld, have you been at it all night?" Shaw said, pushing the door open further.

The man gave no reaction, didn't turn. Shaw thought he'd fallen asleep, hunkered before his easel, and crossed the room to wake him.

"It's not finished," Neufeld said in a thin voice as Shaw reached for his shoulder.

The painting held a scene of last night's tiger attack. The soldier, driven to the ground by that great cat, bloody teeth wounds showing through his tattered sleeve. Both faced out from the canvas toward the viewer, details of abject terror on the man's face and approaching sadistic glee on the tiger's. Their expressions, the details in the background, the man's fellow soldiers too far away to be of aid, one firing his rifle upward in an attempt to frighten the beast away. It all conveyed a creeping, helpless sensation, as if the viewer were personally there but unable to prevent the scene from happening.

"It looks done to me," Shaw said, wondering what else could be added.

"It came in a dream," Neufeld said. "A nightmare."

This last was bordering on dreamy whisper.

"Nightmare?"

Neufeld nodded and his fatigue became more evident. He raised one hand to rub at his eyes. "I ... haven't been sleeping well," he said, leaving a smudge of orange paint on one cheek.

It had been years since his last bout of nightmares. Their return gave Shaw an uneasy impression and he made mental note to keep an eye on his friend. The next painting, a few nights later, confirmed that uneasiness, changed it to dread. It showed a scene he feared, one which his subconscious mind had already expected.

Neufeld's back was once again toward the door as he painted in manic fury. Shaw entered, not trying to be quiet or stealthy.

"Neufeld?"

No response, the man continued painting with great fury as Shaw came up behind him, looking over one shoulder at the scene.

"No," he said. "No!"

On the canvas a gloomy shape skulked between the light and dark, glaring outward. It was indistinct but the face was there, staring. Mouth slack and clawed hands dangling, eyes red. Closer to the viewer was another figure, a soldier transfixed by what watched him. His rifle lay on the ground, forgotten, as he took his first step forward.

"The Maut," Shaw groaned. "It's returned."

That was the missing link for Neufeld's sleep problems. The Maut. Somehow it influenced his dreams.

Sensitive artist type—Lassiter's words from years earlier echoed back.

"That soldier!" Shaw said.

It was the man who guarded the storage building.

Neufeld took a finer brush and dipped it into a cut on his own forearm, then brought it to the Maut's eyes, enhancing that redness. He turned with blank, dazed eyes, bringing one finger to his lips.

"It's not done," he whispered.

"Neufeld," he muttered, a sound closer to revulsion. "Good Lord!"

Shaw debated between staying to help his friend and trying to save the soldier. A brief hesitation. Neufeld appeared safe, despite the self-inflicted wound. Shaw raced from Neufeld's room for his own, pulling the thick curtains aside to look out at the compound. He was sure the Maut would be there, on the edge between buildings with its red eyes, but nothing was there, no monster abiding in the trees.

No guard either.

Only one lonely abandoned rifle on the ground before the storage building.

No sign of the soldier could be found, though everyone searched.

CHAPTER NINETEEN

BANDAGAR, INDIA—MARCH 3RD, 1885

... Despite yesterday's excitement life continues on. Neufeld awoke from a prolonged sleep more lucid and somewhat amazed at the cut on his arm. He is seemingly back to his normal self and remembers nothing of the painting or whatever nightmare provoked it. A mercy to be sure.

He insists on keeping his shift later today, but I shall be sure to keep an eye on him.

Today falls on my scheduled day off. Singh and I will follow our usual habit of strolling through the market in Bandagar, examining the various fabrics and smelling the spices sold there. Occasionally I stop to feel a particularly silky fabric and imagine them replacing all the drapes in the old house. What must it look like these days ...

"Doctor," Singh said, voice low.

"Hmm?"

Shaw continued to examine a bolt of fabric which had caught his focus, lost in thoughts of his mother until Singh placed one hand on his arm. It was about as excited as the boy got and drew his attention back to the here and now.

"I'm sorry, what did you say?"

Singh did not even look at him but rather stared up the path of the market, craning his neck to see past all of the merchants and patrons.

"What is it, Singh?"

He followed Singh's gaze, finding nothing out of the ordinary. More Indian people going about their days in the market, buying and selling. Singh gestured to come closer and he did, struck by how not so long ago he would have bent toward Singh to speak instead of the reverse. True that only an inch or two separated them, but that minor gap wouldn't last. Soon Singh would tower over him. It was enough to bring a jolt of nostalgia. Where had the time gone?

"That man," Singh said, "is Thuggee. From the cave."

Thoughts of fabrics and nostalgia evaporated. Shaw stood straighter, focused. No need to ask anything so foolish as, *Are you sure?* Singh was still no waster of words or given to wild leaps of imagination. The man in question slinked his way through the crowd, paying no attention to vendors or their merchandise.

Now that he'd been identified it was obvious the man didn't belong, was not of the Bandagar people. And in moments he would be out the far end of the market. Too many people traipsed around between them and him.

Or rather, Shaw and him. Singh was already several feet through the crowd.

"Singh, wait."

A hopeless request. Singh had a determined look on his face, the kind he wore when faced with a particular problem needing to be solved.

Though broader of shoulder Singh was able to weave

through the people with better skill. All those years in India and Shaw still could not navigate dense crowds.

The Thuggee exited the market well in lead of Singh, who in turn was many paces ahead of Shaw. The man slunk out of sight, down the street, but Shaw kept his eyes on Singh as the boy passed the market's edge a few moments later. When he reached the same point Shaw rushed forward even as Singh turned the next corner. Shaw bit back the desire to call the boy's name, instead breaking into a sprint which startled many people he passed, apologizing as he went. Around that corner he found Singh already at the next and sped down the lane to catch up. There Singh peered around the corner, looking like an Indian version of Poe's detective Dupin, tracking some villain.

"He went in there," Singh said, gesturing at a house across the way.

It was like any other in the area. One floor with just enough room for a single family if it didn't have too many people. No signs that strange and sinister dealings were occurring inside. Fifteen minutes passed, watching the door and trying to look natural. No others came or went.

It occurred to Shaw that remaining there watching was the worst action they could take.

"If we're seen," he said, "one of two things will happen. Either we will be attacked by these men, which seems the most likely, or they will be startled into running away."

Singh shook his head. "Both."

Given the strategy used at the cave Shaw had to agree. "We need more than the two of us."

Singh looked at the door with regret but nodded. If nothing else he was practical, logical. He knew what these cultists were like, knew the danger of them being in Bandagar. Soon there would be murders, and God only knew who the targets would be.

The two backed away, headed for the outpost.

"The boy is mistaken," Armstrong said, returning to his paperwork.

The commander had been happy to see his nephew at first, but once Shaw started talking about Thuggees and the man in the market, the commander had found items of interest on his desk.

"But—"

"How could he possibly remember one man seven years later?"

"He knows the men who held him prisoner."

"*If* he's telling the truth."

"If ...? Why would he lie?"

Armstrong snorted, a quick burst of derision, and changed course. "We can't frighten the people in Bandagar, sending in British troops on the say-so of one boy."

"We've never worried about frightening them before."

The commander looked up from his papers, bleak expression emphasizing his words. "Leave it be, Shaw. The cult is broken. If any of them *did* escape, which I have come to doubt, they'll be alone and too afraid to act."

"What about the Dhoosar Maut? It's back, too. That can't be a coincidence."

Armstrong rolled his eyes. "I'm far too old for fairy tales."

"But—"

"Dismissed, Doctor!"

Shaw left the commander's office in a disillusioned stupor. What was it Lassiter had said years ago? That the commander believed, but didn't know how to react, how to resolve it. The excuse worked in regards to the Maut but not these cultists. What was his excuse there?

Shaw knew. Destroying that cult was the army's greatest accomplishment since arriving in India. To admit Thuggees still existed would be to point a finger at their own lack of contribution.

Instead they would allow people to die.

Right now soldiers could be headed to the house, catching that man, or men, before they caused harm. Instead Armstrong dared to call into question the honor and honesty of Singh.

It was disgusting. Pathetic.

Leave it be, Shaw, Armstrong had said.

Well, he couldn't, not in good conscience.

But what *could* he do?

"Oof!"

In Shaw's stomping anger and blind rush he'd failed to pay attention and stormed straight into Walsh, winding both of them.

"Hey, doc. Where's the fire?"

"Sorry, Captain," Shaw said, trying to navigate around the man.

"No harm done."

Walsh grinned at the use of his rank and fell into step beside Shaw. Being a captain was still new to Walsh and he was justifiably proud to have risen so far. He didn't brag about it, but hearing himself referred to as captain always made his day.

"Just dropped off one of the recent recruits," he said, cocking a thumb back towards the hospital. "Clumsy lad."

"Hmm, that sounds familiar," Shaw said, only half listening.

The man's smile was infectious to the point Shaw found his annoyance at Armstrong easing off a bit, though by no means completely. He didn't want that sentiment to go away, wanted to remember his righteous anger even if he didn't have any solution.

"You look dismayed, doc."

Shaw gritted his teeth and shook his head once, taking a deep breath to keep that resurging anger manageable.

"Sorry." Walsh raised both hands. "None of my business."

"Oh, it isn't that, Walsh. Just some stupidity you can't help with."

"Ah," the captain countered. "Are you sure? I mean, if nothin' else I can listen."

Shaw took a deep breath and considered. Over the years he and Walsh had become friends, more possible now that the man was a captain. They spoke often about Thuggees and the evidence of their activity. Occasionally Walsh would bring a copy of some Indian paper which had made its way to the outpost a month or more after publication, showing evidence that the cultists were still active. Yes, of course Walsh would listen.

Shaw recounted how Singh had recognized a cultist from years ago and Walsh shuddered. Going a bit past what was proper he then told Walsh about how the commander had ordered him to leave it alone.

"Hmm, Singh is sure though?"

Shaw nodded.

"Yep, 'course he is. That boy has sharp eyes."

"He does."

"Not the sorta people you forget either."

"No."

"Well, you want to go take a look then?"

"I …" He sighed, shrugged. "Honestly? No, I don't. But I feel I should … In the absence of anyone official wanting to."

At the cave there'd been a lot more cultists than what had been expected. If they'd all come at once the soldiers would have been overwhelmed.

"Well, doc. We can check it out, and if there's more than we can handle we'll back out and go for help."

"Are you sure, Walsh? The commander ordered me to leave it alone. It could mean trouble for you."

"Sorry, what was that? I didn't hear the last part." He waved one hand as Shaw opened his mouth to repeat. "No matter, if I see suspicious activity then it's somethin' I'm honor bound to investigate."

He tipped Shaw a conspiratorial wink and came close to getting a grin.

What was he thinking? He wasn't suited to a life of adventure. What if he was forced to kill again … But, what if he didn't do this and someone was killed because of his inaction? Someone he cared about.

"I … owe it to Lassiter," Shaw said.

"Yes, sir, and I owe it to you for savin' my life back then. Can't let you go it alone."

"When?"

"I'm off for a march with my men in a few minutes, so can't be before tonight."

"*Tonight?*"

"Not a fan of the idea myself, what with … *that* … lurkin' out there. Still, it's just from here to Bandagar and back."

Yes. *That!*

A definite link existed between the Maut and Neufeld's dreams. Was there another one?

"You notice how they both came back at the same time?"

"Huh?"

"The Maut and the Thuggees. They both returned together."

Walsh thought about that. "You think they're connected then."

"Yes, though I can't imagine how."

Or could he?

Thoughts of Lassiter's idol barged into his mind, how it had insisted its way into his thoughts and sleep patterns. What had Singh said years back? The idol wasn't the Thuggees only treasure, or their greatest one. They had a book as well, and if that book had an effect like the idol …

No.

Shaw pushed the idea aside, unwilling to believe such nonsense.

Lassiter's killer was just a common murderer, the idol was just a statue, and the Maut was … was …

Oh yes? Do go on, Shaw. The Maut is what?

The Dhoosar Maut was … a mystery that would have some logical explanation in the end. Stepping back he examined that argument, accepting it until a better one came.

"I've got to run," Walsh said. "Meet you outside the hospital around eight?"

Shaw grasped at ideas and came up with one. "Can you bring your men?"

Walsh stopped, smile faltering. "Ah, doc—"

"No, forget I asked."

Walsh going against orders was one thing but he wouldn't ask his men to do the same.

"Besides, if it's just one lunatic we get to be the heroes. If not we come back for help."

Shaw would be happy to let anyone else be the hero.

"I will let one of my men, Corporal Eames, know where we're headin'. Just in case."

Shaw wished he hadn't said those last three words. They chased around between his ears, always retreating before coming back to the forefront again.

Just in case.

CHAPTER TWENTY

BANDAGAR, INDIA—MARCH 3RD, 1885
   ... I was always taught to do what was right, but this is madness.
I'm no soldier, no hero ...

"That's the buildin' then?"

Shaw nodded, tapping his fingers against the sabre at his side. He realized in the dimness Walsh couldn't see any such expression. "Yes."

"Doesn't look like much."

"No."

They studied it from a space between two other buildings across the way. This position was better than what Singh and he had used earlier. Walsh pointed out the bad vantage point that other corner had, how easy it would be to sneak up behind them, so they relocated to an alley up the street. The dimness allowed an odd combination of ability to watch while staying hidden. Shaw still felt vulnerable.

"Quiet enough," Walsh said. "Small too, right? Unless they're stacked back to front there can't be more than a few in there."

"Yes, that *is* true."

And something Shaw hadn't thought of. It was comforting. The house could hold six or seven at most without them falling over each other. Less probably. If they were outnumbered it couldn't be by much and they had the element of surprise ... if the Thuggee was still there. He could have left by now.

"Yes," Shaw repeated, his confidence rising the more he considered it. "Yes, you're right."

"So we wait?" Walsh asked. "Watch?"

"I guess so. I admit this is all strange to me. I'm not the detective story type."

"A doctor and soldier as detectives in India? I'd read that."

"Well, let's survive the night and see if the story is worth writing."

It was the equivalent of whistling while passing through a graveyard, superstitious actions to stave off things that go bump in the night. This was worse though. This was real, not just imagination running amok. Real potential danger. Real unknown threat.

Pale moonlight played hide-and-seek, passing behind clouds and back.

"When do we go in?" a voice behind them said.

Both jumped, Walsh's hand dropping to his sidearm.

The voice had been quiet, with an Indian accent Shaw immediately recognized.

"Singh!" he said, heart hammering.

The boy had managed to approach without making a sound. If that had been real danger—

"Yes, Doctor," he said, as if his being there should have been expected.

As it should have been.

Shaw had wanted to keep him away from this, keep him safe,

but this was a matter of honor for Singh. These people had kidnapped him, forced him to witness unspeakable acts. Singh wouldn't speak about that time. "The past cannot be changed," he would say. These cultists had terrorized his country, murdered his fellow countrymen.

So how did Shaw say he couldn't go in? Singh would just follow, as he had followed them to this alley.

Walsh cleared his throat. "Ah, Singh," he said, the lilt coming through more thickly, as it did whenever he was trying to smooth things over with another. It often worked, made him more endearing. He caught Shaw's eye then looked back to the boy. "It's good that yer here."

Singh made no reply, but he was listening. Subtle signs learned over the years told that. A slight shift to the eyes to refocus on Walsh, a twitch to the shoulders.

Walsh nodded, as if agreeing with an unspoken dialogue.

"We need to go in there, y'see," Walsh continued, gesturing at himself then Shaw. "The doc is leader of our expedition, so he needs to go, of course."

Singh's eyes darted to Shaw then back to the house across the way.

"And I have the gun, so I've got to go with him. For protection, y'see."

Singh turned a fraction more toward the captain, making no response, crossing his arms.

"Now, we need someone out here. Someone we can trust to go for help if we're not back quick like."

The boy breathed in through his nose, slowing his breathing. His eyes narrowed, running through what had been said.

"Can we trust you to be our backup? To go get Corporal Eames and my men if necessary?"

Singh thought it over, not liking what he'd heard but apparently finding no hole in Walsh's logic. Shaw found himself holding his breath until Singh uncrossed his arms, an unspoken gesture of acceptance. He stood without expression or comment until—

"There," Singh whispered, barely a breath.

They spun to follow Singh's gesture. A man with the quick, jerky movements of one not right in the head. He'd emerged from the street's shadows and approached the door.

"Same man?" Walsh asked.

Singh gave one definite nod. Yes, that was the same man. Yes, he was still sure.

"All right then," Walsh said, drawing his revolver.

He held the weapon in hand, pointed upward, finger beside the trigger guard. A glance at Shaw and the soldier stepped into the street, crossing toward the now closed door. Shaw followed, a pace behind, one quick scan to ensure Singh was not following. He couldn't find the boy in the darkness.

Good.

It occurred to him that he was acting the part of protective parent, trying to keep their child away from danger. Maybe he was learning. It's as simple as finding you care about another person more than yourself. Others in life would not treat Singh as fairly, but with any luck having one at the beginning of his life would make the difference.

As they reached the door Walsh stepped aside, allowing Shaw to take the lead. He grabbed the door's handle to push it open. As crazed as these people were, this one didn't bother with locks. Did that betray a lack of forethought, or simply a lack of fear?

Inside all was gloom and shadows, the smell of dust and sweat.

Where had he gone?

Shaw drew his sabre and stepped into the gloom beyond, Walsh now a pace behind. The idea was that Shaw could provide enough delay to any attacker for Walsh to use his gun if needed. As Walsh had said, Shaw was the leader of this adventure. He had a responsibility to at least be in the lead, had insisted in fact.

Leaving the front door open for quick exit if needed Walsh and he started forward, Walsh's left hand resting on his right shoulder so they would know each other's positions. In this way they inched along the inside corridor, eyes adjusting to the gloom until they could make out vague shapes.

The hallway continued.

And continued.

"What the hell?" Walsh whispered. "This is impossible."

Shaw agreed.

The building they'd entered had been a single-family dwelling, nowhere near the warehouse length they'd followed so far. Did it continue into the building behind it? Or slope downward into the ground? Both seemed unlikely. Shaw opened his mouth to respond when his searching hand collided with hard wood.

"A door," he whispered. "Closed."

"Good. 'Bout bloody time."

A note of uneasiness shaded Walsh's words. He was regretting coming in here, and Shaw had to agree. It wasn't the threat of potential danger. No, there was something … off, about this place. The lack of light and the unexpected size, the sensation that they were deeper than expected. It was disconcerting.

Should he suggest turning around? Leaving?

If this door was locked then that would be the end of this search. As crazed as these cultists were, as paranoid as they must be, this would surely be a barrier they couldn't pass.

Yet, if any door were to be locked wouldn't it have been that first one?

"Why *wasn't* that front door locked?"

"I don't know." Walsh was silent a moment. "Seems off, doesn't it?"

They slowed, contemplating.

"Doc?"

"Yes?"

"Forward or back?"

Shaw was more terrified than he'd thought possible. This was no place for a doctor. Why the hell hadn't his "uncle" sent in the soldiers? Damn the man for putting him in this position and—

"Doc?"

He thought of Singh's disappointed eyes if they retreated in failure, if he didn't do all he could. Worse, he saw the boy returning without them, putting himself in danger because Shaw hadn't been able to finish the job.

"Forward."

He grabbed the door handle, thumbing the latch with an inward groan at the lack of resistance. Unlocked. He pushed it into the room beyond. Inside the bleakness was broken by flickering torches which did little to lift the oppressive gloom grabbing at him like a living creature.

"No!"

It was real! Not the shadows but rough hands grabbing at his arms, jerking him forward into the room and to the floor. His sabre clattered away as Walsh let off his first shot. Somewhere nearby a man screamed. The grip on him was gone.

Now, as Shaw's eyes adjusted once again, he could see it. All around were cultists, dressed in the black of night and forming a semicircle.

"Kali," they moaned as one. "Kali. Kali."

Another shot. Another scream.

"Doc, get outta here. There's too many."

He crawled from the room and got to his feet, starting back the way they'd come.

Another shot.

Three left in Walsh's revolver now. Hopefully the threat of death would be enough—

Bang!

Enough to convince them—

Bang!

Enough—

Bang!

The screams of those shot were drowned out by the moans of those still coming.

"Kali."

"Kali."

"Kali."

No, you fools! It isn't Kali you follow at all! It's something worse, something older. Not just a personification of evil, but actual, ancient evil.

Shaw had no idea where the sudden knowledge came from, but he believed it with the same certainty of knowing his own name.

He started to run.

Walsh gave a grunt. The sound of fist against flesh as he punched again and again.

If Shaw had any conscious thought he would have hoped the narrowness of the hallways would allow Walsh to take them one by one. *If* he was thinking.

He was not.

Through the heavy blackness he scrambled, following what should have been a straight path back to the door. Hadn't they left it open? He rebounded off one wall with a pained groan. Then another.

"No!"

They hadn't made *any* turns. The hallway had run a straight line from the door … hadn't it? He collided with a corner, the sharpish edge biting into one shoulder, numbing it.

"Where am I?"

Strange sounds in the distance, buzzing and whirring which

drilled into his brain. The smells of death. Then the floor was gone from under his feet and he tumbled.

A wedgelike shape ground into one side and Shaw knew he was falling down stairs.

A heavy bounce, his left leg folding underneath him with a blast of white pain and a snap like dry wood. Another bounce and his head slammed against solid ground, robbing him of consciousness.

CHAPTER TWENTY-ONE

BLACKNESS.

Absolute and smothering.

Pain bit through it, rousing him.

Shaw's eyes fluttered.

Blurry shapes. A hint of movement.

He'd been … falling?

How long?

Minutes? Hours?

Where—

"Kali."

"Kali."

"Kali."

"No!"

His eyes went wide, wild, and he struggled to rise but found shifting his left leg caused a spike of pain which threatened to rob him of consciousness again. He closed his eyes against the pain and nausea, waiting for them to recede.

The leg was broken, and badly.

Not that there was a good way to break a leg.

The thought made him want to giggle and Shaw knew hysteria was close. He swallowed it, forcing the panic away, and opened his eyes again.

The blurs resolved themselves. Torches placed in holders every few feet illuminated the wide room, cultists arranged in a semicircle swaying to their chants. Behind them was a door—that final one they'd opened?

He lay on some flat, elevated surface. A table?

"Kali."

"Kali."

"Kali."

"No!" he shouted, his hoarse voice not rising above the incessant chanting. "It's *not* her. It's ..."

Only he didn't know what this was, depicted on the idol, and on the cave walls. This heinous *monster*!

No. Not a *thing or a monster*, but a *god*. Like Kali, but more ancient. More evil.

Evil.

Did ants perceive humans as evil when they were stepped on?

The cultists gawked as if he were some delicacy, at least two dozen of them. How did this building hold so many? It wasn't possible.

As impossible as not being able to find his way down a straight hallway?

"Kali."

"Kali."

"Kali."

With gentle effort Shaw turned his head right to see more gloom and Thuggees, further on another door leading deeper into this unending house. To the right ... Oh, the view there made him wish he'd lost consciousness again. Walsh lay on a second table five feet away and facing his direction. The eyes were wide and bulging, his uniform pulled away at the neck where an angry bruising tattooed his throat.

"No," Shaw said, barely a whisper. "God, please no."

But God wasn't listening ... not any god whose attention he wanted to attract.

Walsh was dead. Dead, and it was Shaw's fault. The life he'd taken at the cave paled in comparison.

Shaw turned his neck back to center, away from Walsh's staring, accusing eyes. An accusation that might be only inside his own head but well deserved nonetheless.

A massive shape stepped toward him from the waves of Thuggees and Shaw tried to recoil. This was more monster than man. Huge, a gorilla in size, while his face held a dead expression which he'd seen before. This man-thing held up both hands, as if in prayer—and for all he knew that's exactly what the gesture was.

One hand, the right, was the expected human shape, the other a dead-white claw, and Shaw knew where he'd seen those dead eyes.

The Dhoosar Maut.

What did this mean? Shaw forced attention on other Thuggees, seeing none with such ... what, deformities? Mutations? This man was a monster, in form as well as size, as much so as the Maut.

How could a beast like this exist? Had the ... had the Maut crossbred? It was an obscenity which Shaw couldn't contemplate.

He ... It closed both hands into tight fists, the knuckles cracking. That dead, slack face stretched into a smirk. Shaw's insides shriveled, stomach trying to retreat, brain wishing it could lose focus.

Soon he would share in Walsh's fate. They'd been biding their time for him to be awake.

It was no less than he deserved.

He should have persisted with his uncle, insisting he investigate. If he'd pushed enough surely that would have gotten the building searched. Walsh would still be alive.

Could've. Would've. Should've.

The least he could do was die with defiance in his eyes, take the opportunity to spit on one of these monsters if the chance came. If he could rise he would give them a hard time of it but that was impossible, held prisoner by his broken leg as much as by these Thuggees. In short time he would join his friend in whatever afterlife might exist. Would it be quick? This monster's hands were like slabs of meat.

One day Singh might be this size.

Singh!

"No."

He *couldn't* give up and die. To do so would be death for Singh. No one at the base would look after the boy, make sure he was fed and healthy, taken care of.

"No!" he repeated. "Please, I have a ..."

A what? A son? No, that wasn't quite right. But saying he had an orphan boy he watched out for wasn't sufficient to describe what the boy meant either.

Would it matter what was said? How many others had given the same emphatic plea before dying, had begged for their very lives? Nothing would stop this beast from strangling the life from his body.

The Thuggees he'd heard of were inhuman, worshipping murder, but this thing ... Was there a better word than monstrous? Obscene?

The chanting ceased.

A gloved hand came to rest on the huge man's shoulder and he stepped aside, lunatic grin remaining in place. In that space stepped two others, one man and one woman.

A woman?

Shaw's mind whirled, grateful to latch onto a subject which was not his own mortal danger. From all he'd been told by friends in Bandagar the cult avoided women, both for killing and for inclusion ... but why the hell should they? Was Kali not female? The cultists all followed her. A female cultist made perfect sense.

He came close to giggling once again and knew how close to raving he was. Did it matter in the end if he was killed by the man, the woman, or by whatever that hulking brute was?

Both man and woman wore the robes of their cult, but cleaner, paired with equally clean, black leather gloves. He held a bulky object and Shaw's gaze dropped to his hands.

Another flash of black leather.

A book.

The pair came closer, stopping within two feet of where he lay, one to each side. The man stood, unsmiling, looking as if he wanted some reaction from Shaw. Was he expected to beg? Shaw wished he had more strength, more self-respect in him than that, but knew the begging would come.

This man glanced toward the female cultist, though her attention didn't waver from Shaw. What was their relation? Husband and wife? No, the two shared some slight family resemblance. Siblings?

She held a strength in her stare, and no glimmer of the outright madness that the other chanting lunatics had. The man? A little. Yes. But not her. She was lucid, calculating, determined.

She was no one's subordinate.

The man turned toward her and gave a bow of subservience, raising the book on flat palms. Now she focused on him, waiting. The silence went on for a second, two, before he looked up into her eyes. A silent message, a warning, passed between them and the man gave several nods before returning to the tome.

Message given, she once again turned back toward Shaw. "You have the idol."

Her English was accented but the words were clearly spoken. She'd obviously had an education. The words themselves were not a question, nor accusation. Merely a statement of fact.

"I ..."

She leaned closer, face inches away and sniffed. "Oh yes, you have touched it. Held it."

"Yes." Shaw agreed, though wondered on the insinuation that it could be smelled on him.

A soft chuckle, without any real humor, and she stood upright again. "We knew one of you kept the idol after the cave, but couldn't determine who." She shrugged. "Kali is patient. We watched all these years, of course, but saw no sign of who possessed it ... or that any of you were ready."

"Ready? Ready for what?"

"We knew," she continued, ignoring his question. "In Kali's time the holder would be directed to us, and here you are."

Shaw cleared his throat, eyes going to the left and the hulking man-monster there, looking at Shaw as if he were some bug to be crushed rather than a person.

"I ... Yes," Shaw said. "I took the idol, brought it back to the outpost with me."

Another man, behind the monster and to his right translated these words to the cultists, who all moaned. Thankfully they did not resume chanting.

"I carried it back, in my pocket," Shaw said, mind seeing the idol and the words on it once again. "Kept it there until ..."

An image of Singh bubbled up, replacing the idol. Shaw narrowed his eyes at the woman, staring into her face.

"Why? Why kill Lassiter for the idol only to abandon it?" He aimed for the words to come out as terse demand, sounding like a plea to even his own ears. "It doesn't make sense."

For a moment it seemed she would not answer, just continue

on to some other topic. "Not abandoned. The idol was passed on, as is its nature."

Shaw shook his head. "I don't understand."

The leader smiled indulgently, as if Shaw were a slow-witted child.

"Your friend—Lassiter, was it?—touched the idol. A great honor," she said. "Any who touch the idol are marked for service to Kali, another privilege. Your friend refused to join us, refused to serve Kali. This marked him for death, as the other doctor had when he abandoned his duty."

Other doctor? Middlemarch.

"His duty? The idol—"

"After your friend's murder our discovery at the cave was inevitable. This served our purposes. We wanted to be found. Our brothers sacrificed themselves so the next Britisher would find the idol, and be ready."

"Ready?" he repeated. "Ready for *what*?"

Shaw barely whispered but the woman heard, all the while the other translated, whispers running through the crowd.

"Ready to *read*," she said, and before Shaw could respond, "The idol softens the English mind, unable to believe in anything you can't touch or see. The idol makes you more receptive to great Kali's teachings. The writings on the idol speak to you, corrupt you."

The writings. Yes.

Shaw had no words, though he hardly needed them to keep her explaining.

"You must be strong to have endured the idol so many years without joining Kali."

"Years ...?"

Hopelessness surrounded him. Mad cultists. Broken leg. Walsh dead. And yet ... a glimmer. They didn't know every-thing. He propped himself on his elbows, weight leaning to his right leg.

"I don't have your damned idol."

The man holding the book drew in a breath. The woman's eyes narrowed. Translation hissed out, snaking through the room with volume rising at each subsequent person. Moans began again. The woman raised one hand and all sound ceased.

Shaw *had* made the right choice in sending the idol away. Though he wondered now on what he'd done to the poor devil who'd received it at the Museum.

"I'm happy to have deprived you of your treasure," he spat.

The woman considered then shrugged, accepting what could not be changed without much reaction. It was disappointing. Shaw wanted her to wail for the loss of the idol, to demand it back. Anything.

She gestured and the gloved man brought the book forward. It reeked of an evil beyond the mustiness of ancient paper. Sulphur and excrement and blood. Leather bound and black as midnight, etched designs in the cover. One clasp of tarnished silver was set at the middle to keep this book sealed, though this was now undone.

In preparation to be opened.

Shaw shook his head, raising his hands to ward off whatever lurked inside. The movement drew a gasp of pain as too much twist was applied to his broken leg. It was a short distraction, diluted by his fear. He didn't want a closer look at that book, couldn't, his mind refused. *This* was the book Singh told him about. *This* was the greater treasure, that greater evil.

"The idol has done its task and shall return to us in time," the woman said, allowing space for the man to approach.

He rubbed one finger along the raised leather design on the book's cover.

"We wish to read this book," she said. "Oh, how badly we wish it. But we cannot. Most of my Thuggees are illiterate, and those who are not are simple, and join Kali too quickly if they try."

Join Kali?

They go mad!

"*You* haven't looked inside," Shaw said.

"No."

"I ..." The man tapped the book's cover with splayed fingers. "I have seen ... some."

He sighed, hand tracing the design again with abject longing and reverence. The woman stared at him, waiting, but nothing more came.

"We cannot join Kali yet," she continued, gesturing to the man, then herself. "We have our own tasks. It is why my cousin and I wear gloves."

A cousin. Yes, that fit.

"We've abducted educated men, scholars, writers, historians. Some, so fascinated by the writing inside have gone too deep too quickly on touching the book. They wanted to know more, but Kali has her secrets and guards them well.

"This book will bring the Kali-Yuga. A time when Kali will walk the earth once more to rule my people. Each attempted reading brings us closer, each helps wear away the veil between worlds, just as each death in Kali's name."

"But ... But ..."

The woman laughed. A single note that was there and gone. "You have been told the Thuggees seek to prevent Kali's rising." Her voice was soft, but it pulled all attention in the room toward her.

Shaw nodded.

The man holding the book grinned. "That is the way of old Thuggee."

"No doubt they would consider us abominations," she said, then leaned forward, hands behind back as if to impart some great piece of wisdom. "Why should we prevent great Kali from rising?"

"The great goddess shall return and free us," the man with the book said, "Reward us."

This last was said with a half giggle, more suited to a child performing mischief than an evil cultist. The woman's eyes went to her cousin, lingering a moment.

Shaw shook his head. This creature they prayed to would not return to free the Indian people. It would crush them without a thought, as it would crush any obstacle that came in its way. Unless … the reward they sought was madness.

Why would anyone *want* to go mad?

She gestured again and this time the man opened the book, pages falling open on their own. His eyes went to whatever lay inside, growing wide, lingering. Beside him the huge man-monster inched closer to peer over one shoulder. All others moaned in horrible ecstasy. The man ran one gloved finger down the page, teeth peeling back in a grin, eyes huge.

The woman cleared her throat and the grin vanished, tearing his gaze from the page with a soft cry. The man's breathing was labored and a sweat had broken out across his forehead.

"My apologies, Ananya," he mumbled, not looking toward her. Then in a low whisper only Shaw would have heard, "Oh, how I envy you."

With obvious effort he turned the book to face Shaw.

It was an instinctive reaction but Shaw looked and wished he had not. The picture was of a terrifying creature. Tentacles dangling from a horrible mouth. Head bulbous. Wings spreading behind.

The distortion of Kali on the cave walls.

Lassiter's idol.

All around the picture, surrounding the margins, were words which Shaw immediately averted his eyes from. Too late. They pulled up a memory of those on the idol, his finger tracing it again and again that entire march back from the cave.

Oh!

Those words!

Mad words. Words of neither English nor Indian Sanskrit. Something other, older. He closed his eyes tight against them, refusing to look at those in the book. They assaulted his mind from without, like a madman hammering against a flimsy door. The lock could not keep this intruder out.

Those words were etched into the paper of his mind.

Demanding to be read.

His jaw was grabbed, soft glove brushing against his chin. A smaller hand. The woman, Ananya. Did she mean to hold his face while forcing his eyes open? Shaw pressed them together tighter, trying to push her hand away. If they expected him to look—

"Cthulhu."

What? That word. Where had it—

No! *He'd* said it. How …?

And what did it mean?

A name. *The* name. This tentacled, horrific god. Its name was—

"Cthulhu!" the woman's soft voice agreed, close by his ear.

Her grip released his jaw.

"Cthulhu!" she repeated to the mob, ecstasy in her voice.

The contradiction between this name and Kali didn't give any cultist distress. They moaned in ecstatic response.

A rough slap shocked his eyes open, a backhand from this woman. The book came closer, held vertical by her cousin. Soon it would be pressed against the flesh of his face, at which point he would lose his mind forever.

Ananya's piercing eyes remained on him. "Don't fight it."

"No, please … I can't …" He focused anywhere but on that book, refusing to look at the words, or the drawing. One glimpse had been more than enough. "Please. I can't … ca—ca —Cthulhu!"

The word burst from his throat as a scream without any

bidding of his own. His eyes shifted from the woman to her cousin then back, all the while aware of that book's presence, so close. So close. Its closeness was vile, loathsome, like bloated maggots crawling across his face, his eyes, his lips. Shaw recoiled as much as possible, struggling to ignore the whispers inside his own skull.

"That is not dead which can eternal lie!" he said through clenched teeth.

The Thuggees swayed in time to words.

"Kali."

"Kali."

"Kali."

Word after word babbled from his mouth then, without knowing what was said, knowing this would be his existence now. A drooling madman like those others who'd had their sanity devoured.

With each passing moment he cared less and less, his words becoming delirious shrieks closer to animal noises than narration.

"It is enough," Ananya said. "His mind is ready."

"Ready?" he screamed. "Ready? Ready?"

Ready for what?

But he knew. This was simply the beginning, a warm-up. There was more!

"Rest for now," she said, close to his ear. "Soon, you shall read the words to raise Kali."

"No. No, no, no, no, no! Please!"

The open book remained before his eyes, the cousin's sweaty-faced glare on Shaw.

"Suresh!" she said, a hint of warning to her tone.

The man, Suresh, jerked and closed the book.

Shaw lay panting and sweating, delirious with horror, the pain of his leg a distant welcome voice which barely cut into the fog. Sanity was a spiral, a track his mind rolled along, coming closer and closer to the bottom. When it reached that point he would be done.

Mad.

He teetered on the precipice.

A sharp sound broke into the delirium. Unexpected. Far away.

A crack.

Then a shout.

They called him back.

A second gunshot rang out and the man, Suresh, staggered and fell, taking that damned book with him. Thuggees spun toward the door, broken inward, soldiers with pointing rifles there. Another crack and a second man fell. One more and the huge monster of a man raised his clawless hand, exploring a wound that had appeared in his opposite shoulder. It seeped a liquid more black than red, oozing like syrup. Whatever passed for its blood.

It did not fall.

The room descended into madness.

And Shaw did not care, for he had already seen true madness.

The book was out of view but he could perceive the influence of those cursed words invading his mind. He thanked whatever god existed that he had not been forced to touch it.

Cultists surged forward, rushing toward the soldiers who held their rifles pointed into the room. Each would fire, then retreat to reload while another two took their place. One man held a revolver which he emptied into the advancing wave of cultists, dropping one after another.

Not all advanced though.

"It's a distraction," Shaw mumbled. "Like at the cave."

"Shield me," Ananya ordered, barely glancing at the hulking brute.

He acknowledged with a slight bow and stepped between his

leader and the danger. She bent, retrieved the tome, and turned to leave.

"No!"

A hand appeared next to Shaw, pulling a body behind it. The cousin, Suresh, forcing his feet under him, blood coursing from a shoulder wound similar to the huge man. He held one hand to the wound, staring at the book.

Ananya spared him a nod and pointed across the room toward the other exit. "Go, cousin."

Suresh took the book and went, wound forgotten, while the woman turned back for a brief moment, focusing on Shaw.

"Goodbye, Doctor."

No! He wanted to scream. *They know who I am!*

Or *was* he screaming?

One last look toward Shaw with that expression, all the more horrible for its lack of insanity, then she pivoted and was gone, following her cousin through the other door. Three others joined her with man-monster remaining between them and the bullets. Somehow this greater target didn't take another hit while ensuring their escape.

No! Ensuring the *book* would escape.

"Hey!" Shaw screamed. "They're getting away."

Yes. Now he was screaming.

Bang.

Bang.

Bang.

None of the shots reached those passing through the far door.

"Hey," he repeated, with less volume.

They're escaping with the book.

A thing of nightmares.

Which had almost robbed his sanity.

And he'd only seen ... one ... page ...

One.

One.

One.

One ...

Like the effects he had seen from morphine or opium, the world around became unreal. Shadows and thoughts consumed his mind, gnawing at his soul.

Oblivion came and finally, mercifully, robbed him of his senses.

CHAPTER TWENTY-TWO

ONCE AGAIN SHAW'S EYES FLUTTERED OPEN, LIGHT BLINDING HIM. The comforting smell of clean linen rose to his nose. His vision cleared to reveal he lay on one of the hospital beds he'd so often stood over, only now he was the patient.

Singh waited nearby, arms crossed and impassive, waiting.

Shaw drew in a deep breath, mind whirling and sifting through the memories until it landed on one piece he would have rather stayed buried. "Walsh!"

"Gone," Singh said, coming closer.

It was all the answer he needed. Walsh was gone and he already knew that, just as he knew it was all his damn fault.

There would be time for recriminations later, though.

"The book?" he said, trying to push himself up and wishing he hadn't as a cannon-shot of pain blasted through him.

Singh placed a hand against Shaw's chest, stopping him from rising further ... a feat he was nowhere near capable of. "It escaped."

It. Not they. Not the cultists.

It all came back in a rush. The book. What was inside.

Everything!

No.

No, no, no, no, no, no, no!

Why couldn't he have left that alone?

"I saw it," Shaw said, eyes widening, remembering. "I saw *inside* it."

Singh bolted upright in alarm, removing his hand from Shaw as if burned. "Inside?"

"Yes. Yes. Yes. The drawing. I saw *Him*!"

Now Singh took a step back, shaking his head.

"Oh, yesssss … that dread, tentacled god." His voice rose from hiss to shout. "Cthulhu!"

Doctor White rushed from the ward's further end to watch goggle-eyed from beside Singh.

"I saw it!" he shouted at them.

What's more, he could still sense it.

Oh yes, the book was out there!

It probed at him too, at all of them. Death surrounded them, sucked at their very souls. Time eroded the human race, bringing them closer to the day when *Cthulhu* would walk the earth once again.

Shaw brought his hands up, one on either side of his head, feeling like it would explode if he didn't.

White glanced at Singh who grabbed Shaw's arm, holding it steady. The doctor pulled a syringe from one pocket and expertly inserted it into Shaw's vein. He didn't fight it. Why bother? All was inevitable.

The morphine concoction entered his system and soon he found his eyes rolling up into his head.

Darkness took him to a dreamless sleep.

Only … not dreamless. Not quite.

The morphine was a weaker mixture, enough to put him under but not enough to rob him of thought.

Mists surrounded him, with silent inhuman faces watching him. The great eyes of that tentacled nightmare watched him, judged him. An awareness of being examined and declared unfit, unworthy, a disappointment.

The thought of its unholy displeasure was terrifying to contemplate.

Singh once again stood over his bed—or was it still? He'd changed neither position nor expression.

"Tell me you've slept," Shaw rasped, mouth drier than a cracker. "Water, please."

Singh poured a glass then helped him sit up. Shaw ignored the howling complaint from his leg and gulped greedily, as if days had passed since the last time he'd drank.

Had it been days?

"How long?"

"Since last night," Singh said. "It is almost noon."

More than twelve hours unconscious. Morphine robbed time so effectively, so completely.

Thirst taken care of, Shaw turned attention to his leg. It was broken of course, he remembered that from the night before—that and other information he knew better than to consider. A heaviness dragged at the leg and he pulled back the sheet to view the cast, starting mid-thigh and reaching all the way to his ankle.

"Broken," Singh said, as though informing him what to expect for lunch. "The bone splintered and lacerated the skin."

Not *just* broken then.

A wave of revulsion flashed through him at the mental image. It was a wound he'd treated in others, more than once.

Still, it was a different matter when these things happened to oneself, harder to disassociate the point of view and look with a clinical eye.

A break of this sort took at least three months to heal, more likely four or five.

He *was* alive though.

"I have you to thank for the rescue?"

Singh shrugged. "I started back as you passed through the door."

"You knew two people wouldn't be enough."

"No, but I knew having too many would be better than too few."

"Well done."

The reason he was alive, or not barking at the stars mad, was because this boy looked at the situation and saw better than adults had. Only he wasn't a boy, not really. He'd seen and experienced too much. He might be only fifteen but that only meant he wasn't quite a man either. Not in terms of years, anyway; in terms of experience he might be older than McCready.

"Your raving is gone," Singh said, watching his face.

Shaw thought about that, searched for any remnant of those sensations, that madness which sucked at him like the ocean tide. It was distant, as if something dreamed.

There'd been a name … No! That was better not considered. Calling a name could lead to a reply.

"It seems to be."

"Most I have seen do not recover."

How did one recover from madness?

"My god, Singh. I saw the one page, and that just a glimpse," he said, taking a deep breath. "That book is evil. Pure evil. More so than the cult, or even the idol."

"You did not touch it."

A statement, not a question, but Shaw shook his head.

"This is why your mind has returned."

The concept, the very thought was more madness, but how could he deny firsthand experience? Only ... he'd done that before, chose logic over fact. Not this time. Any lingering doubts on the nature of that book were gone from his mind.

"They escaped," Shaw said.

"Yes."

"The *book* escaped."

Shaw thought back, trying to remember details while being careful not to fall back over an unseen precipice of madness.

"Five escaped," Shaw said. "No, six. One had a ... a claw, like the Maut."

Singh settled into the one chair, listening.

"Their leader is a woman."

It was all information Singh undoubtedly knew, but he allowed Shaw the chance to sort his thoughts.

"Well, Shaw," Neufeld said, arriving at his bed. "Seems you're fully awake."

Neufeld looked exhausted. Was it just the extra tasks from being a doctor short, or more? Horrible nightmares and terrifying paintings. When Neufeld closed his eyes did he see what Shaw had seen last night? Was he—

Shaw stopped himself, the raving at the outer edge of his consciousness, waiting. With effort he retreated from those thoughts, focused instead on Neufeld and another reason for guilt. Shaw had intended to keep an eye on the doctor and keep him from hurting himself.

"How are you feeling?" Neufeld asked, eyes on Shaw and truly caring about the response.

Only, Shaw didn't know *how* he felt. His basic concept of the world had been destroyed and the events of last night left him with too many options on how to feel. Stupid. Hurt. Scared. Ashamed. A need to hunt down these last cultists and the book for the greater benefit of humanity. Was there a name for that?

Mostly he was filled with a great heartsickness for Walsh.

Another friend gone.

Shaw grunted a noncommittal reply while Neufeld made notes on the chart, eyes sympathetic. He then leaned forward as if checking Shaw's eyes and said in a low voice, "Armstrong and McCready were here. Asking when you'd be awake."

Shaw closed his eyes and nodded.

"I suspect they have questions."

When Shaw opened his eyes again Neufeld was gone.

"The book, Singh. We have to find it. Find them."

Singh considered and gave a shrug.

"Where would they go?" Shaw asked.

"Out of the area."

"Are you sure?" he asked, then gasped, positive he'd found the answer. "The cave?"

"No."

"Where then?"

Singh shook his head, his message trickling through. The cultists and the book were gone.

Shaw leaned back, frustrated and angry. Twice they'd had the chance to stamp these maniacs out and capture that book, destroy it. But they hadn't known ... *he* hadn't known ... the depths of the evil they were dealing with. Much more than just the evil of man.

If only Walsh and he had taken others with them, or brought soldiers and left them at the doors. Then they would have the cultists, *and* the book ...

Was that true though?

The soldiers had arrived, surprised the cultists, and still those five had escaped with the book. The one way they could have gotten them all would have been to surround the house, gone in from all entries. Even then, if there were some other secret exit ...

Shaw made a disgusted sound. "It's maddening."

Maddening.

Maddening.

Yes. Something to that temporary madness he'd experienced on waking. It echoed. Familiar. Like a madness he'd experienced before. Only how could he have experienced madness and not …

Of course!

When he'd encountered the Maut, it had drawn him to it, drawn his soul away. Afterwards he had been out of his mind for a short time. The madness brought by the Maut was reminiscent of that brought by the book.

"How are they related? How?"

Singh cocked his head to one side and rose to his feet, gaze shooting past Shaw then back. "I shall investigate."

Without anything further he left.

Shaw followed where Singh had looked, already knowing what approached. Armstrong and McCready. He prepared for what was to come: questions and accusations, recriminations and punishment.

Would he be placed in prison? He *had* defied orders.

"Well, you've had quite the adventure," Commander Armstrong said, taking the chair Singh had vacated.

He sounded as though he spoke of a vacation Shaw had returned from.

McCready stopped at the foot of his bed, arms crossed and scowling.

Shaw looked at the commander—finding he could no longer consider him "uncle"—and gave a nod, shocked to find tears brimming his eyes, waiting to spill. He was suddenly the small child in front of an adult after some ill-advised experience both forbidden and terrifying. Armstrong placed one hand on his shoulder and patted in a there-there gesture, meant to be comforting.

"How's the leg?" the commander asked.

Shaw thought about it, muttered, "Not so bad."

"Oh, yes?" McCready jumped in. "Once that morphine wears off then you'll be feeling it."

The tone of voice said, *And it's exactly what you deserve.*

"Hmm, well, Shaw," Armstrong said, voice soothing, drawing Shaw's attention back. "Why don't you tell us all that happened."

For a moment Shaw hesitated, ashamed by the death of Walsh, then he took a deep breath and launched into the story. No point in denial since most of it was obvious already, and it wasn't in his nature anyway. He hammered on the point of how he'd come to Armstrong first, telling him of trouble, asking for help. The commander waved it aside. Inconvenient. Inconsequential.

There would be no acceptance of blame on this man's part.

"Hmm, so six escaped?" Armstrong mused at the end of his account.

"Yes."

"Well, six madmen can't very well topple an empire, eh?"

McCready grumbled, "I would say the cult is broken for all time."

Shaw snorted at the hollow words, said before in his presence and meaning as much now. Looking from face to face he saw the same blind acceptance of the sentiment as that time they gathered in the commander's office.

"A minor resurgence," Armstrong added, ignoring Shaw's reaction. "A few throwbacks to an earlier time."

Shaw saw it now. This was a conversation already held between the two, rehearsed before coming to his bedside. His part was to fill in the silence with agreement, parrot back the words.

One important part he'd kept to himself was the book. How could he explain an item of absolute evil, or the existence of ancient gods? *He* hadn't believed until seeing with his own eyes. They would think him mad.

Would they be right?

"You need to search for them," Shaw said.

Armstrong's gaze flicked to McCready and back. "Of course, of course."

They wouldn't. Not any more than they already had, and he wouldn't convince them of the true danger without sounding like a lunatic. They would search the way they had after Lassiter's murder: send out patrols, look in obvious places.

Singh was right, though: The Thuggees would be gone. They had no idol to trick someone into taking this time, no reason to be found.

"Captain Walsh died a hero," Armstrong said, changing topic. "Brave man."

The mention of Walsh was like a physical jolt. Painful.

The tears threatened to return.

"Walsh. He … It was my idea. I—"

"Rest," Armstrong said, giving another there-there pat. "You've had a traumatic experience, but you'll be on your feet soon enough."

As if to emphasize it the commander rose to his own feet and, giving a quick farewell, left.

McCready stayed, staring. His mouth worked, eyes narrowed.

Ah, here would come the reprimands and recriminations.

"What were you thinking?" the older man asked, not waiting for a response. "You are a doctor, one of *my* doctors. You're here to save lives and treat injuries, not run off on hairbrained adventures."

Shaw opened his mouth but McCready was already on to his next verse. Also rehearsed?

"If you want that sort of life, transfer to the army. This can be arranged if you prefer shooting guns to treating those who do the shooting. The death of Captain Walsh is on your conscience, as it should be. If not for you that brave man would still be alive."

That brave man.

Brave, but so much more. Walsh was a man who did the right thing, even if it was inconvenient. A man who stood by a friend and followed him into danger, not because he was ordered to as a soldier might be, but because he listened to the facts and came to his own conclusion, because he'd been needed. Yes, Walsh was brave, but it was the courage of his convictions that were bravest.

"He *was* a good man," Shaw said.

McCready lips pressed into a tight angry line.

"And I will remember his bravery and friendship forever."

What more could be said? Shaw lapsed into silence, thoughts swirling. Walsh's sacrifice. Armstrong saying the cult was broken. The idea that they certainly were not. The book. The *Book*! An evil more malignant than anything McCready had encountered in all his many years.

"What were you thinking?" McCready repeated, summing up the argument, then turned to go. Message delivered.

"What was I thinking?" Shaw asked.

McCready turned back, surprised. As was Shaw, not realizing he'd had any more to say on the subject. Words did spring into his mind and they fit the situation, saying all that needed to be said about Armstrong and McCready's inaction, about Walsh's sacrifice.

"I was thinking of words John Stuart Mill said." He took a breath and summoned the words to mind, hoping he could get them right, or at least their intent. "He said: *Bad men need nothing more to compass their ends, than that good men should look on and do nothing.*"

McCready's lips vanished, pressed together so tightly.

"*That* was what I was thinking," he said. "And it was something which Captain Walsh believed, too."

CHAPTER TWENTY-THREE

BANDAGAR, INDIA—MARCH 5TH, 1885

... We didn't destroy the cult, and the greater threat of that book is still an active danger, in the wrong hands. No, for all of my grand talk about doing what is right there is nothing to show for my actions except a dead friend and my own broken leg. The price is too high.

McCready was right. I'm no soldier, no adventurer. Just a doctor ... and a fool ...

"They have disappeared," Singh said after his second day of searching, no note of surprise in his voice.

Disappeared?

"Magic?"

Aloud it sounded ridiculous and Shaw closed his eyes against the thought. It would seem he was now prepared to believe anything.

"No," Singh cut into his thoughts. "Kali does not give power. Kali takes."

"Not Kali—"

"The name matters less than what is done in her name."

"Yes. Yes, you are correct."

Would there be a day when this boy no longer educated him?

"I returned to the cave."

Shaw pushed himself up straighter, with effort, the wound screeching like an iron spike dragged across sheet metal. He gasped and gritted his teeth against the excruciating pain.

"Morphine?" Singh asked, glancing for Doctor Barrowman.

Shaw shook his head. There was a danger of dependency where that was concerned, he'd seen it before. It plummeted from help to want to need. Morphine. Opium. Cocaine. Where would it stop if that door was opened? No, he would accept the drug as a last resort.

"The cave?" he prompted.

Singh shrugged. "Empty."

"Has anyone been there?"

"Not for years."

Nowhere nearby. Not at the caves. No sign of them.

"Then ... they *are* gone," Shaw said.

Another shrug.

Sometimes that impassive attitude of Singh's irked him. Nothing riled the boy, looking at everything with a calm, logical perspective that Shaw only wished he could achieve.

Back to the matter at hand.

Gone.

But where? Gone from Bandagar and the outpost only meant they were someone else's problem. People who might not be as aware of the danger.

Still, what could be done until and unless the cultists returned to this area? Shaw racked his mind and came back with a truly unsatisfying answer.

Nothing. They could do *nothing*!

Nothing against the Thuggees.

Nothing against the book.

His mind whirled round and round, like a storm, searching for some small piece to latch onto.

"The madness," he said, not realizing it was still in his thoughts.

Singh cocked his head to one side, a gesture that had become his equivalent of one raised eyebrow.

Shaw's thoughts were a mad jumble, whirling in a storm. Fragments of ideas, snatches of near understanding, unrelated concepts sliding together … No, not quite together.

"This madness," he said, mulling it over. "The madness from that book."

Familiar madness.

Yes.

"Similar to the Maut's, but greater."

Similar madness? Are there distinct types, like the flavours of food?

Yes, there must be.

"You think the two related?" Singh said.

The same words Walsh had said two nights ago about cult and Maut.

Thuggees. Maut. Book. Even that idol. All related.

"Yes."

Singh lapsed into silence, following his own thoughts.

More troubling than a possible connection to the book, an inconsistent fact which continued to peck at Shaw's thoughts. "Why are some driven mad, while others are torn apart?"

Again Singh had no response.

"What do we know? The Maut draws people toward it, staying in the shadows, only coming out at night. Why? Fear of discovery? No."

"The light."

Shaw looked up at Singh. "The light …? Yes … Yes! An aversion? A weakness?"

Another shrug and more silence. One of the boy's best qualities was allowing a person to think when he had nothing to add himself. Most people filled in silence with their own blather.

Light.

Yes.

Shaw leaned back against the pillows in search of some position which wouldn't cause agony, considering this concept. At the moment this could be nothing more than theoretical puzzle so any concept would do as well as another. If it kept his mind focused on anything other than the need for morphine for the next minute or two then it would be a welcome diversion.

CHAPTER TWENTY-FOUR

BANDAGAR, INDIA — APRIL 6TH, 1885

... The first month has passed. Slowly. Grudgingly.

Life around me has returned to normal while I remain confined to this bed in the hospital ward. McCready ordered two months of complete bed rest while my leg is kept under observation.

One more month.

After which, if I am up to it, I'll be able to help around the hospital once again, as well as permitted to make the transition back to staying in my own room. I have already resolved that no matter the pain involved I SHALL make that transition.

Meanwhile I've filled an entire notebook with sketches and plans on a solution for the Maut. This distraction, I will freely admit, has grown to an obsession. The Maut fears the light! This is just a theory, of course, but it has merit. It feels true.

The best idea in my notebook cannot be carried out alone. Certainly not by someone with a limited mobility ...

Bandagar, India—April 15th, 1885

... Six weeks has crawled past since my injury. Each day like a month.

Singh does his best to look after my needs while I do my best to find some sense of calm and allow my leg to heal.

I've been lucky to avoid infection in my wound, thanks—I am convinced—to McCready's insistence on following Lister's teachings. There is that at least, though by now the pain should have eased off, not completely of course but it should be somewhat better.

It is not.

This isn't unheard of, though it is disheartening. Concerning. Worrying.

Worst of all is the fact I can do nothing except wait and hope to walk normally once again. Optimism, I must hold on to that, but it is easier said than done.

Most of my visitors, other than Singh, have been fellow doctors, both on and off duty. Even White and Adamson have come by to show support, keeping all snide comments to themselves. Thankfully they never stay long. I'm sure the underlying motive to their visits is to see the curiosity piece on display, and chuckle over my discomfort when they are alone again. Perhaps I don't give them enough credit. Neufeld comes on a regular basis to chat and keep my spirits up, or try at least, but this confinement to bed is driving me mad.

No! Madness is not something to speak of so glibly. Not anymore.

I'm afraid I am not the best of company to my visitors. Perhaps that is why Commander Armstrong no longer stops by ...

Bandagar, India—May 2nd, 1885

... McCready's two-month prescribed course of recuperation is coming to an end. Tomorrow, with the aid of a wheelchair, I shall be allowed to make hospital rounds once again, to actually be of some use.

Neufeld, on his last visit, had the haunted eyes I associate with his nightmare stages. On seeing my concern he lifted both sleeves to prove he had not inflicted harm to himself again. He claims to be in control and is bewildered by what he'd done the last time.

It is indeed his artistic side making him more susceptible. Not because he is "sensitive," as Lassiter said all those years ago, but because he is open to input from all around him. He looks at the world with different eyes.

His nightmares prove the Maut is back in this area, and I fear that means it's only a matter of time before Neufeld does do harm to himself again.

Tomorrow I also return to my own room. At which point Singh will track down Corporal Eames and ask him to visit me.

It seems I am not done playing the fool just yet …

———

Walsh had spoken favorably of Corporal Eames often. One of his most trusted men and in line to become captain himself one day.

No doubt at all existed in Shaw's mind that Eames and the other men hated him for what had happened to his commanding officer. He accepted their hate, deserved it.

Shaw stared out the window, dreading the coming confrontation but accepting its necessity. He should have given Walsh's men the chance to speak their mind before now and get it off their chests, asked at least Eames to come to his hospital bed. Now the resentment will have festered and grown.

A knock at the door was followed by Singh coming through with Eames following. The man looked left and right as if expecting a trap.

"You wanted to see me, sir."

"Yes, Eames, I did."

Where to begin?

The hardest part first.

"Eames, I am sorry."

The corporal's face went from wary to confused. "Sir?"

Shaw took a deep breath and let it out in a barely audible sigh, not able to look the man in his eyes. "I'm sorry. Sorry to you and the other men, for the … the death of Captain Walsh."

"I … Sir, may I speak plainly?"

"Please do."

Here it came. The true feelings. The blame and recriminations, the insight into how these brave men felt about him. It was no less than deserved.

"We … me and the lads. We're the ones who are sorry. We should have gotten there sooner."

Shaw's own confusion encouraged Eames to continue.

"If we'd reacted quicker when he came to us." Eames nodded toward Singh. "Then we would have maybe saved the captain, and …"

Eames looked down at Shaw's leg.

Shaw digested this bit of information. Guilt, it seemed, was in abundance to spread around.

"Everyone blaming themselves," Shaw said. "Not what Walsh would have wanted, is it, corporal?"

"No sir. I suppose not."

Shaw brushed fingers along the cast of his wounded leg, looking down before speaking again. "I … have an idea, Eames. It's a bit on the mad side, but if it works we may be able to get a little back for the captain."

"From the Thug … I mean, these … villains?"

"You can call them what they are, at least in this room. Thuggees, plain and simple."

Eames's mouth quirked at the corner. "Yes, sir."

"Don't try that with any other officer, mind you."

Eames shook his head.

"No, not the Thuggees, I'm afraid. Not yet. They're out there but we don't know where."

Eames's eyes narrowed, "Then who—?"

"The Maut."

Corporal Eames took a step back and gave a low whistle. His eyes shifted from Shaw to the window then back again, as if planning his escape. "And they're connected?"

"I think so," Shaw said. "They seem to come back at the same time."

"Hmm ..." Eames considered this, staring out the window before answering. "And you say you have a plan?"

"I do." With a deep breath Shaw prepared to tell his mad idea, sure that Eames would think him just as mad. "The Maut can't come into the light. It's a weakness and with hope the light actually hurts it. In either case, we lure it forward then cut off its retreat with a light source."

The corporal absorbed the idea, clear enough except for the one vague part which might be tough to swallow. "Lure how?"

"Well, we give the Maut some bait, but prevent that bait from going to the Maut when it calls."

"And this bait is?"

"Someone who can't go to it. Say, someone confined to a wheelchair."

Singh, silent until that moment, sucked in one quick, surprised breath.

It took Eames less than a day to recruit five other men who'd all been part of Shaw's rescue months ago and fill them in on the idea. Each immediately jumped at the chance to be involved.

The plan itself was simple.

It involved Shaw in his wheelchair left at the opening between hospital and dining hall, where he'd encountered the monster years earlier.

The bait.

Outlining it all for Eames while in the safety of his room it had been easy, logical, rational. Now, two nights later, in the gloom of night and strapped to his wheelchair it felt like ill-conceived lunacy.

The wheels of his chair were locked. The chair's belt, in place to prevent patients from falling out, was fastened tightly, secured far behind him where he wouldn't be able to reach. Between him and the trees, still between the buildings, a tiger trap had been dug for the Maut to fall into, a temporary electric light installed and ready to be turned on. Three soldiers crouched around the far side, ready to rush out with torches and force the Maut on into the trap.

Then, if it *could* be killed with lights that's what they would do. Second-best option would be holding it prisoner until a better idea came. Armstrong would have to listen when confronted with such physical proof.

But ...

Lunacy. Lunacy!

He couldn't do this for as many nights as it took. The Maut was certainly in the area but that didn't mean it would come to the outpost.

So many parts of this plan had major faults. He saw that now.

Would the Maut be aware of the trap and not come?

Could the soldiers resist its influence?

No. This was insanity, it—

Shaw pivoted in his chair, looking at Eames and Singh who concealed themselves in front of the hospital. The remaining two soldiers waited in front of the dining hall. He opened his mouth to call them, to tell them to come free him.

The plan was off.

He couldn't do this. He was afraid.

Terrified.

And ... everything had gone silent. No birds. No crickets.

His gaze shot back around toward the murkiness between buildings.

Movement in the shadows.

"No!"

But yes.

There could be no doubt on what approached. Its call wormed into Shaw's mind.

"No." This time barely a whisper.

The Maut shambled forward, coming from the trees' edge. Its attention focused on him. Grey, leathery flesh sagged from it, the flesh of the dead. Its black eyes drilled into him. Probing.

Shaw's brain screamed, wanting to flee, while his body twitched in a desire to go to this monster. Fear and hopelessness grasped him roughly, as if with those awful dangling claws.

"Nooooo," he repeated one last time.

Once again he struggled to rise, not caring a whit for any further damage that would do to his leg. His hands fumbled, clawing to release the belt which would allow him to go, all the while terrified that he might find a way.

"No. Please no."

The Maut shambled closer, closer, stopping on the edge of the trap the soldiers had dug that afternoon, right arm close to the ground. Its dead eyes bored into Shaw's, his soul shriveling.

Why wouldn't it take that final step?

It knew. It knew!

All their plan. Everything.

It knew!!

The Maut took a step back.

Shaw bucked against the bond holding him, struggling to be free.

Light!

It sprung up behind the Maut, illuminating the space between the two buildings. Nowhere close to the light of day but enough to force back the shadows. Three soldiers came from the tree side holding lit torches, adding to the illumination, but not nearing the Maut.

No! This was the part of his plan that was so flawed. So dangerously, stupidly, flawed.

Those soldiers would be drawn in by the Maut!

Indeed, all three stopped, dropping their torches into the dirt before them. None drew nearer though, hesitant, as if stunned and forgetting what they'd planned to do.

As the Maut focused on those three soldiers Shaw felt its influence ease on himself. The need to go to it had eased, but the terror remained. It could affect him and the soldiers but couldn't draw in that many. Of course! It would have done so before now if it could.

The monster's eyes shifted with the slowness of honey pouring. Left. Right. Back.

It hesitated. Nowhere to go.

Yes! They had it!

Trapped!

The Maut looked toward the trees, now behind that light, behind the torches. It turned toward Shaw again, taking one step. A low moan came from the creature, haunting, growing in pitch to a shriek. It pierced the night and carried on the air.

A wisp of steam rose from the Maut, its skin hissing, bubbling.

Yes! He'd been right. The light *was* its weakness.

Could they force it into the trap? Now—

In the space between heartbeats the Maut dissolved, like dirty ice, its liquid oozing into the ground to leave a greasy puddle behind.

The soldiers on the far side of their trap roused, shaking heads and looking around. One stooped to retrieve his torch while staring at where the monster had been a moment ago.

Shaw's mouth dropped open as he eased back into the wheelchair. The influence of the Maut had left him, the desire to go to it vanished with the monster itself.

"Hah!" Eames whooped rushing up beside Shaw. "It worked, doc!"

Singh, too, came to stand behind Shaw's wheelchair, releasing the belt holding him in place.

Yes, it certainly appeared to have worked as they'd planned. So, why was he so uneasy? That sensation crept up his body like a spider.

"Something is wrong," he said.

"Behind you!" one soldier on the compound side of the tiger trap called.

Those on the far side spun, torch making an arc of light.

There, in the spot it had occupied earlier, was the Maut. Reformed and solid.

Unfazed.

Unmoving.

It stared that way for a second, two, eyes looking past the soldiers to lock onto Shaw. Then it stepped away into the trees and was gone.

"Don't let it escape!" one soldier said, raising his torch and dashing forward.

"No!" Shaw had no idea what the man hoped for but going into those trees wasn't any sane way to do it.

"Stop!" Eames called, in tune with Shaw's thoughts.

The soldiers did. Whether it was from their comrade's call or what came next Shaw would never be sure, and in truth it didn't matter.

Emerging from the spot where the Maut had disappeared came a man, hollow-eyed and vacant expression, cheeks sunken. Muttering words no one but those closest could hear, he advanced toward the three soldiers.

"Halt! Who goes there?," one said, pulling the rifle from his back.

The others copied the action a moment later, all three pointing their weapons at the approaching man.

Shaw knew him.

He was one of the many mindless men haunting the back alleys of Bandagar. One of those insane people he'd tried to help.

Continuing forward, continuing to mutter, the man raised his arms.

"Hold it!" the soldier repeated.

The man continued on.

Two of the soldiers on that far side fired their rifles, dropping the man.

Nothing supernatural there. No rising from the dead to attack again.

Just a dead lunatic.

As dead as Shaw's plan when the Maut reformed in the trees. At least no one had been hurt—

More movement in the trees as two other human shapes emerged from the shadows, equally dull-eyed.

Four more came on their heels. Hands raised and silent.

The last soldier with a loaded rifle on that side fired and missed. The madmen surged forward.

"Get out of there," Eames yelled.

Two of the soldiers turned and fled, the first leaping the trap with fair ease.

The second stopped at the hole and looked back for his friend. "Wilson!"

Wilson had reacted too slow, falling under the wave of attackers which grew with each second. These lunatics ripped at the downed soldier like wolves on a sheep, tearing him apart.

"Davies," Eames yelled at the final soldier. "Come on!"

Davies tried a standing jump across the trap but the rifle threw his balance off. He crashed through the sticks and leaves covering their trap, hitting the bottom with a grunt.

Eames rushed to the edge, calling over his shoulder to the soldiers on the compound side. "Shoot them!"

"But we'll hit Wilson."

"Wilson is dead," Eames hissed. "Shoot!"

Sure enough, the madmen rose from the remains of Wilson, leaving a pool of blood and flesh where the man had fallen. They started forward, gaining speed, as if the soldier's death had filled them with energy.

The two soldiers with loaded rifles fired and one attacker fell while the others continued their advance. Eames extended one arm into the trap, reaching for Davies.

"It's Baker," one soldier said.

"Baker?" Shaw said, then saw who they meant.

Baker, who'd been immortalized in Neufeld's painting. The soldier who'd guarded the storage building and gone missing. Baker advanced with the other lunatics, dead-eyed and drooling. They all rushed to the edge of the trap; those who'd ripped Wilson apart were coated in blood from fingers to elbows, more across their faces.

"Davies!" Eames shouted. "Get on your feet and grab my hand. Move your arse!"

Whatever slowed Davies became his doom. The lunatics spilled into the trap on top of the soldier. His screams as he was torn apart echoed off the building's walls on either side. Still other madmen came from the trees.

The three soldiers now on this side, having had the presence of mind to reload, fired again. Two bullets took down the same lunatic. The last missed.

"Get the doc out of here, Singh," Eames said, drawing his rifle and firing into the trap.

Singh released the chair's brake and jerked it around, heading for the hospital's door and jouncing him painfully as they went. Shaw gripped the arms of the chair to stop himself from being thrown free.

The gunshots and screams had drawn other soldiers from the barracks.

"Attack!" someone yelled. "We're under attack!"

The soldiers came in varying states of dress, weapons at the ready, though none looked prepared for what they saw. All had thought the outpost a safe place.

The last Shaw glimpsed before passing into the hospital were lunatics trying to leap across their fellows in the trap.

From outside came the bang, bang, bang of rifles.

Shaw placed his head in his hands and waited for it to end.

CHAPTER TWENTY-FIVE

BANDAGAR, INDIA—MAY 6TH, 1885

... Two more dead, because of me.

Two more who will not see England or anything else.

With nothing to show for the cost once again. The Maut had simply dissolved and reformed.

I am done ...

Armstrong took the occurrence as an attack from radical reformers against the outpost's presence. If he wondered what the tiger trap between buildings was all about he never mentioned it, at least not to Shaw. What he made of the soldier Baker returning was likewise a mystery.

The attack was repelled with minor loss of life on the outpost side—only Wilson and Davies. For Shaw those two dead soldiers were a heavy weight, like an elephant on his conscience. Without him and his plan those two men would still be alive.

Eames came by Shaw's room after investigations and cleanup had completed.

"McCready was right," Shaw said, shaking his head. "He told me that I am a doctor, not an adventurer."

Eames shrugged. "It was a sound plan."

"A sound plan? Two men died!"

Eames looked at Shaw a moment before taking the seat across from him, leaning forward. "Wilson and Davies were soldiers, Doctor. Death's a part of the job. We do what we've got to sometimes. We did what we set out to."

"No. The Maut escaped."

"It did," Eames agreed. "Next time though—"

"Next time?"

Eames nodded. "You were right, doc. The Maut has a weakness. It can be defeated."

Shaw had a comment on his tongue but swallowed it. The cost of human life was distinct between soldier and doctor, or the way that cost was looked at in any case.

He sighed, continuing in a low, tired voice. "I've seen enough death, Eames."

The corporal got to his feet. "Fair enough, doc. You've done the planning, let us do the rest."

The soldier crossed the room, ready to leave, but stopped with one hand on the doorknob and turned back.

"One question. What were those people who attacked us about? I knew Baker before he disappeared and he was a good man, but he attacked us like those other lunatics."

Shaw had considered that over the previous sleepless night. It was an answer to the one part of the Maut which had bothered him. The inconsistency.

"I think ... Well, the Maut pulls people in," Shaw said. "Drives them insane."

"Yeah, I can believe that."

"But it also uses them as a defense, like a porcupine's quills. If the Maut is threatened it calls out to them."

"That moan?" Eames asked.

"Exactly. It draws in whatever lunatics are near to tear the threat apart."

"Huh." Eames digested that information, storing it away for further use later, and gave a shrug. He left without another word.

———

A week later, an Indian man was murdered in Bandagar. Strangled in an alley between two houses.

The Thuggees *were* still nearby. Had they left the area then returned, or simply gone to ground and waited?

Armstrong and McCready refused to consider this murder as more than mere coincidence.

Only a native. Nothing for them to be concerned about.

Two nights after that another man was murdered, the same manner but farther away. On the path, halfway to Hyderabad. Word traveled among the soldiers to remain in groups at night, a rule which had been eased over the quiet years since Lassiter's death.

"Surely you see these ... lunatics are still here?" Shaw demanded of Armstrong on one of the commander's increasingly infrequent interactions with him.

"Nonsense! They are long gone."

"But—"

"Nonetheless," the commander cut in before Shaw could get too agitated, "it seems something might be happening which needs an eye on it."

Armstrong stepped up patrols, having groups of four pass through village and outpost throughout each night.

The murders ceased, as quickly as they'd started, validating Armstrong's opinion that there were no more Thuggees or anything strange, odd, or terrifying in or around the outpost. It was an opinion Shaw lacked evidence to argue against and Armstrong wouldn't have listened anyway. The commander had taken the defense of the area as far as he was about to.

CHAPTER TWENTY-SIX

BANDAGAR, INDIA — MAY 22ND, 1885

... As I told Eames, I am done with Thuggees, Mauts, and plans. Done!

I came to India to be a doctor and that is what I shall focus on, to the best of my current abilities.

I hobble around the hospital, attempting to perform duties I'd managed without conscious effort before the fall. Now something as simple as doing rounds is a monumental task, even with Singh's aid or that of my new companion, the wheelchair ...

Bandagar, India — July 5th, 1885

... The pain and discomfort has not changed one jot from that first day, not by any noticeable amount at least. Placing too much weight on the leg without one of my crutches to aid it results in a blast of stunning agony.

McCready has delayed the removal of my cast by another month on this account.

I've had a severe compound fracture, after all, and couldn't expect it to heal overnight—or so McCready, Neufeld, and even Barrowman remind me. It's a prognosis I would have given a patient myself, only this is me and I'm having difficulty looking at it in such a positive light.

I stay in my room when not at the hospital, interacting only with Singh ...

Bandagar, India—August 4th, 1885
... Today I get this damn cast off. Finally!
Then we shall see.
We shall see....

Neufeld worked with deliberate care to remove the cast while McCready observed. Singh, too, was present for the momentous event. The atmosphere in the room was one of hope and fear, mixed with the chalky smell of cut plaster.

"There you go," Neufeld said, snipping through the last of it. "Take it slow, Shaw. Tentative movements first."

An angry-red scar started half an inch to the right of his knee and continued down the side of his calf to halt close to the heel. The fibula had been broken, splintered, and he was lucky not to have also destroyed the knee. Shaw rotated his ankle and gasped at the stunning amount of pain that simple motion returned. He sucked in a sharp intake of breath through clenched teeth.

"Pain?" Neufeld asked.

Shaw nodded, glancing at McCready, who watched from one side, arms crossed and evaluating.

With that spike of pain Shaw lost confidence in being able to put weight on the leg at all. That was the purpose of the day though. He needed to see, needed to know for sure. Scooting to the edge of the bed, he placed his uninjured foot against the floor and leaned in preparation to—

"Ahhhhhhh!"

Pain beyond anything ever experienced slammed into him, would have thrown him to the floor if Neufeld had not been on one side to catch him. Singh rushed forward to take his other arm. Shaw was afraid to so much as twitch. He had barely brushed the floor with his foot, hadn't put any weight on that leg at all. Another assault like that would hurl him into unconsciousness, but standing there with the leg dangling was only marginally better.

"It's all right, Shaw," Neufeld said. "Let's ease you back down."

They helped him onto the bed where he writhed among the remnants of his cast, sweating and gasping. When he'd broken the leg at least he'd had the mercy of passing into unconsciousness, and again when they'd set and cast it.

"Your leg hasn't healed properly," McCready said.

Those were the most unnecessary words Shaw had ever heard. At least McCready was able to keep the *You deserve it* from his tone, though not from his eyes. That last, Shaw would admit, may have been his own imagination.

"We could re-break your leg, re-set it," McCready continued, "but the way that bone had splintered, it's a wonder you can walk at all."

"You were expecting this," Shaw said, getting his gasps under control.

"Expecting? No, not exactly." McCready was silent, contemplating. "I saw the possibility for complications in the wound though, as I'm sure you did. Your leg had not only broken but twisted afterwards, causing further damage to the bone."

Shaw took a deep breath and glared at his traitorous leg, probing for the pain with his mind. Yes, he'd seen this possibility, but had ignored the evidence, even when the pain had stayed constant rather than easing.

Several years ago, while still in medical school, he'd seen a wound like this. A man who'd been run over by horse and carriage, at least one hoof and probably both wheels. He'd never walked right again.

When Shaw looked back, the judgement was gone from McCready's eyes—imagined or not—replaced with concern. That frightened Shaw more. For McCready to show concern meant circumstances were indeed grim.

The head doctor came forward, uncrossing his arms, and looked Shaw in the eyes. "Whatever you decide you will most likely walk with a limp the rest of your life."

Shaw took another deep breath and focused on the two doctors, forcing himself to sit up. He wished to be free of the patient status and speak as an equal. Difficult when talking about oneself. He glanced at Singh then back, shook his head.

"We all know that rebreaking the leg won't make a difference, not the way it was fractured. I doubt I could do it again anyway, even under morphine."

No surprise or recrimination in McCready's eyes. If anything there was agreement. "We will give it another month to improve now that the cast is off."

Shaw nodded.

"But if it doesn't—"

"Yes, I understand."

McCready let the rest drop. If the leg didn't improve in the next month then Shaw would be discharged from the army and sent back to England.

CHAPTER TWENTY-SEVEN

Bandagar, India — August 6th, 1885

... At the urging of Doctor Neufeld I have begun experimenting with a cane, doing short jaunts with it while in my room mostly. No matter the result in a month I shall need it. Each time I place too much weight on my leg over the cane I am greeted by an agony which I have nothing to compare it to.

I came to India to make a difference, now I can't even make my bed.

Meanwhile I have more waiting to look forward to, and less optimism to do it with. Optimism. The luxury of starry-eyed dreamers and ignorant people who don't know better ...

Bandagar, India — August 18th, 1885

... My skill with the cane continues to improve, though it's an accomplishment for which I only feel the deepest bitterness. I've learned to get to standing position using it, to put my weight on it rather than my leg. I can even get down a short hallway or from one room to another within the hospital.

Neufeld assures me I will get used to it in time.

I assure him I do not wish to get used to the damn thing.

The only one not lavishing pity on me these days is Singh …

Bandagar, India — September 4th, 1885

… And so my one month's reprieve has passed.

As I expected my leg has not improved and in a little over two weeks' time I shall board the monthly ship to England. Just like that life as I know it is over and at the tender age of thirty-four I find myself cast out from the army. A reject. A cripple …

"You are alive," Singh said.

Shaw snorted, deep into his own self-pity and self-anger. Angry at himself for ever entering that house. Angry for being so stupid and careless as to fall down those stairs. Angry that he was being discharged back to a country he hadn't seen in almost a decade and which was no longer home.

Singh shrugged, willing to allow him to wallow, a difference from everyone else who wanted to point out how much there was left to life—All the while thanking the powers that be it was he and not them in this situation. Singh stared back, not dropping eye contact but without any judgement behind those eyes.

For once the stoic, emotionless outlook angered Shaw beyond reason.

"Alive," Shaw repeated, his voice the disgusted tone of one who'd bitten into rotten fruit. "Alive?"

Singh stood, silent, impassive.

"This is *not* alive, Singh. This is existing. This is marking time until death comes to reprieve me."

No reaction, no change to his expression.

"Alive is not bloody well enough!" Shaw shouted, slapping

one open palm against the desk in their shared room. "I want to walk again, without pain, as I did months ago. I want to sleep without waking in tears every time I shift. Is that so much to ask? Is it?"

He gripped the cane in both hands, twisting them around the wood and wishing for the freedom to break the damned thing against the table, or throw it out the window … But he couldn't. This cane was a necessary reality now.

"The cultists may as well have taken me, pressed their damned book against my face, and taken my mind and soul as well as my body. At least I would know nothing. This is … This … I …"

Still Singh betrayed no change of expression, but his eyes didn't waver. Shame burned through Shaw and he placed both hands over his face, struggling for control. He took one deep breath and released it slowly before dropping his hands.

"I'm sorry, Singh. You're the last person I want to take this out on."

Singh took the chair opposite. "If alive is not enough then what else do you have?"

Shaw's face clouded, angry again in an instant. Another deep breath, swallowing the first instinctive retort to give the question serious thought.

No, alive was *not* enough.

What else was there though?

What could an invalid possibly do?

"What is at the core of your being?" Singh asked. "What makes you who you are?"

A blankness filled Shaw's mind. It wasn't a question he'd ever asked himself, or even thought of in any abstract way.

An answer prowled the edges of his thoughts, elusive. What was it?

What made him Doctor Archibald Shaw?

Doctor.

Yes.

"I'm a doctor, damn it."

He *was* still a doctor wasn't he? Having all the skill and knowledge which went with it. He was returning from abroad, wounded but still capable in that regard.

"More. You are a good doctor. You care about others."

Did he though? Did he still care?

That answer came back without hesitation. Of course he did. His body had changed, not his soul.

So, what options for a good doctor who cared?

"I … I'll return to England, start my own practice. Use the skills I've honed while here."

"Yes," Singh said, as if it was obvious the entire time.

It was, or should have been if he'd looked at it from outside his own self-pity.

His immediate to long-term future planned, Shaw started, realizing his change would be an even greater one for Singh.

"You'll come with me, won't you, Singh? Back to England?"

Now the boy's expression did change, eyes shifting. A tinge of sadness, subtle but there. A shake of his head. "No, Doctor. My place is here."

The depths of disappointment surprised Shaw, more profound than any disappointment over his leg. To be parted from Singh was unthinkable. He'd come to depend so much on him, both as his confidant and friend. This boy was his …

Well, Archie old boy, what exactly is he to you?

Simple. Singh was family. The only family he'd known these past years. He couldn't just leave the boy here, but was it fair to convince Singh to leave the land where he'd been born and where he wanted to stay? No. Singh was old enough, wise enough to make his own decisions, had been for some time.

Shaw opened his mouth to speak but found the words wouldn't come.

"I'll go with you to the ship."

Shaw looked toward the window so Singh wouldn't see the true emotion behind his eyes. Losing the ability to walk without pain was one thing, losing Singh was a distinct misery which wouldn't be anywhere near as easy to recover from.

Two weeks until his entire world changed.

CHAPTER TWENTY-EIGHT

HYDERABAD, INDIA—SEPTEMBER 19TH, 1885
... And so, my journey back to England begins.
Another trip to foreign soil ...

"Your servant can't ride up here."

Shaw stopped, leaning on the cane he'd come to resent so completely. Singh stood behind him, motionless and prepared to catch him should he tumble backward.

The man who'd spoken, a conductor judging from his railway uniform, glared in their direction, arms crossed and eyes narrowed. He blocked the aisle so they wouldn't do anything so nefarious as to sneak an Indian aboard an Indian train in India.

"Servant?" Shaw said, putting on a mask of confusion. He glanced at Singh then back to the conductor, a mask of comprehension as if this were an obvious and understandable mistake. "Oh! No, no. This is my son."

Singh made a slight sound and Shaw counted it a victory to have surprised him, though couldn't look back to relish it. Any expression would have been smoothed over before he could turn anyway.

Ah, well.

Instead Shaw maintained eye contact with the conductor, preparing for war over the point of Singh riding in first class.

"Look here ..." the man started, then paused, taking in Shaw's appearance.

Shaw knew what he presented. The army uniform. The cane. He held the respected position of doctor and an apparent battle veteran having received permanent wounds in the service of Her Majesty. He also could not get around without aid, obviously.

A sympathetic picture.

The conductor exhaled, dismissing his undoubtedly cutting words before reluctantly stepping aside to allow passage. "Be warned, if you plan on going to the dining car I wouldn't expect the same understanding that I've shown."

Shaw wanted to tell the man exactly where to place his understanding, but would rather ride in comfort for the next thirteen hours. Instead he nodded his own understanding. The conductor would find some way to explain Singh's presence for other scandalized white passengers as they boarded ... not that there would be many given this was the overnight train to Bombay.

They took their seats.

"Your son?"

Shaw shrugged. "Close enough."

Singh had a strange look and Shaw worried he'd given unwitting offense, that Singh suspected he was being made fun of.

Shaw leaned forward on his cane. "You are a fine young man, and I would be honored if it were true."

A brief smile twitched the corner of Singh's mouth as he turned to look out the window, and that hit Shaw like a hammer. Damn, but he was going to miss Singh. He'd become the most important person in all parts of Shaw's life, the one constant, the person that could always be relied on.

"What will you do once I'm gone?"

Singh tried to raise one eyebrow, cocked his head instead.

"Not that you need me," Shaw rushed to add. "It's just ... you've spent so many years helping me and that's bound to leave a vacuum. You'll have more time now."

Singh's eyes shifted. "I will continue to study. Meditation. Yoga."

"Good. I'm happy to hear that."

"Are you? Why?"

Shaw thought before answering. Why *was* that of importance to him? "Well, I suppose because it's a part of you. I see how it makes you happy."

"It makes me whole."

A sudden realization came to Shaw that all these years he'd gotten his assessment wrong. Singh didn't have an impassive nature, nor was it an absence of emotion or some stoic outlook. Singh simply had a sense of calm. He was at peace.

"You've been a good friend, Singh, and more."

"Friend?" Singh considered the word. "Yes, you are a good friend as well, Doctor Shaw."

"You *can* call me Archibald."

Singh shook his head. "I think not, Doctor."

Shaw laughed, the first genuine one in what felt like months. "First name Doctor, last name Shaw. Is that how you see it?"

A second quiver of near smile. "Yes. Just so."

With a deep breath Shaw forged ahead with his next question. "Did I do right by you, Singh?"

Another cock of the head. "How do you mean?"

"Well, after the cave. Should I have done something different? Given more effort to a search for your real family? Found someone in Bandagar to raise you?"

Singh was quiet for so long Shaw thought he might not

answer but finally Singh shook his head. "I had a better life than most orphans. Food. Shelter. Education. Friendship."

Shaw blocked the ghost of Lassiter's remarks from his mind. He knew what his friend would have said and didn't care. He was happy to have done what he could and if Singh was content with that then so was he.

"Perhaps that was unfair to other orphans," Singh said. "It gave me the chance to learn from the holy men in Bandagar."

It was enough to know Singh didn't have any regrets. Shaw still wished he was coming back to England with him but respected Singh's desire to stay in India. They passed the thirteen-hour trip in conversation, both realizing this would be one of the last for them. Shaw would be able to reach him by post, but then what? A conversation with months in between each correspondence? That would not be near the same.

That and the upheaval in his life created an uneasiness in Shaw's soul which he tried to ignore, yet it played against his nerves as they rode, like a violinist scraping his bow across the strings, slightly out of tune. An uneasiness wore at him, a sense that something here was out of place.

A danger?

He looked around and saw nothing which could be considered a threat, and shook his head. Too many encounters with Thuggees and the Maut. Too much death.

He wouldn't miss that at all.

The conductor arranged for food to be brought, a light dinner, when he saw Shaw's trouble in navigating the swaying train. He appreciated the gesture but it still irked him. Singh appeared unconcerned.

"One day, Indian people will ride in whatever car they wish."

Shaw looked up from the food he'd been prepared to bite into. Singh had said the words low but with emotion, as if making a promise.

"You think so?"

Of course he did. Singh didn't speak without reason and Shaw knew it.

Singh nodded.

Possibly. With the work Allan Octavian Hume—another saviour of the Indian people?—had done founding the Indian National Congress earlier that year it held some promise at least.

"I hope so, Singh. I truly do."

They rode in silence for many miles, watching the country go by as the sun set. Shaw remarked at how little it had changed over the years. It was still as beautiful and wild as years earlier.

CHAPTER TWENTY-NINE

IN BOMBAY THEY RENTED A HOTEL ROOM, MORE SPACE THAN WAS needed but since the place was owned by Doctor Patel's cousin they'd been given an excellent bargain.

Though it was close to noon and approaching lunch time Shaw wanted to explore, to stroll through the marketplace as they often did in Bandagar. In reality he wanted to escape the fact that in less than twenty-four hours he would be saying goodbye to Singh and India. Remaining in the hotel room contemplating those facts was more than he could endure.

After a short side trip to purchase his ship's ticket it was obvious the task of strolling through Bombay would likewise be more than he could endure, this time physically rather than mentally.

"Damn it," he muttered, leaning against a wall and taking all weight off his leg. Not that the cursed thing dangling felt any better.

Light pressure on his bad leg was becoming bearable a good deal of the time, but traveling any real distance was more than was possible. He should have known better after that brief horse and carriage journey from train to hotel—a cab ride which had left him recovering in their room for more than an hour.

He'd resolved to go back to England and give meaning to his life but wasn't even able to stroll a few blocks. McCready told him this would improve in time, once he toughened up that leg it wouldn't be so bad.

Some days Shaw believed him.

Not today.

"Doctor?"

"I'm fine, Singh," he said. "Just wondering how I'll get around aboard that ship."

Singh said nothing, staring at Shaw, which told him the answer was obvious and he should be able to see it for himself. Ah, yes. Of course. There would be many aged and infirm passengers on the boat and they somehow managed. If they could, he could.

"I'll be fine," he said, realizing his previous statement could be taken as an attempt to give Singh guilt about leaving Shaw to his own devices. He didn't want that, as he didn't want Singh worrying about him once he was gone.

"Shall we return to the hotel, Doctor?"

Shaw turned back the way they'd come, gritting his teeth in annoyance. Though the marketplace was as close as two streets away it might as well be in the New World.

"Sorry, Singh," he said, taking the offered arm. "I know it's inconvenient to drag me back and forth."

"It is what it is, Doctor."

"Just another part of life?"

"Just so."

At times Shaw could appreciate the outlook, though he was far from being able to adopt it as his own. Still, Singh's calm demeanor at least blunted the edge of his self-pity.

Singh guided him back toward their hotel, and the slow-moving, steam-powered elevator ride awaiting them. The two-floor journey took ten minutes of jerking, shuddering movement, but was more dignified than being carried like luggage up the stairs. Shaw suspected that this time, once in the room he would stay until it was time to leave for the ship tomorrow morning. Meals could be arranged to be taken in the room, a reality he must get used to in time.

He sighed as Singh eased him into one of the reading chairs in their room, knowing from experience the relief wouldn't last.

"What did you wish to get for your mother?"

"My mother?" Shaw looked up at his friend, opening his mouth.

How exactly did one go about telling something which should have been shared long ago? He'd kept it to himself too long, stupidly unable to share it.

"You don't need to run my errands."

"Need?" Singh shook his head. "No, but I shall go."

It brought a smile to Shaw's face, infrequent these days. He'd told Singh so much about his mother over the years until the young man must have felt as if he'd met her. Oh, if only that was possible.

It was a silly impulse but Shaw wanted a bit of India to bring back with him. Some spice to keep in a jar on the shelf of his future office and take down to sniff at whenever he missed this country too much. He explained as best he could and Singh left with one quick nod.

Staring out the window held his thoughts for ten minutes or so, mulling over the use of language to best describe the scene, realizing that, yes, boredom was an issue. He should have asked Singh to find him some books for the ship. Ah, well, surely there would be a library aboard.

He had no idea how long he remained like that, watching people pass on the street below without paying any real attention. Movement in the hallway, the scuff of a foot against floor as someone stopped outside the door rather than passing. The sound drifting through brought a happy expectation to him. They could play a game of chess, though he was meager challenge for Singh these days.

The positive atmosphere slid away.

Something was wrong. Out of place.

A flash of danger passed through his mind, much as the brief sensation had on the train. This time he couldn't explain it away as easily.

The knob rattled, then turned, the door swinging inward to reveal not Singh but—

"You!" he said.

Framed in the doorway was the cult leader, Ananya. The woman he'd encountered months earlier in Bandagar. The person responsible for Walsh's murder and his laming.

"Yes, Doctor Shaw." She stepped uninvited into the room.

Eyes narrowed and lips pressed into a grim line. She'd discovered his name, the sound of it from her mouth unpleasant.

Behind her came the hulking man-monster, stooping to pass through the door. His normal hand—for want of a better word—and his claw clenched into fists at his side. Two human cultists came last, closing the door behind them. Their leader advancing to stand before Shaw, her beast of a servant one step behind.

"How did you find me?"

"We never left you," she said. "All these months one was always nearby to watch, waiting for you to be alone. We accompanied you from Hyderabad, took the same train to Bombay."

So the danger he'd sensed on the train had been real.

"Stalking me?" he said, anger rising like bile. "Haven't you done enough?"

Shaw shook his cane for emphasis.

"No."

The calm, matter-of-fact statement in response to his indignation deflated Shaw. She pulled a chair closer and sat facing him.

"The idol chose you."

"Chose me!" He wanted to say it was ridiculous, but he'd seen much more incredible incidents since arriving in India. "I'm glad your damned idol is back in England, out of your reach."

Ananya stared at him, a smile at the corner of her lip for the briefest of instants. One human cultist repeated the word *England*. She waved a hand, pushing it aside as inconsequential.

"You are the only educated man who has returned from looking into the book. You read the words. Understood so much."

He shook his head.

"Your mind is ready, Doctor."

"No!"

He didn't want to think about it.

"You are needed," she said. "Valuable."

"No. No!"

"Yes."

"*You* read it! Or your cousin." Shaw's eyes grew wider, pleading.

She ignored it, shook her head. "My cousin thinks he can look in the book. Quick glimpses. He has grown incautious but I shall not."

Shaw shook his head again, the way a child might with their parent, knowing all power belongs to that other person.

"You will come with us."

She returned her chair to the desk. Man-monster stepped forward and grabbed Shaw by his shirt, pulling him from the chair with a screech of pain, cane dropping to the floor. He found himself flipped over the brute's opposite shoulder, facing the door.

A door which swung inward.

"Singh!"

He stood frozen in the door, shocked, a paper bag in one hand.

"The traitor," Ananya said.

"Run, Singh!"

Singh did not.

"These are the ones who escaped," Shaw jabbered needlessly. "From under the house in Bandagar."

Who else would they be?

Man-monster threw Shaw to one side, his landing painfully on a bed mere luck. The two human cultists flanked the giant henchman while their mistress stepped backward.

Singh outweighed the two humans by many pounds, taller than either by almost a head and broader of shoulder. The man-monster in turn outweighed Singh. He ... *It* raised both arms, clenching the fingers of its unclawed hand, eyes narrowing. Singh's own muscles rippled under his robe.

The first cultist, slightest of them all, rushed forward, impatient. If he wanted his chance before their more massive companion waded in, it was ill-advised. Singh dropped his parcel and grabbed this man by the bunched up front of his disheveled robe, pulling the man forward to meet his other fist. It collided with the cultist's face, mashing his nose flat with a wet crunch. He staggered back, into the hulking cultist's path, tripping him.

Seeing his two companions down the third man attacked, screaming words which neither impressed nor frightened Singh. Instead he punched this man on one side of the head near the upper jaw, knocking him sideways and to the floor. This man collapsed on the tiled floor, shaking his head, trying to clear it from the solid blow.

Singh's skill astounded Shaw. He'd certainly never taught Singh to fight, couldn't have even begun to in all honesty. Was it from his friends in Bandagar? Or from his time with the cult, and earlier?

All three cultists rose to their feet, the third still shaking his head while the first let the blood from his broken nose flow freely. Before any could regain complete composure Singh grabbed the abandoned parcel, rushing forward in a half crouch. He looked as if he would go for the massive one but instead shifted and caught the most dazed of the three around his waist, driving him into the window's frame, Singh's shoulder in the man's stomach. The cultist dropped like a sack of rice, gasping for air while Singh spun toward the others. The broken-nosed cultist took a step in front of their leader, keeping her safe. The two circled toward the door while man-monster remained between them and Singh.

"It's a distraction, Singh."

Singh nodded, seeing that fact for himself. The two in back continued their retreat, leaving their more brutal friend to deal with Singh, and abandoning the last cultist under the window. The same familiar technique. Distract while others got away. Only in this case the man-monster was undoubtedly expected to do more than just make a sacrifice. His job was to kill Singh and take Shaw according to the original plan.

It raised both hands, clenching fist and claw to intimidate Singh. It didn't work. Singh launched his paper-wrapped package at the thing's face, exploding in a fine yellow cloud. The orange-ginger scent of turmeric filled the room, the monster gasping for air. Singh rushed forward, going first left then right, before planting a fierce punch on the huge man's jaw. It staggered a step, then shot out the clawed hand with a speed that should have been impossible for its size. It grabbed Singh around the throat and departed somewhat the expanding yellow fog, holding him against one wall. The monster's normal hand joined the first in a stranglehold.

Ananya with her broken-nosed cultist had reached the doorway and passed through, stopping on the hallway side to watch events transpire, ready to flee should events go unbelievably against them. The look on her face showed how likely she thought this was, but this woman was cautious, strategic.

Shaw rolled off the bed, crying out in agony as too much

impact was forced onto his leg. Still, he hobbled forward in a half crawl, giving himself no other choice. He grabbed at the cane, discarded on the floor. Between it and the bed frame he forced himself to a wobbling standing position.

The man-monster paid him no heed—why should he?—dismissing him as less than a threat, focused instead on strangling Singh.

"Fine then!" Shaw howled. As a battle cry it left much to be desired.

He staggered forward the few steps and once again put all weight on the strong leg.

At the door Ananya hissed a command at the bloody cultist beside her. He rushed forward.

Too late.

With a graceless motion Shaw brought his cane up, around and down with all the force he could muster, across the back of the huge cultist's head. A crack like thunder and the cane snapped in two, as his leg once had. The momentum threw him to the ground.

"Ahhhh!"

Hands grabbed at Shaw and he thrashed out, catching the cultist in his broken nose by sheer luck. He staggered back a step and fell.

When Shaw looked around again that beast still had Singh in a stranglehold, but the impact of the cane had had some effect. Singh pulled in a rattling gasp and kicked with one leg. Monster or not, it seemed to have the same tender areas other men did. The grip loosened more.

More than half the length of wood remained in Shaw's grasp. Splintered as it was the cane would never hold him up again, but it possessed another use. Without thinking too much Shaw placed his good leg against the ground for leverage and stabbed upward with his makeshift weapon. It caught the hulking cultist under the ribs and punctured the skin there, driving inwards but nowhere near deep enough to do real damage. The monster jerked left, whipping the cane from Shaw's grasp even as other hands grabbed at him. The broken-nosed cultist.

Too late again!

Shaw's action had succeeded. Singh leapt free and danced around the monster's grasping claw to grab at the cane still poking from his opponent's side. With better leverage and better legs Singh drove it deeper, burying it to the handle in that beast's side.

The dazed cultist struggled to rise from his spot under the window, still sucking in air. He looked about, wobbly on his feet and unable to be of much help to the man-monster.

Singh pushed and twisted the splinter of cane, steering the huge cultist toward the window. Increasing momentum, catching their dazed companion in the rush. With a howl of agony from the man-monster the three collided into the window as one, cultist, man-monster, then Singh. Between Singh's force and the monster monster's and cultist's weight the wood cracked, the glass shattered and gave way. Dazed cultist went through the window and was gone, a meaty thud coming from below seconds later. Man-monster teetered, pinwheeling arms to gain balance, fighting his own weight. Singh let go of the cane, starting to step away, but even as he did the leathery claw of man-monster shot out and grabbed him by the robe.

And both disappeared through the window.

"Singh!"

Shaw fought the hands which held him, trying to scramble from his spot on the floor, trying to make his way to the window.

"Singh!" he screamed. "No!"

It was too late, Shaw knew that. Singh, his boy, was gone.

And now they would take him, keep him, force him to look on that book.

He couldn't do it. Couldn't!

Better to join Singh out the window to splatter against the street below.

The woman commanded something and Shaw glanced over one shoulder. The bloody-nosed cultist rushed for him.

"Leave me alone!"

The man grabbed up the shorter end of Shaw's shattered cane and brought it around to connect with the side of his head.

Blackness followed.

CHAPTER THIRTY

PAIN BROUGHT THE WORLD BACK TO SHAW IN A RUSH.

His eyes shot open to find Ananya looking at him with emotional detachment. One hand squeezed the lower part of his left leg, fingernails digging into the flesh. He shrieked with agony, a bright glittering pain that turned the world before his eyes bright white.

"Stop!" he gasped, trying to bring his arms up, trying to retreat.

Unable to do either.

Ananya let go. Her cousin, Suresh, stood to Shaw's other side, holding the book in an embrace like some obscene lover. The man appeared well past exhausted, eyes haunted circles, his cheeks sunken. The two waited while Shaw got himself under control and looked around, coming to grips with the situation.

He was in a plush, wingback easy chair. A thick leather strap, similar to those used in asylums, circled his chest. Shifting one arm only succeeded in pulling his other, one lengthy belt which passed underneath the seat securing left wrist to right. His legs were free and straight out on a matching ottoman.

From what he could see it was a modest room though well-lit

with electric lights. One door in the wall a few feet's distance sat half ajar.

Low moaning came from behind them. A murmur of voices.

They were not alone.

Memory came back like the crack of a whip.

No.

"Singh!" he wailed at the woman. "You killed him!"

"Another death to weaken the veil."

"Another …?" This wasn't some random, unknown person. This was Singh, this was his boy. "Go to hell! You *and* your mad goddess."

Hand snaking out she grabbed and squeezed his leg again, pulling a gasp from Shaw. He writhed in the seat, tears springing behind clenched eyes.

"Manners, Doctor Shaw."

The pain continued until he opened his eyes, looked at her. Once Ananya had eye contact, and an understanding that all power was hers, she released her grip.

"You are the guest of honor tonight, Doctor, but that will only allow so much."

She looked past him and gave a nod. Hands grasped both sides of the chair back, rotating it and bringing another cry of pain as his leg was yanked from the ottoman to bang against the floor. Another message of power from Ananya. He gritted his teeth against the agony until it dragged to a stop. The two Thuggees who'd turned him brought the ottoman around and unceremoniously plunked both legs back onto it.

Easier for her to reach out and punish him.

His plush confinement perched atop a raised stage, two feet above a room much more extensive than he'd first imagined. A ballroom of sorts. The walls were decorated in paper of gold and burgundy, doors on each side surrounded by ornate framework. Windows lined the left side of the room, floor to ceiling, where that door led to a garden of magnificent flowers and shrubs.

Where the hell was he?

A nicer lair than the house in Bandagar, or the cave. That much was evident.

Assembled in that room were those he'd heard moaning. They swayed and chanted, each wearing a black robe with hoods up to obscure their expressions. Thuggees. More than those at the cave, more than what had been in Bandagar. Fifty or sixty in all.

All faced in his direction.

The guest of honor.

"The veil is worn thin," Ananya said, speaking for all to hear. "Today we raise Kali."

"Kali."

"Kali."

"Kali."

Shaw shook his head, fingers digging into the chair's arms. He bit back a whimper which had perched on the edge of his throat, denying her that slight satisfaction.

Ananya levelled her full gaze on him. "Your mind is ready to read *the* page."

"The ... the page?"

"The page which will destroy that veil forever and allow Kali access to our world."

"No," he whispered. "This is madness."

"Yes," she agreed. "Glorious madness, and all shall be rewarded."

Shaw shook his head.

"Oh, yes," she whispered. "And you too shall have her reward, Doctor."

Rewarded with madness? Shaw's thoughts turned to Singh, to the boy he'd saved from execution only to watch die anyway. His grief was unbearable. Madness would be preferable.

Ananya spoke to the assembled Thuggees, voice rising and full of righteousness. "There are those who want to prevent

Kali's return, to regrow the veil. That is old Thuggee and not our way."

"Kali."

"Kali."

"Kali."

A noise from the back interrupted their ecstasy, starting as slight but growing, rising above the chants and moans. It worked its way through the room. The robed cultists parted respectfully, a familiar shape staggering through, step by step until it stared up at them.

The man-monster.

Shaw's splintered length of cane remained embedded in its side, the blackish blood flow having slowed. Surely that wound was fatal! If that wood were pulled free would it not bleed to death? The man-monster waited, giving its mistress a slight bow. The right arm, the normal one, dangled uselessly by its side.

"We are complete," she said.

Man-monster turned, filling the space between Ananya and all others, as was its place. The chants resumed, filling the ballroom.

"Kali."

"Kali."

"Kali."

Ananya raised one hand and Suresh shuffled forward on Shaw's other side. His attention was elsewhere, looking miles away over Shaw and his cousin. He held the corrupt book in his gloved hands, one below and one above. The upper hand caressed the cover's leather gently.

"Suresh."

No reaction. His hand continued to trace the raised figures of the cover.

"Suresh!" she repeated.

"Mmm?" His gaze swung around. A shake of his head, then

another. A bow to Ananya. "Apologies," he said, voice a hoarse whisper. "It ... is difficult."

"Not long now, cousin."

"No. Not long," he repeated. "Not long. Not long."

The gloves, it seemed, were no longer keeping outright madness away. Not for Suresh.

"It is time," she said, nodding toward Shaw.

"Time. Yes." Suresh looked down with haunted, mad eyes. He leaned in close, lips beside Shaw's ear. "There is one page. I can almost read it. Last night ... Last night ... I. Read. Three. Words."

Yes, Suresh had read some words for certain. Willingly. And it had cost him his mind.

Did that make the difference? What had Ananya said? Some embraced the language of the book enthusiastically and went too quickly into the madness.

Could he do that? Give his mind and save humanity?

It was a sacrifice he found himself willing to make. With Singh gone he'd lost his last reason to survive. But ... would he go mad fast enough? Maybe not. He'd resisted once before, come back from the edge.

He could end up doing exactly what they wanted.

Suresh stood, holding the book flat. It opened, as if from some non-existent hand, pages riffling. Shaw clamped his eyes tight, refusing to look at where that search would end, knowing closed eyes would not prevent his involvement. If this woman wanted his eyes open she would grind his flesh and bone until he complied.

Then in his madness of seeing the page he would babble the words to condemn the world. No, madness was *not* definite enough. He had to ensure he didn't speak ... couldn't speak. Could he do that?

Only one way occurred to him ...

One grim, insane possibility.

Without a tongue he couldn't pronounce the words.

Without his tongue … Yes.

He would sever it. Clamp his teeth into his tongue and saw through.

Could he do it? Did he have it in himself?

Probing his own internal resolve he found that he did.

He had to.

That was it then.

Fine.

Fine!

"Kali."

"Kali."

"Kali."

Inside his mouth Shaw pushed his tongue forward as far as possible, clamping teeth into the strong muscle, prepared to saw through with all his strength. If he couldn't finish, he would at least choke on his own blood.

Now!

"Stop this madness!"

A stern voice. Commanding. Accustomed to being obeyed.

Shouts of panic from the Thuggees. Anger.

Ananya made a noise of disgust. "Not now."

A faint hope of rescue forced Shaw's eyes open.

All the Thuggees had turned, backs toward him and the stage. They continued to gather closer together, regrouping to face the invaders who gathered just inside the open garden door. Thirty Indian soldiers glared hatred at the Thuggees, poised ready to charge in. Still more came through the doors.

In the lead of these soldiers was a man in colorful silk robes, wearing a headdress with one magnificent jeweled feather at the center.

"Prince Kanwar?" Shaw said, teeth releasing his tongue.

The Prince of Hyderabad! Here!

The man would have no real power in Bombay. He was far

from home and had brought soldiers into another province, an act which could be viewed as invasion.

Ananya levelled a gaze on the prince, a slight smirk to her lips. "You will not stop me."

Shaw clamped his teeth back around his tongue, ready for any outcome.

The Thuggees organized, lining up between their leader and danger. The soldiers were outnumbered but better trained. Shaw knew the power of sheer fanaticism though, had learned that lesson years ago.

"Oh, but I will stop you, my sister," Prince Kanwar said. "This ends now."

Sister? *Sister?*

"You have perverted the beliefs of Thuggee," he continued. "Defiled the book."

The soldiers held no rifles, no weapons. Each flexed their hands, ready to charge.

"I will have back what is mine," the prince said, looking toward the book.

Suresh took a step back, tilting the book away from Shaw and back toward his own view.

"Cousin, why do you follow her?" Kanwar said to Suresh. "Why give your home to this madness?"

Another step back. A narrowing of the eyes. Suresh flipped pages—One. Two. Three—until his eyes grew wider, his face determined, haunted.

"You are weak, Kanwar," Ananya said. "Refusing to allow Kali's return."

"Madness!"

"Yes," she agreed, the very picture of calm. Then to her Thuggees, "Kill them."

"Forward," the prince commanded.

Both groups rushed together, each pulling out lengths of rope, weighted sashes, garrottes. The weapons of strangulation.

"Now, Doctor Shaw," Ananya said. "While we have time."

The sounds of hand-to-hand combat began.

To the left one hooded cultist caught Shaw's attention. This one didn't charge for the soldiers like the rest but instead headed for the stage.

Man-monster stepped in his way, giving a low growl of warning.

A traitor? One of the prince's men?

This man went to the right but when man-monster followed to block he changed direction and grabbed the length of cane still protruding from the creature's side. The hooded man pulled it free with a squelching gush of blackish blood. Man-monster made a grab, but with one useless arm the attempt was easily dodged. It fell to one knee, making a mad swipe with the clawed hand which raked into the man's robe, shredding one side. Blood continued to jet from the monster's wound. One arm braced against the floor. The creature looked up at its mistress, an apology on its face, then fell forward and lay still.

The man leapt onto the stage, Ananya taking one step back. She bared her teeth but the man ignored it, pulling a knife from inside his robe and facing Shaw. The knife swept down, starting to saw through the leather straps holding his arms.

"What …?"

"Rest easy, Doctor."

The voice. Could it be?

"Singh?" Shaw whispered. "Is it you?"

Singh said nothing but finished cutting the strap and turned to the thicker one surrounding his chest. Shaw twisted in his seat, crying out with the pain, looking to see whether Ananya was about to attack.

She was not. Her eyes focused on the room, darting to Shaw, then her cousin. Again her mind was calculating, forming an updated plan.

All around, men were locked in combat, hands around each

other's throats, choking. The sounds of battle were eerily subdued, both sides trained to kill in silence. There were grunts as some were strangled, the sounds of fists on flesh as others attempted to be free.

Shaw looked to his other side, searching for Suresh, and found the man with full attention on the book, lips working.

He was reading. Reading. Reading.

More than just three words.

The lights flickered, dimmed.

Shadows grew in the room's corners, seeping inward.

"Stop!" Shaw said.

"Suresh!" Ananya yelled. "No!"

Sweat poured down the man's face in a river as his eyes widened. He twitched. Words spoken through clenched teeth.

"Dhoosar Maut!" a voice cried out.

The sounds of combat lessened. One man screamed.

"Dhoosar Maut," another said. "Dhoosar Maut."

Another scream. Soldiers and Thuggees jumped to their feet, the battle forgotten as the strangled cry of "Dhoosar Maut!" raced through the room.

A shape flickered within the shadows of the farthest corner, coming forward to the edge.

"No," Shaw muttered. "Oh, no."

Terror welled in him.

How had it gotten here?

Suresh continued to spit out words. The flesh of his hands where they held the book smoked and sizzled. Ananya— Princess Ananya—turned toward her cousin, then back to the Maut. Her mind worked and with a nod she stepped forward to the stage's edge.

"We have called you here, Dhoosar Maut," she said, "to witness the rebirth of Kali."

The soldiers shrunk back from the shadow and the monster

there, toward their prince, while that man's eyes remained on his sister, making no advance.

"Yes!" Ananya hissed. "Kill the unbelievers, Dhoosar Maut! Kill them all!"

The Maut made no further movement into the room, but glared at all with its dead eyes and slack jaw. Body stooped, the right arm hung at one side, close to dragging against the floor.

"No, sister," Prince Kanwar said. "Dhoosar Maut does not obey."

Kanwar said the words with such simple certainty, the voice of a man speaking from experience. The prince took a step back toward the garden door, then another.

Princess Ananya also stepped back, one shake of her head, her confidence dissolving.

The terror from the Maut was incredible, the draw irresistible. It was more than he'd thought possible. The Maut had always affected people who were alone and Shaw thought it *couldn't* affect more. He thought—

"No," Shaw whispered.

Another creature stepped from the deepest shadows, this one closer to the stage, to their left.

Another Maut. A second one. It wasn't just—

Then a third on the farther side of the auditorium, near the garden door where Kanwar had been. Through the windows Shaw could see him and two soldiers rushing through the flowers.

Each creature lounged in similar manner, but with slight differences. One stooped left, another right. One held a claw of leathery grey, a second in black. One's eyes were a lifeless black and another's red. They stopped on the edge of those shadowy corners, looking into the room from their positions, boxing Thuggees and soldiers in. Paralysis coursed through the room, infecting every man there. All stood rigid, staring at these creatures, struggling to have their will back. The labored breathing of each the only sound.

Horror clear on each and every face.

Still Suresh continued to read.

"We. Must. Go," Singh struggled to say. "Now."

The strap fell from Shaw's chest, freeing him to go to one of these Mauts. Singh grabbed him roughly and lifted, throwing Shaw over one shoulder and heading for the back door.

"Stop, you fool!" Ananya said, grabbing the book from Suresh, slamming it shut. "What have you done?"

Suresh glanced around, hands up as if still holding the book. A runnel of saliva dripped from one side of his mouth to his robe. He gurgled something which might have been words, at least in his own mind, then turned toward the shadows behind them. Suresh stepped toward the fourth Maut, coming from that corner.

Every hair on Shaw's arms rose up in terror as shivers dashed through his body. He wanted to go to the monster, struggled to make Singh let him go. All the while his mind repeated one fact over and over.

More than one Maut.

More than one!!

God knew how *many* more.

As he and Singh passed through the back door, soldiers and Thuggees around the ballroom stepped unbidden toward the nearest Maut, terror the only emotion.

Ananya and the book were already gone.

CHAPTER THIRTY-ONE

OUT THE BACK, THROUGH THE NEXT ROOM. FORWARD. FORWARD. Increasing distance from those monsters and their influence. A painful, bouncing nightmare for Shaw which he endured because the alternative was unimaginable. Singh continued to barrel from room to room until a door led them through an entry and out of the house. Even then Singh didn't stop, kept going until they passed through a gate and stood in the street.

"Stop!" Shaw gasped. "Please!"

Singh spun, looked around, ready to continue fleeing but finding no danger lurking nearby. No pursuing Mauts. No mad cultists. Back the way they'd come was a wide, sprawling mansion, the lights inside flickering ... flickering ... failing. Inside the Mauts devoured the sanity of both sides' Thuggees, preparing to lead them away.

"Yes," Singh said. "Yes, of course. Rest."

One last look then Singh eased him down onto a low stone wall, gently propping his bad leg out straight against the stones.

Singh remained in motion, scanning the surroundings and staring past Shaw toward a much busier street ahead. The young man relaxed, their path chosen, and pulled off the black robe, discarding it. He turned back, watching Shaw massage his aching leg.

"Singh," he said, looking up. "I'm ... I'm so relieved to see you. I thought ..."

But he couldn't finish.

"No, Doctor. I survive."

"How?" Shaw asked. "When I saw you go out that window ..."

He shook his head, again unable to put words to his thoughts.

"The first cultist fell to the street," Singh explained, then gestured back the way they'd come. "That other ..."

"The man-monster?"

"Man-monster?" Singh cocked his head to one side. "Yes. He fell on the first man while I grabbed the window ledge."

The thought of Singh dangling two floors above the street brought Shaw's heart into his throat.

"When I pulled myself up you were gone, but I followed this man-monster once he rose again."

"Singh, I—"

"We should leave, Doctor. I do not think we are safe."

"You are not."

Both Shaw and Singh jumped and found Prince Kanwar only a few feet away, eight soldiers accompanying him. Shaw held out one hand to keep Singh back, to stop him from maneuvering between him and the danger of the prince.

"Where is my sister?" Kanwar demanded. "Where is *my* book?"

Shaw shook his head and the prince glared, storming forward until barely three feet separated them.

"That book is mine, and I *will* have it back."

Shaw wished he could retreat, wished there was somewhere to retreat to.

"Ananya stole it along with an idol from my collection. Sacred items."

Shaw nodded, not thinking it wise to tell the prince the idol was far away now. "She … wants to raise Kali."

The prince chuckled. "That is not Kali in the book."

"No."

"I do not wish to awaken that elder god and watch all I love destroyed. Neither do I wish Kali to walk the earth again for that same reason. For generations we have killed to prevent her return."

The prince gestured at his men, who drew closer, glaring, hands clenching. These were old Thuggee, as Shaw had suspected.

"If you don't wish to raise … that … monster," Shaw asked, looking to distract the man, delay him. He was painfully aware that he couldn't hope to protect Singh and held no hope his friend would leave. "Then what good is that book?"

Again the prince chuckled. "There are other rituals, other creatures which can be summoned." Here he gestured back to the building they'd fled. "Ones which can be commanded … with possession of the book."

Singh tapped some object against the small of Shaw's back, out of the prince's view.

"With these creatures," the prince continued, "we will force you Britishers out of India."

The gears of Shaw's internal clock turned and one thought which he'd wondered on since his first day became evident.

"*That's* why you want an outpost at Bandagar."

"Very good, Doctor." The prince gave a half smile. "Call it a test."

"A test?"

"My father created your outpost to show we could all live together, British and Indian, to make India a better place."

"Your—"

"Before he was murdered for not denouncing the Sepoy Mutiny quick enough."

"Oh."

"I was placed on the throne in his place, giving a great show of being welcoming to you British. Meanwhile I started reading what I'd found in my father's private library, experimenting."

"*You* raised the Maut!"

Kanwar stared back, not favoring the outburst with any response. Nor did it need one. Shaw expected revolt here one day, for the Indian people to take their country back by force, but this ... this was insanity.

"You would sell your soul to drive us out?"

"If that is the cost, yes," the prince sighed. "But Ananya and her so-called 'new Thuggees' interfered. They, much like you British, are a pestilence. Both need to be removed from this country."

"I ... am leaving India."

"Doctor Shaw," Singh murmured, pressing the object more insistently against his back.

"No, Doctor, *you* will not be leaving." The prince shook his head then turned to Singh. "*You* however may join us."

Another poke. Shaw reached back to find what was jabbing him and felt cold metal thrust into his hand. He grabbed it, finger sliding through the trigger guard.

"I would die with Doctor Shaw before living with you."

The prince raised one eyebrow. "Such loyalty is commendable, and is your prerogative."

Shaw didn't wait for the soldiers to take the first action but whipped the revolver from behind his back, levelling it at the prince.

"Don't move!"

The shout was overenthusiastic, bordering on panic, and lacking in any real menace, but the gun said enough. The prince raised one arm to halt any action by his men.

"Tell them to get back," Shaw said.

A narrowing of the eyes then Kanwar shrugged. "Do as he says."

The soldiers hesitated.

"My prince—" one started.

"Do not worry," Kanwar said. "This man will not shoot without provocation."

No, not without provocation, but to protect Singh he would fire without reservation.

The soldiers backed away two steps, murder plain in their eyes. Murder in the name of Kali. Eight soldiers and six bullets. The others would be performing this same math. Still, a standoff unless they could guarantee their prince's safety.

"Time to leave," Shaw said over his shoulder.

Singh scooped him up in both arms, carrying him while backing away. Shaw didn't care about how he was carried or the pain which came from it. He focused on keeping the threat of that gun where all could see it.

One soldier came forward and muttered to Prince Kanwar who shook his head, then turned to head in the opposite direction.

"Do not let our paths cross again, Doctor."

Singh carried him another block, toward the busier street, while both looked back the way they'd come. No soldiers followed. Prince Kanwar would be more concerned with finding Ananya and the book at the moment.

Reaching the new street Shaw could endure no more and begged for another rest, slipping the gun into his pocket. The two settled on some steps, their backs to a wall, wary for danger.

"Where did you get this?" Shaw patted the revolver in his pocket.

"From your trunk. I suspected it might be needed."

It was some quick thinking, and during a time when Singh was rushing but … "Why give it to me? I doubt I would have hit more than one of those soldiers if they'd attacked, and only then because they were grouped together."

"I do not know how to shoot."

"Oh."

Of course he didn't. Shaw had taught him about medicine and math and history, not weapons. Most days he was glad for that.

Shaw twisted badly and hissed in a breath against the pain. "Are we far, Singh? From the hotel, I mean."

The hotel! There would be a difficult conversation with Doctor Patel's cousin, Mr. Gupta, on the damage to their room.

"A short ride by carriage," Singh said, standing. "I shall find one."

"Wait." Shaw raised one hand. "The prince cannot get that book."

"No."

"We have to find it before him."

"Yes."

Shaw looked at his leg, knowing he would be worse than useless in any search, he would be a hindrance. Now he needed to ask this fifteen-year-old to take on the responsibility of an adult. Worse! To hunt for an item of such evil that most adults would never know of its existence.

"Can you do it? Find Ananya first?"

"Perhaps." Singh said crossing his arms. "What then?"

"We …" Shaw hadn't thought that far ahead. "Well, we take the book from her. Somehow."

Singh was good enough not to allow any dubious expression to show. "I shall find a cab," he repeated.

"No! Please. I'll be fine."

Singh looked down at Shaw's leg, then back into his eyes.

Without a cane he would not be going anywhere until Singh returned.

Curse this leg!

"Go on, Singh."

"Will she come back to take you again?"

It was a prospect he hadn't considered. Yes, of course she would, though with the prince on her heels it wouldn't be today. Would it?

All Shaw could do was shrug in answer, then pat the pocket holding his revolver again. He hoped the gesture appeared more confident than he felt. "It's fine."

"Hmm …"

Without further comment Singh took off at a jog. Shaw shifted his weight, getting more comfortable. He hoped no one would come and insist he leave this spot.

Less than five minutes passed before a one-horse carriage stopped nearby. A chill ran along his back, knowing it was there to take him.

Ananya? One of her endless group of followers? India held no shortage of miserable, forgotten, disaffected men for her to recruit.

The door opened and Singh jumped out, rushing over to Shaw, helping him rise.

"Singh, you shouldn't have—"

"It is already done."

No arguing with it. The gesture had been made, the time used for it already gone. Better to be grateful for it, and he was … though it was a perfect example of him being a hindrance, a delay.

Singh placed him inside the cab.

"Singh!"

"Doctor?"

"Don't … put yourself in danger."

"I've heard you say: All it takes for evil to win is for men to look on and do nothing."

"Yes. Yes." Shaw agreed. "But you see, Singh. Another way for evil to win is if they kill good people."

"Good people?" Singh considered this, as if the thought in relation to himself was a new thought. "I shall be careful."

With that the young man slammed the cab door and left, heading back toward the mansion they'd just escaped.

Now the doubts came. The fear. Had he sent the boy into horrible danger?

No! Singh was resourceful, intelligent. He would be fine. He had to be.

The ride was not comfortable, but slightly better than being carried across someone's shoulder. Without a cane to stabilize himself, Shaw found the bouncing of this cab greater than their earlier ride from the train station, and more painful. At least it was brief.

At the door to the hotel he was met by Doctor Patel's cousin who rushed back inside, returning with two sturdy youths. They helped Shaw from the cab and through the lobby, depositing him with gentleness into a comfortable chair next to the elevators. The hotel owner sat next to Shaw, dismissing the two helpers.

"Oh, Mr. Gupta," Shaw said, looking up at the man. "The damages to your room, I am so sorry. I'll pay, of course."

The man made a gesture, dismissing the concern as irrelevant. "Vinod told me of the troubles in Bandagar, Doctor. The Thuggees," he whispered this last word. "This was more of the same?"

"Yes."

Gupta's expression became more grim and he muttered a word Shaw wasn't able to translate. "The police have come about the dead man on the street."

Shaw sighed, nodded.

"I will look after it, my friend. You rest."

Shaw was left alone in the chair, a place he expected to occupy until Singh came back, but within ten minutes the hotel owner returned with a wheelchair. Shaw had no idea where it had come from or how the man had gotten it, and was too grateful to ask. As if asking would make the illusion disappear.

One of the sturdy youths came with him and the two helped in a painful transfer from chair to his new seat. Shaw gritted his teeth against the irony that he should now miss his cane, though he doubted his ability to use one just now.

"Help the doctor to his room," Gupta asked, then turned back to Shaw. "Your belongings have been transferred to another room."

An overwhelming gratitude filled Shaw toward this man he'd known less than a day. As good and caring as his cousin.

The new room was next to the previous and had the same view of the street below. He passed the next hour watching people pass, hoping for Singh, vigilant for Ananya, and Kanwar or anyone who looked vaguely Thuggee. Every person looked a likely suspect.

He took the revolver from his pocket, placing it on the table where it could be grabbed easily. His mind soon rolled around to another subject.

The Mauts. Mauts!

Who knew how many of those monsters!

One by itself was able to affect one person, draw them in and destroy their mind. Horrible enough. Four of those monsters could paralyze and an entire room of fifty or sixty men. Did they affect everyone between them?

Shaw shuddered. If they hadn't left when they did …

"Oh!"

One fact dawned on Shaw and he slapped the table. He and Eames *had* destroyed the Maut … A Maut anyway. His plan *had* worked. That Maut in the trees had been a second one. It hadn't stood right, stooped in the other direction. He saw that now …

Just as he saw how fortunate they were the two hadn't arrived together ... Corporal Eames needed this warning on what multiple Mauts meant. Who knew how many Kanwar had raised around Bandagar?

After scribbling all he knew about the Mauts and addressing it to Eames, Shaw's mind returned to the book. What *could* they do once Singh found Ananya? Could Shaw call on soldiers from those stationed in Bombay? Armstrong would possibly vouch for him, if he was careful to not use words such as Thuggee or cult. Yes, certainly a favor could be called in if he pushed, but that favor was thirteen hours away by train.

Could Mr. Gupta round up some help? Certainly the man held no love for the Thuggees and would know others who felt the same. Once Singh found Ananya's lair they could surround the place, go in by *all* entrances while leaving a few outside to catch the inevitable escapee who would flee with the book.

That could work.

It was the best they could do.

A second hour inched past before a noise in the hallway drew attention away from his thoughts. A scuff of soft-soled shoe against tiled floor. Fear escalating in the space between heartbeats Shaw scrambled for the gun, vowing Ananya would not take him without a struggle.

He levelled the revolver at the door, at chest height of a normal sized person.

Yes, if he'd had this last time they wouldn't have taken him so easily.

His hand shook.

The door opened to reveal Singh and Shaw let his pent-up breath loose, lowering the gun. His young friend crossed the room and held one hand out, a length of wood in it.

"What's this?"

"A cane, to replace your broken one."

Shaw rubbed his fingers along the smoothness of the wood.

Teak, he thought. It was simple, undecorated but gorgeous at the same time, of higher quality than the other. This would not break over someone's head. Again he marveled at the irony of missing a cane.

"You went shopping?"

Singh shook his head. "I followed her trail through the market."

"Yes?"

"And lost them."

Shaw gritted his teeth in frustration. The statement was unnecessary, of course, an oddity in itself. If Singh had not lost them he wouldn't have returned, and would not have bothered to stop and purchase a cane.

Singh held out a paper bag. Shaw looked at it, one eyebrow raised.

"The spice, turmeric, for your mother."

"Ah. Yes."

Thoughts of the yellow cloud blinding the man-monster came back, as did thoughts of his mother. Shaw opened his mouth to speak but Singh looked away, leaning against the window frame, arms crossed and staring outside.

"What next, Doctor?"

What next? A fair question, and one which he had no answer to. What *could* be done?

He knew what could *not* be done. He couldn't pretend this evil didn't exist, couldn't close his eyes and leave this problem for someone else, for Singh.

No.

Shaw reached into the inner pocket of his jacket, drawing his ship's ticket out and holding it toward Singh. "Take this. Trade it for passage on next month's ship."

Singh cocked his head to one side.

"Please," Shaw added.

Singh took the ticket, a quiet statement on his face to say that his unspoken question had not been answered.

"I can't leave yet." Shaw took a deep breath, leaning to one side to favor his leg. "Ananya is still in Bombay, somewhere, and so is that damned book. If we can't find her, then we wait for her to come for me. Once we have the book, *then* I can return to England."

And if it took longer than a month he would trade that ticket in too, and again until the job was done. Whatever it took.

"The book needs to be destroyed, Singh. Only you and I know it."

Singh considered. "Sikhism teaches we must live an honest life and care for others."

"Yes! And we must pay our debts," Shaw said. "I owe a debt to Walsh for saving my life. And I owe a second one to Lassiter because I couldn't save his."

The ticket vanished somewhere inside his robe, a feat which always fascinated Shaw given there was no outward appearance of pockets or storage.

"An honest life," Singh repeated, staring at Shaw a moment longer before pulling the other chair out and sitting on it. He gazed into Shaw's eyes. "Your friend Lassiter died because of the idol."

Shaw nodded, having assumed as much since the day at the cave, and confirmed by Ananya in the Bandagar house. Lassiter had died alone and afraid. Had Singh and the man Shaw thought his father still been nearby when ...?

Had ...?

No.

Shaw turned his gaze back on Singh, a dread thought turning like gears in a clock until all hands pointed to midnight. He sucked in a brief shocked breath, refusing to believe.

"No." Shaw shook his head, rejecting the thought. "Not you, Singh."

"It was the next stage of proving my worth," Singh said, less confession than telling of fact. "My partner held him."

Singh looked away, toward the floor. Some guilt or remorse lodged there after all.

"Oh, Singh."

The young man got to his feet without another glance and headed for the door. "I shall trade in your ticket."

Then Singh was gone, leaving Shaw with his thoughts.

Swirling, whirling, impossible thoughts.

Singh had killed Lassiter.

Murdered.

Had Armstrong and McCready been right all along? Should Singh have not had that second chance?

"No!"

Shaw knew him, knew the Singh now. The Singh then was different, in an impossible position, owned and controlled by the Thuggees. That didn't excuse the actions, but he was only a boy at the time, was barely more than that now.

More swirling, whirling, impossible thoughts.

He would follow a chain of thoughts, only to find himself returning again and again to the beginning.

Singh had killed Lassiter.

Another hour crawled past, he in the same position, body still but brain in constant motion.

He knew Singh! He'd spoken with him, taught him and learned from him. Slept in the same room as him and left himself vulnerable to the boy. He watched Singh changing his life, searching out better teachings than Shaw could give, becoming a better man than Shaw could hope to be.

Ah, he saw it now. That was the beginning of Singh's path to redemption, the holy men in Bandagar. It was why he would return to them once Shaw was gone as well. He was trying to atone.

An honest life, Singh had said.

The door opened and Singh stepped inside, surprising Shaw. He was lucky it hadn't been Ananya. They would have caught him without defense.

Singh handed over the updated ticket and stood before Shaw, unmoving. "I am prepared."

"Prepared?"

"For the authorities. You will call them to take me for punishment."

Shaw jerked upright, this fresh shock overpowering the pain.

Call the authorities?

Had that idea briefly occurred to him?

"Sit," Shaw said, gesturing to the chair Singh had occupied earlier. "Please."

Singh did so, arms against those of the chair. Back straight and eyes forward. The condemned man anticipating sentence.

The quest to punish Lassiter's murderers warred with Shaw's quest to keep this boy—this man—safe and healthy. "I think we have a job to do."

"Of course, Doctor. We will find Ananya and then you can—"

"And then I can do nothing."

Singh cocked his head.

"What happened, what you did, was years ago. You were a child."

"That does not excuse it."

Shaw shook his head, realizing it echoed his own earlier thought. "No, but it's up to you to make amends."

Singh's eyes flicked back and forth, mind working. "The Khalsa—a group within the Sikh religion—believe in defending the faith, even at the expense of one's own life."

It was the second time Singh had spoken of his faith and beliefs. "You are Sikh then?"

Singh continued as if Shaw hadn't spoken. "From the Hindus I have learned Raja Yoga for mental control and meditation. And Karma Yoga to eliminate selfishness."

This time Shaw kept his mouth shut and let Singh continue at his own speed.

"No, Doctor. I am neither Sikh nor Hindu … or perhaps I am both. My mission in life contrasts from either: To find and destroy this book, even at the cost of my life."

"At which point you will have made amends?"

Singh looked at him with eyes which pleaded for an answer and Shaw was reminded this was still only a fifteen-year-old boy.

"I cannot condone what you did."

Singh sighed, a quick shake of his head.

"But if you help destroy this book I believe you *will* have gone a considerable way to making amends."

Singh thought about this and his shoulders relaxed, muscles unclenched, as if a burden had been removed. The thought fit in with his ideology and was a rationalization he could live with. Shaw found that he too could live with this, and in the end Lassiter would surely be happier in destroying a greater evil than punishing one that no longer existed.

An honest life.

An honest life.

The words returned again and again, slapping at Shaw's own conscience.

Too many secrets, and not all of them Singh's.

Shaw placed one hand on the spice-filled bag and tapped it softly. "Thank you for this."

Singh nodded and Shaw rushed on, before losing his nerve.

"My mother … died," he said, hands wringing together.

A cock of the head.

"Earlier this year. In February."

Confusion then hurt crossed Singh's face. This was not a secret one kept from a friend and Singh had every right to feel betrayed.

"It was a difficult time." Shaw wished he could get up and

pace. Instead he gripped the arms of his chair. "Not a topic I was able to talk about. I believed if I kept writing to her it somehow wouldn't be true. Then when I had accepted her death too much time had gone by. I felt foolish."

Singh was silent a full minute before focusing on Shaw again, connecting eye to eye. "I am sorry for your loss."

The sting of tears filled Shaw's eyes and he wiped them away without embarrassment, only a gratitude toward this young man so much better than himself.

"So you see, I have little to return to, and a greater reason to stay."

Singh nodded and the two lapsed into silence for some time before Singh spoke again.

"We wait for Ananya to come back for you? This is our plan?"

"I ... Yes. Unless we discover where Ananya is holed up which seems unlikely in a city this size."

As far as plans went it wasn't much of one, but it was all they had.

And Singh did not need to point out the one glaring problem in the plan: What if Kanwar found her first?

CHAPTER THIRTY-TWO

BOMBAY, INDIA — SEPTEMBER 20TH, 1885

... *It seems, Mother, that I will not be returning to England after all. Not yet.*

I'd actually thought I was finished with all of this madness, thought I could return to England and a normal life of medical practice where all was explainable through science.

But, no. I've seen too much.

The days of experiencing the world in such simple terms are gone. Done.

The destruction of this book is a higher calling than a medical practice. What is the point of healing people's bodies if their souls are destroyed as easily ...

Shaw woke the next morning to find Singh gone.

He grabbed his cane and hobbled around the room. No note. No explanation. Bed barely slept in.

At the door he rested one hand on the knob, debating. Go out or not?

Had something happened to Singh?

Had Ananya found him?

Worse! Had that, ruthless, monstrous god—

"No! Don't even think that name!"

It took five minutes to travel to the elevator, by which time Shaw realized he should have taken both the wheelchair and the revolver. All he had was his cane, and no intention of heading back.

Another excruciatingly slow ride down to the lobby.

"Good morning, Doctor Shaw," a voice greeted as he stepped out.

He turned to see Mr. Gupta.

"I can't find Singh."

"Singh?"

"Singh! My boy!"

Shaw envisioned the picture he presented, swaying in the lobby wearing his pyjamas and gripping his cane. He looked and sounded frantic, unbalanced, and forced himself to calm down.

"Yes, of course." Gupta placed a hand on Shaw's arm, steering him back toward the elevator. "I saw him earlier, just before sunrise."

"Sunrise?"

Singh hadn't been gone long then. He could still catch the boy.

A twinge of pain in his leg told him how wrong he was on that.

"I ... I ... I can't lose him," Shaw said, voice low.

The hotel owner made sounds of agreement and pressed the button for the second floor. The two rode up together.

"I am sure Singh will return soon."

"Will he?" Shaw looked at the man, wishing he agreed. "You know what these Thuggees are like."

"Yes. Yes, I see, my friend. I will have my two workers search for him. How is that?"

Those two could look for Singh much quicker and effectively than he could. Shaw agreed, defeated by his own body, and allowed himself to be guided down the hall and back to his room. This would have to do, though admitting it froze his soul.

Thanking the hotel manager he managed to cross the room and fall into the chair. Here was where he would bide his time.

Shaw placed the revolver in his lap, staring at the door. Minutes ticked by, each one like a full lifetime. Looking at his watch convinced him it had stopped, but time simply crept by too slow for him.

Should he get dressed and go himself?

What if Singh came back while he was gone?

No. He would at least wait to hear what the other two searchers found.

An hour. Then a second one. The sun was high in the sky when a step came from outside the door. No effort to be quiet, sneaky. Shaw gripped the revolver, ready to swing it up and shoot.

The door opened.

"Singh!" Shaw breathed out the word.

He dropped the gun back into his lap and struggled to stand without success.

"Where have you been? I was afraid that ... afraid ..." He stopped himself, knowing if he continued he would embarrass himself with tears of relief.

"I couldn't sleep."

"You ... Why didn't you leave a note?"

Singh breathed in and out, once, twice. His entire attitude distracted. "I had an idea. I might not be able to find Ananya, but maybe the prince could."

"Kanwar?"

Singh leaned in the door frame. "I thought he could lead me to her."

"Yes, of course. Smart." He leaned forward in his seat. "You found him?"

Singh nodded.

An excitement rose in Shaw. "You followed him, didn't you? Followed the prince to Ananya."

"I followed his soldiers."

Now Shaw did stand, forgetting, then ignoring, the agony. The revolver clattered to the floor. "Kanwar has the book! Is that what you're telling me?"

Singh's gaze came up, a shake of his head. He stooped, retrieved the gun and returned it to the side table.

"Where, Singh? Where is she?"

"On the ship. Her and one other."

"Ship? What ship?" Only one came to mind. "The ship to England?"

"Yes."

Memories of that exchanged ticket crashed in on Shaw.

"Well … Fine, then. Fine!" Shaw gripped his cane tighter and hobbled toward the door. "Let's get to that dock, Singh."

The ticket could be replaced, and all avenues of escape would be known on a ship … unless they jumped a rail into the ocean.

"Doctor."

"Surely we can round up some soldiers for help. No … scratch that. No time. We can get aboard and find them."

"Doctor Shaw."

"Corner them, bring them to the captain and—"

"It's gone."

"Gone?" Shaw stopped, leaning onto the cane while looking into his friend's face. "What's gone?"

"The ship. An hour ago."

"No." Shaw deflated, sagging against the door frame. "Gone!"

Singh rushed to his side and took an arm, helping him back across the room and into the chair.

"Gone!" Shaw repeated, closer to a shout this time.

Ananya was headed for England ... where she would replace her need for Shaw with some other Britisher. It might take time but one item Britain had was an abundance of British.

"I arrived too late," Singh said, "as did the prince's men."

"Well ... that's something at least. Small favors and such." Shaw lowered his face into his hands. "It's my fault, Singh. I chased her there when I told her where the idol was."

The next ship to England was a month away, and in that time Ananya and her Thuggee would have landed in England and fled like rats into some hole. Oh, there would be signs. People like that didn't disappear without clues.

But what could *he* hope to do about it, an army doctor with a bum leg? It was hopeless. He couldn't chase someone down a street, much less across England.

This task was too great, too overwhelming.

And no one else for the job. As he'd said to Singh last night only the two of them knew about the evil of this book. He drew in one long breath and let it out through clenched teeth, coming to terms with the inevitable.

"I will find it, Singh," he said, knowing his voice lacked any substantial strength. "I will find that book and destroy it. Somehow."

"We."

Shaw narrowed his brows in confusion. "We?"

"*We* will find them."

He stared at the young man a full minute, afraid to say the next words but knowing he must.

"Your place is here, Singh. You said so yourself."

"I also said my mission is to destroy this book."

"Your studies."

"Will continue."

"I ..." The words wouldn't come. Shaw nodded his gratitude.

In the morning they would get a second ticket for Singh on the next ship, and a more spacious cabin to share.

CHAPTER THIRTY-THREE

Bombay, India—October 21st, 1885

... Mother, I do wish I were returning home to you, though considering all I've learned of the shadowy world around us and the dangers to body, mind, and soul—forgive me for saying this, Mother—I am happy to know you are beyond this danger. No, happy is not the correct word. Relieved.

We are on our way, a month behind Ananya and the book. I can only hope that delay will not doom all humanity. Only Singh and I are aware of this danger and no one but madmen would listen to our ravings.

We are on our own.

The shores of India are now out of sight, probably forever. I left England in search of a new life and grand adventure. I found that, losing so much more in the process. Lassiter. Walsh. My position in the army. My ability to walk normally. Worst of all I've lost my blissful ignorance, my ability to believe in a logical, rational world.

Have I accomplished anything?

The Thuggees still exist.

The book. An item of incredible, ancient evil is loose in the world.

Mauts are still out there, lurking in the wild, summoned by

Kanwar in Bandagar, and Suresh in Bombay. Who knows how many of them, who knows how many driven insane and dragged along as mindless slaves.

And where did that grotesque half-breed man-monster come from? Are there others? Most probable.

So, I repeat: Have I accomplished ANYTHING?

Across the cabin a young man meditates on his bunk.

Singh.

The one accomplishment I can show for my time in India.

That is enough.

THE DAMNED VOYAGE

April 10

The Southampton docks were bedlam, people shouting and gawking, cursing and rushing. Beyond all this a stream of first-class passengers boarded. The ship would soon be under way, to where I neither knew nor cared. I needed to be aboard.

Gusts of warm, brisk wind forced their way around us, and I shifted more weight to the ever-present cane. To my right, Singh, companion and best friend for more than a quarter century, stepped closer to offer support. I took an equal step away, which was met by a resigned shrug. Singh never *had* understood stubborn English pride.

"It is here, Doctor Shaw," he said.

It was. I'd felt the damned thing calling to me, insisting, as soon as we'd arrived. "Yes. It's aboard the ship."

The two thieves must have boarded earlier with the lower classes.

A brief sigh escaped me. This mad adventure was better suited to someone half my age. At sixty-one I should have been in front of a fire, penning memoirs no one could ever read.

Memoirs of death, madness, and an ancient evil mankind was better off not being aware of.

Singh stepped into the crowd, one hand under his robe on the concealed dagger. Always ready. People took one glance at the massive Indian's emotionless face and created a path while I followed in his wake.

The first-class passengers boarded in a steady stream across what was more wooden bridge than ship's ramp. At the base of this bridge I plucked at Singh's robe, stopping him from forcing his way to the deck above. He turned.

In 1878 I had helped rescue Singh from a final holdout sect of the Thuggee cult, a cult we had thought long broken, destroyed. Now, three decades later, no trace of that orphan boy remained, having become a man of solid muscle and determination.

And now I had to leave him.

"I'll be taking this voyage alone, old friend."

A flicker of anger passed over Singh's face, arms crossed over thick chest. At six-and-a-half feet, the man towered over me by almost a foot.

"You need to go to London," I said, holding up one hand. "In case I fail."

Singh's expression didn't change and I nodded my understanding. Aboard that ship were two men who had stolen an item he had vowed to keep safe, as he had vowed to keep me safe. Now I was asking him to abandon both.

Perhaps he understood English pride better than I thought.

"Go to the prince's son," I continued. "His father knew the dangers of this book and so does he. Warn him it's loose in the world again."

Prince Albert Victor was dead now, as were most of the group that had come together in Whitechapel twenty-four years ago. They'd done their duty, retrieved the book and earned their rest, all except myself and Singh, of course, who were charged with keeping it out of the wrong hands, and Kosminski who would rave in an asylum until he died.

"He may be illegitimate," I said, "but he will have the resources to help."

"He will listen better to you."

"Perhaps, but I couldn't endure the carriage ride, much less handle the horses. I only made it here through your skills."

I'd walked with a limp for more years than not and forgotten what it was like to *not* carry a cane. Getting about was not a problem, controlling a carriage would be. On top of this, the breakneck trip here had taken its toll, though I struggled not to show it.

"The book calls to you, Doctor," Singh said. "Will you resist when it's in your hands again?"

"My leg is lame, not my mind," I snapped.

Missing last night's sleep had made me irritable and short-tempered, and Singh's blunt words were too close to the truth. The damned book *did* call to me, *had* called ever since I'd opened it and read those few words twenty-four years ago. We'd followed that calling over the space of miles, from Cambridge to here.

Would I be able to resist?

I closed my eyes and calmed my mind.

"You've taught me well, Singh. How to meditate and block the voices."

Singh heaved a deep sigh, the only sign he would give of his frustrated resignation. He knew this was too important, that precautions needed to be taken.

"How will you get aboard?" Singh gestured toward the deck above.

Fair question. We'd had little money in the house, certainly not enough for a first-class ticket. I'd taken all we had, grabbing my doctor's bag as an afterthought. There was one possibility as I saw it.

"Ships like these allow first-class passengers to have friends and family, even their doctors, go aboard to see them off."

All these well-heeled passengers milled about, chattering their inane conversations, making sure not to give the appearance of being in line to board the ship. They were far too important to queue up.

Singh strolled the length of this line that was not a line, acting like one of many dock workers. The rich ignored him. Twenty passengers along Singh stopped, made a sharp about-face and headed back. Where he'd turned stood an elderly woman, some aging dowager, stooped and wrinkled, perhaps ten years my senior. She fanned herself against the unseasonal heat while waiting to move forward, alone.

"Best of luck, Doctor," Singh said as he passed.

I headed for the woman.

"Good morning, madam. Archibald Shaw at your service."

She started and glared around at this intrusion. I waited for my appearance as a plump older gentleman to register as unthreatening. My receding grey hair and squared lenses completed the image of a latter-day Ben Franklin. Her glance dropped to my doctor's bag then back to my face, a smile cracking her features.

"Oh, Doctor. A pleasure."

"The pleasure is mine," I assured her. "This heat is quite unbearable, is it not?"

That was sufficient to get her going on a lengthy diatribe of problems, starting at her sore feet and working up, leaving out none of the aches and pains of age. I offered her an arm for support and we ascended the ramp side by side. It had been years since I'd practiced medicine, but I still recognized this lonely woman for the hypochondriac that she was. She would have a bagful of medications when what she needed most was someone to listen. I made sympathetic clucking noises and tut-

tutted in all the right places, trying to identify the perfume she wore. L'Heure Bleue?

In the course of the one-sided conversation, moving slowly up the ramp, I was able to discover the ship was headed for New York after a couple of brief stops.

Reaching the deck above we found no less than the captain waiting to greet us. My companion introduced herself as Mrs. Penelope Hooper, then the man held a hand toward me, a dubious expression on his face which was quite understandable. My style of dress hardly measured up to first-class standards.

"Captain Edward Smith, sir."

"Doctor Archibald Shaw."

The other man's expression changed, the smile more genuine. Everyone trusted a doctor. He appeared ready to continue the conversation but a crowd had accumulated behind us in our slow journey here. These guests requiring the captain's attention worked in my favor as too much scrutiny from this man wouldn't do. We moved on.

On the docks below there was no sign of Singh, on his way back to London already. I was well and truly alone, a thought which both saddened and frightened me.

My new companion continued chattering on about her medical woes while I half-listened, scanning the passengers around us until I saw one that would suit my purpose.

"I beg your pardon," I said as Mrs. Hooper took a breath. "I'm afraid I see a patient of mine I must speak with. May I look in on you later?"

"Of course, Doctor," she said with a smile.

The man ahead had about an inch height over my own five foot eight, but I beat him by ten pounds in weight. Other than that we were similar in build, and he seemed to be alone.

He would do.

Only the amount of passengers making their way through

the halls slowed him, but it was enough to keep pace. I was able to catch up as he reached the door to his cabin.

"Excuse me," I called.

He gave a jump and turned toward me, an annoyed expression on his face which quickly passed.

"My apologies, I didn't mean to startle you. Ship's doctor."

"No harm done, Doctor. Can I help you?"

"A couple of routine questions if I may?"

"Oh, of course. Please come in," he said, opening the cabin door.

Everyone trusted a doctor. Of course it was easier if that doctor looked like someone's grandfather.

Glancing left and right I followed the man inside, allowing the door to close behind me.

The cabin was decorated in mahogany paneling and furnished better than my house. A bed with nightstand, a heavy wardrobe, a sitting chair, and a table with two chairs for taking tea. This would be one of the smaller first-class cabins, still a most comfortable way to cross the Atlantic.

I placed my bag on the table.

"What can I do for you, Doctor? Not to be rude but I do still need to change."

"Yes, of course," I said, glancing over at the massive chest at the end of the bed. "You are traveling alone?"

"I am. On my way to New York for business."

I gave my most disarming expression, recollecting the basics of doctoring, building the trust of the patient. "First time across the ocean?"

"Yes." The man shrugged. "Traveling in style."

He glanced at the clock sitting on a chair-side table. As his focus changed I drew the sword concealed inside my cane, thrusting it forward in one fluid motion. The blade pierced the man's heart, a killing thrust.

He looked at the sword protruding from his chest, expression changing from surprise to rage.

"Fall, damn you," I said, withdrawing the sword and stepping back.

Blood gushed from the wound, but not shooting out as it should have. Not the immediate killing stroke after all, but fatal nonetheless.

The dying man rushed at me, hands outstretched. We landed on the floor, him on top with hands closing on my throat, his blood squelching between us. My sword skittered across the cabin, stopping against the bed's leg. Strength left his grip, but not quickly enough. My lungs burned with the need for air while my heart pounded an irregular, terrified throb in my ears. With each beat the world went more grey, moving toward black.

Singh, I'm sorry old friend. I failed.

It would be up to him now to find the book and keep it out of the wrong hands. God knows we'd tried to do that over the years, moving from place to place, keeping away from those searching.

The black deepened, then receded back to grey. The man's grip on my throat relaxed, and I gasped. The world came back into focus and I pulled one rasping breath into a burning throat. For several minutes we lay on the floor, the dead man's weight pinning me until I mustered sufficient strength to move. Rocking him back and forth I eventually rolled him to one side. With the weight off I was able to draw more air into my lungs.

"Damn."

How had I missed the artery, the entire heart? But raising my hands, so unaccustomed to precision work now, I knew how.

I lay on my back a long time, exhausted and hurting, needing a rest but having so much to do. Using what strength there was left, I crawled to the sitting chair and pulled myself upward with the help of that heavy furniture. Halfway to standing, I slumped into the chair. My head leaned back and eyes closed even as I tried to get moving again.

Perhaps a few minutes' rest then.

Bastard.

My eyes opened and I focused on the dead man's face. "That I am, my friend."

You're no friend of mine.

"Why don't you cross over?" I muttered, the room fading.

Then everything slipped into the blackness of unconsciousness.

The door to the small room laid before me and on the other side was the next woman I would question. It was a vast conspiracy, a spiderweb of cheap, brazen women, weathered and beaten down by fate, ready to grasp anything to give meaning to their lives.

The last woman had given the address for Mary-Jane Kelly.

Nearby, hidden in an alley, Singh and the others waited, making sure I would not be disturbed.

When the door opened and I saw the young lady on the other side I almost lost my nerve. This was no old whore in her declining years. This woman was lovely.

"And who sent you then?" she asked in an Irish lilt.

"Annie."

The lass started, blonde hair bouncing around her face. "Annie's dead."

"Yes, she is," I responded, stepping forward.

Mary-Jane Kelly did not die easily. It took hours for her to convince me that she was not part of the cult.

By then her death was a mercy.

My eyes snapped open.

I was cold and clammy with the sweat of nightmares, my body still thrashing against the soft upholstery of the reading chair.

Nightmares.

I hadn't medicated before napping and those damned dreams, those memories, had taken me by force.

Aches and pains echoed through my body, unaccustomed as the muscles were to such strenuous work and of sleeping in a chair.

My glance drifted to the clock beside me.

"8:30 PM?"

I bolted to my feet, all aches forgotten. It had been a few minutes before noon when we'd entered the cabin.

"No! I've slept more than eight hours."

In that time the ship had not only launched but had come and gone from its first port in France.

You sleep well, for a murderer.

"You don't understand," I said, looking at the dead man's body. "The thieves could have disembarked in France. I would never catch them now."

I stood still, listening for the presence of the book.

"It's still here," I said.

Of course it was still aboard, the nightmare alone should have told me that much. Without the book's presence I would have had a peaceful sleep.

Twenty-four years ago, when I'd brought the book home from Whitechapel, I succumbed to curiosity. I opened it, read from it. The first word threw me into convulsions. I read on, unable to stop. Another word. A full sentence. The words leaping from my mouth in lunatic screams.

Ph'nglui mglw'nafh Cthulhu R'lyeh wgah'nagl fhtagn.

Singh had batted the book from my grasping fingers and I

collapsed, spending the next weeks raving about ancient evils that no human mind should try to comprehend.

Those words still echoed inside my mind.

I tried to strangle you while you slept. The voice was hateful. *I couldn't touch you.*

"Of course you couldn't. You're dead. All you can do is observe."

The angry spirit gave a long mournful groan.

Using the furniture for balance, I made my way across the cabin to retrieve both sword and cane, then headed for the dead man. I wiped the sword against his chest.

My favorite jacket.

"You've no use for it now."

The front of the man's jacket, like the shirt underneath, was a mess of sticky blood. An inside pocket held a billfold which in turn held his ticket for this voyage. Both had been narrowly missed by the sword thrust. I pocketed the billfold after wiping it against the man's jacket, and opened the ticket.

Bastard, the voice said.

"So you've said and I didn't deny it." I read the name on the ticket. "Stephen?"

I will kill you.

"No, you won't. You can't even touch me."

You're a monster.

"Perhaps."

Stephen was silent a moment before replying in a low whisper. *Why me?*

"Convenience. I needed a cabin, ticket, and clothes. You were close enough in height and weight."

You killed me for my luggage?

I felt no desire to explain to this spirit, but if it would give him the closure he needed to move on … "No. I killed you to stay aboard this ship, and I would kill a hundred more like you to get this book back."

Stephen sobbed and I wondered at a ghost's ability to cry but left it.

There were some unavoidable tasks before I could leave the cabin to start my search. The sleep had done wonders and I found myself full of energy, though also full of aches and pains. Heading for the trunk, I flipped the lid up, throwing contents onto the bed.

Not enough to have murdered me? Now you vandalize my belongings?

I didn't reply, continuing until the trunk was empty. Now it was light enough to be dragged across the cabin, my left leg giving complaint, but I'd lived with that pain enough years to ignore it. Once it rested next to Stephen's body, I tipped the trunk onto its back and opened the lid, then getting onto the floor next to the dead man, I used my good leg as a brace and rolled him inside. Rigors had set in, giving trouble with the bending of limbs, but there was no need to be gentle about it. In the end Stephen fit inside his own trunk.

A choke of outrage had initially come from the disembodied voice, but Stephen had since fallen silent, as if at a loss for words. That wouldn't last.

Getting the proper leverage to flip the trunk back turned out to be more difficult. The trunk needed to be rocked back and forth several times before rolling back onto its bottom.

Stephen laughed meanly. *You are too old for this.*

"I'm fine," I snapped.

A sensitive topic. I look forward to your heart attack.

I stayed silent. Stephen couldn't affect the physical world but words had a power of their own.

My clothes looked as if I'd been in the operating room, catching Stephen's dying blood between us. I washed up in the water closet, then changed into some evening clothes from the jumble on the bed. The fabric was of excellent quality, much better than what I'd been wearing.

Is there nothing of mine you will not violate?

"Why should this matter to a dead man?"

Well, it does.

A knock sounded on the door and I jerked in surprise.

Come in, Stephen yelled. *Quick. Help!*

"No one can hear you," I said in a low voice, then louder, "Coming."

Gathering my ruined clothes, I threw them into the chest, covering Stephen's upturned face, then closed and latched the lid. On the way to the door, I inspected the cabin. All seemed in order.

Outside was a young man in ship's uniform, smiling as the door opened.

"Good evening, sir," the man said. "I will be your steward for the trip. My name is Thompkins."

This man murdered me, Stephen screamed. *Get the captain.*

I greeted the steward, forcing a smile onto my face though Stephen's shrillness hammered my brain.

"I knocked earlier," Thompkins said, "but there was no answer."

"Ah, yes. I took a nap. It has been a long journey."

Damn it! This man is a lunatic.

"You need to see my ticket?" I asked.

"Oh, no, sir. We'll ask for those after leaving Ireland tomorrow."

"Of course," I nodded, trying to appear the experienced traveler. The last time I'd been on a ship was as a doctor in the army, traveling to India and back.

The thought of India reminded me of Singh. Damn, but I missed the man. So many years I'd relied on him.

"I wanted to introduce myself," the steward continued, "and to see if you needed anything."

"I suppose I've missed dinner?"

"Yes, sir, I'm afraid so, though the *a la carte* restaurant will still be serving. Or, I could bring food to you."

"Perhaps just some tea. I want to stroll around first though. Say in an hour?"

"Yes, sir. I'll leave it on your table if you aren't back yet."

"Thank you."

The steward left, retreating down the corridor.

He couldn't hear me.

"No, I told you as much. Only I can hear you." I stepped into the corridor. "You will find you are confined to this room as well."

A lie, but, with luck, one Stephen wouldn't test. I needed time to think and couldn't have the dead man following me around the ship, moaning about his fate.

Damn you.

"I've been damned a long time."

And now you've damned me, too.

"You're not damned, you're dead."

Stephen fell silent and I reached for the door's handle.

Please don't leave, he said.

I stopped. Stephen's personality had an annoying inconsistency. Depressive. Hateful. Now pleading? Was it an inability to cope with being dead?

There is a voice ... It whispered to me all day, telling me unspeakable things.

"A voice? That is the book you're hearing."

I knew the power of that whispering. I'd heard it, resisted it, for years, but with a tie to the physical world which this spirit did not have.

Yessss, Stephen sighed.

I felt unsure if he was responding to me or not.

"Stephen, where is it?"

Silence.

I waited, hoping for a response, until it grew obvious none was coming. Unfortunate.

"You are correct, I am not your friend," I said to the empty cabin. "Let me give you some advice as if I am, though. Move on to the afterlife."

With that I left, closing the door on the morose spirit.

First class occupied an incredible amount of the ship and, moving at my speed, it took some time to travel around it. Even after my tour I'd seen no more than half of the deck, though did discover the name of the ship which meant little to me.

While moving about I'd became more certain of the book's location being somewhere below my current deck, on one of the lower-class levels, but could not get an idea of how far away or whether it was closer to front or back of the ship. I would need to get closer, but that was a different problem.

Passage to the lower decks was marked by waist-high locked gates, each of them attended by stewards ensuring no one made the social faux pas of mixing with the wrong class.

I continued my investigation, hoping for another way below to present itself.

Around me a vague atmosphere of gloom and despair had descended on the ship like a fine mist. At this point, few would be aware of it, but that wouldn't last. Below, it would be worse. In all likelihood the book would be in the lowest levels. It called to the uneducated and backward, the psychotic and disturbed, the easily swayed.

And which was I?

It had called to the Thuggees in 1878. The cult was a throwback to a more brutal time of Indian history, a final holdout against the purges. The cultists hadn't been able to read the book, but from the illustrations inside they concluded the book would bring about the Kali-Yuga, a time when their brutal goddess would rule the world. What they presumed to be the many arms of Kali were the tentacles of a much more ancient, more terrible god.

At that time I was a doctor in the army, knowing little of cults and nothing of ancient, sleeping gods. My regiment assaulted the cult's cave hideout, intent on wiping them out. The Thuggees threw themselves at us in a fanatical wave before being broken. These sacrifices played their part though, giving time for several of their number to escape out the back, leaving behind the too old and young.

One of the initiates left behind was a boy of eight taken from the streets of Bombay, already on his way to learning the art of assassination. I took on the job of rehabilitating him.

As I educated Singh, he educated me, telling me about the cult and what had happened within that cave, telling me of the profane book, an object of pure evil that only the highest in the cult were ever allowed to touch.

It was true. Inside those caves there had been a tangible malevolence that was more than simply the evil of men. The book was a danger, but the remaining cultists had fled with it and the army declared the Thuggees broken for all time.

The book was forgotten until our return to London.

Shaking off the memories of those more carefree times I headed for the a la carte restaurant the steward had recommended. The smell of cooked beef and melted butter set my stomach rumbling.

When was the last time I'd eaten?

I ordered the first item on the menu, something which would come quickly, then watched the people around me. The passengers acted as one would expect, chatting with friends and family, enjoying the novelty of being aboard such an incredible machine. Occasionally there were furtive glances on one of their faces, eyes darting as if expecting some unseen danger. They would then return to what they were doing, unaware of their brief unease.

These would be the more sensitive people. Artists and romantics.

The food arrived, a hot beef sandwich, and my focus changed for the next fifteen minutes. It had been some time since I had enjoyed a meal so fully … enjoyed anything for that matter.

Sipping an after-dinner port, my thoughts returned to the book and thieves. Speed and mobility was their advantage but aboard a ship, even one this vast, that advantage became less relevant.

Only if I was smart about it though.

They couldn't know I was aboard, but any search of the lower decks now would draw attention. All they would need to do, if they became suspicious, was keep ahead of me and disembark tomorrow in Queenstown. Without Singh I couldn't give chase.

I wandered the deck, thinking, planning.

Tomorrow, after the last port of call, I would find a way past the steward and into the lower decks. There would be some way, and if not, I would create one. For now I would wait, and I was skilled at that, having done little else for the past twenty-four years, guarding the book while waiting for death to come.

Standing at the rail, watching miles of water pass without truly seeing it, I found myself starting to doze and was surprised to see the time close to midnight. The decks around me had cleared off in April's chilly night air.

How long had I been standing here?

Sighing, I headed toward my cabin. "Better to sleep in bed."

With luck Stephen would be gone.

Five steps toward the cabin, a wave of overwhelming fear and horror slammed into me like a train. It gripped my heart and squeezed. Staggering against the rail I stopped myself from falling to the deck.

I knew this sensation.

"No! Oh, God damn it, no."

One of the thieves was reading from the book.

Then it was gone, as quickly as it had come. The reader had been interrupted after only a word or two.

I waited for more but none came.

Behind me the door closed with a soft click. Inside the cabin, the chest had been returned to its place at the foot of the bed, and a silver serving tray with teapot and cup had been delivered. I'd forgotten about that. Not much hope of it still being hot.

Ooooohhhhhhh, the mournful groan came, filling the cabin.

Damn. I should have known better than to hope Stephen would have moved on. Mary-Jane Kelly had haunted me a full year before going wherever the dead go.

What have you done to me? Stephen said, his voice pure misery.

We both knew the answer to that question, but I wasn't sure he was even talking to me. No, something had changed in Stephen in the past few hours.

The moaning increased, coming from every corner. A disembodied wailing.

The darkness. The evil. IT PULLS ME.

Of course! The thieves had read from the book, awoken its power. Stephen, being all spirit, took the brunt of that influence, greater than the most sensitive artist would experience. Earlier it had been whispering to him, but now it was screaming.

Oh, God! It's driving me mad. I am damned!

Something hit me across the back, staggering me forward. The pillows from the bed were on the floor behind me.

It's pulling me apart!

The teapot lifted from the table and hurtled across the cabin, crashing against the entry door. Next, the clock soared past, missing me by a foot and colliding with one wood-paneled wall. I dropped to the floor, my leg screaming at the sudden rough treatment as the cabin came alive with every object not secured. The two chairs from the table. The silver serving tray. Cream and sugar containers. The soap flew from the water closet, shattering against the table and showering me with soap splinters. I too felt myself being pulled upward and crawled under the bolted-down table, grabbing it as an anchor.

The damned book had awakened an ability in Stephen, turning him from ghost to poltergeist.

Chairs, clock, teapot, soap splinters, and more, all flew in a swirling maelstrom around the cabin, accumulating objects. Across the room the trunk flipped onto one side and stayed there.

Stephen's screaming increased to the point where I needed to choose between holding onto the table or covering my tortured ears. If anyone could have heard those wails they would have been breaking down the cabin door.

The long scream became a word.

Cthuuuuuuuuuulhuuuuuuuuuuuuu.

"Oh God!"

I opted for covering my ears and was immediately pulled out from under the table.

"No!"

The scream ended, cut off mid-syllable, and I returned to the ground with a bounce, fighting to catch my breath.

"St—Stephen?"

No response.

Another full minute on the floor, recovering, watching the objects around me.

"Stephen?" I repeated.

Still nothing.

With the help of the table's edge I was able to get upright again.

The room was still.

Stephen was gone.

Absently, I moved around, cleaning the damage while thinking about what had happened.

Cthulhu.

That word chilled my soul to the core, more thoroughly than a winter's night would freeze my body. I knew the name, remembered it from the words I had read.

I shuddered.

Stephen had connected with the force of madness and power that was the book, and his soul had been destroyed because of it.

"No," I whispered, making my way to the sitting chair.

I collapsed into it, my thoughts resting on grim subjects. Killing innocents was a horrible but necessary task at times, and as I'd told Stephen, I would kill a hundred like him if need be.

Being responsible for the destruction of an immortal soul was too cruel a weight to bear.

I closed my eyes, slipping into a meditative state and calming my mind, focusing past the constant whispering.

In time, sleep did come again.

Dreams of sleeping gods lying in their sunken kingdoms.

Deeper and deeper I descended into the stygian blackness, past pale loathsome things swimming. Things which had never been seen on the surface.

A pyramid of dense obsidian, ancient when the Valley of the Kings was young, came into view, each brick etched with a language as dead as the god it held.

No. Not dead. Sleeping.

"That is not dead which can eternal lie."

Through an opening massive enough for a ship to sail, along ink-

black corridors where I could see nonetheless, until I came to face the
pyramid's sole inhabitant.

Eyes opened, glaring at me, shriveling my soul like a raisin.
"COME!"

April 11

Standing at the rail of the ship, I watched those disembarking, wondering how many had planned such a short voyage and
how many had horrendous nightmares they'd taken as premoni-
tions. The artists among them would have for certain.

Nightmares. If theirs had been half of mine, they were wise to
leave. The morphine in my bag would have provided a dreamless rest, but I'd allowed myself to sleep without it. I knew better.
Singh had been able to push the book's influence from his mind
through meditation, but the best I could manage that way was to
subdue the voices.

I stifled a yawn.

Tenders shuttled people back and forth, the docks at Queenstown being unable to accommodate the ship. This gave only
one avenue of departure.

None of those milling about, preparing to depart, were the
thieves I chased, not that I expected them to leave without some
sort of push. There was more to this than the cultists reclaiming
their evil tome. They had an agenda, some reason to cross the
ocean. Were they headed for one of those cursed New England
towns heard only in whispers? Innsmouth? Dunwich?

"It is beautiful, isn't it?"

I turned toward the source of the voice to see Captain Smith
also looking at the tenders. He stood with the excellent posture
and bearing of the career sailor, one hand on the rail, the other
by his side. The man had an air of authority and power which
came as much from personality as from station.

"It is indeed," I agreed, though unsure whether the man spoke of the ship or the sea itself.

The captain breathed deep of the salty air, serenity clear on his face. "So much comes together to make a successful voyage. Ship and crew, the course laid, even those tenders below. If all works to plan, then most of it is not noticed by the passengers."

It all seemed to be running like a German train.

"I apologize, Doctor," Captain Smith said. "Get a sailor talking about the sea, and he drifts away."

If the pun was intentional, the man gave no sign. I was more focused on the fact that he remembered I was a doctor.

"How is Mrs. Hooper?" the captain asked.

"Mrs. Hooper?"

"The lady you boarded with. I had assumed you were attending her."

"No." I shook my head, forcing a smile. "Just two slow-moving people coming up the ramp together."

"Ah, I see." The captain nodded, watching the proceedings below. "Please excuse me, Doctor, I have tasks to attend to before we sail."

"Of course, Captain, you must be quite busy."

I felt happy to see him go. Though he was an amiable sort, having the attention of the most powerful man aboard ship made me uncomfortable.

A few steps and the captain turned back. "Doctor, would you join my table for dinner tonight?"

Damn it. More attention, and not the sort that could be rejected.

"Thank you, Captain, I would be honored."

After departure from Queenstown, I headed back toward my cabin, frustrated.

The gates between decks remained closed with stewards always at hand. I had tried the direct approach, simply asking for entry and when the steward explained this was impossible, I demanded. The man offered to call the captain and I'd relented.

Thoughts of killing the steward and forcing my way through itched at my brain, but too many people milled about. Even if I wasn't apprehended immediately and *could* retrieve the book, then what? It wouldn't be destroyed. I'd tried enough times over the years to know the damned thing didn't burn or tear, and submerging it in water didn't even smudge the ink.

No, once it was in my possession again, I would need to wait until New York. That meant retrieving the book as quietly as possible. A murdered crewmember couldn't be left on the deck, or even thrown overboard, without complications. Second class would also have a gate and steward blocking my way into steerage.

Killing had to be a last resort for now.

I needed to return to the cabin and think on this.

As I neared it, a wave of pure malevolence dragged me from my thoughts.

All around, passengers went about their regular business. Nothing strange. I slowed to a stop and another man some thirty paces away did the same, making a show of searching through his pockets. In all outward manner he appeared a typical first-class passenger though overly tall and thin to the point of malnourishment. The clothes hung from his frame, yet one finger tugged at his collar as if the shirt were too tight.

I continued forward, as did my chaperone, a consistent distance between us. There could be no doubt he was following me, and was the source of the terrible sensation as well.

At my cabin door I stopped, turning to face the man who again came to an abrupt halt, his eyes darting. A full half minute we stood this way until he shook his head several times, like a man fighting to clear his mind, and stepped toward me.

That loathsome sensation increased, wrapping around me like some great, constricting fist. Evil and corruption accompanied this man in an aura reminiscent of the one surrounding the book, coming off the man in erratic waves, like the heat from a fire.

I was looking at one of the thieves.

How had *he* found *me* though?

Gripping the head of my cane I was ready. The man stopped in front of me, staring down with piggy eyes. One sinewy hand reached over and rubbed at his opposite arm, but he made no move against me.

This was no casual evil surrounding the thief. He was not a man who cheated the poor or beat his wife. No, he had a blackness to the center of his soul and it was one I recognized.

He had read from the book, just as I had, and he'd found me by following that shared link. The same link that allowed me to recognize him.

Now what? He'd still made no threatening move.

"We gots the book," he said in the twang of the uneducated.

A faraway quality rested in those eyes, worse than an opium sot, a look I recognized from years earlier after coming out of my own ravings.

"We gots the book," he repeated.

Was he boasting? Taunting?

No, he waited for a reply.

"Yes, I know," I improvised. "Where is it?"

"Safe. Safe ... yeah, safe."

"Yes, of course," I said as if that all made perfect sense. "Where is your partner?"

A glimmer of normalcy flickered in the man's eyes and he spoke as if I were the lunatic. "Wit' the book. Keepin' it safe."

Of course he was. The other thief had not read from the book and could be trusted with its keeping.

"Was lookin' fer you. Goin' to yer cabin."

"Right. My cabin."

Why would he ...? A flash of insight hit me and I almost gasped with sudden understanding. This man wasn't coming to *my* cabin at all. Another conspirator was aboard the ship. Because of our shared link and his confusion, this man thought I was the other.

Thoughts swirled in my mind. This thief had knowledge that I didn't. If I could get him inside the cabin ... "We can't talk out here."

The taller man gave his head one quick shake, eyes darting again as if surrounded by people trying to eavesdrop.

No one who passed spared the briefest glance at my companion. It seemed that clothes, no matter how ill-fitting, did make the man. Was that how he'd been able to get into first class? Surely he needed more to get past the steward. Perhaps this unknown conspirator had greater influence than I did, enough to allow a steerage passenger into first class.

I reached for my door handle.

"Where you goin'?"

"My cabin."

Confusion creased the expression of the thief's face. "On A deck."

"I beg your pardon?"

"Yer cabin. It's on A deck."

Suspicion replaced confusion and his hand darted into the jacket he wore. The motion reminded me of Singh and I knew there was a concealed knife.

Damn.

"Oh yes. My cabin was changed at the last moment," I tried. "Very inconvenient."

The mind worked behind the thief's madness. My advantage was disappearing and I threw the cabin door open, backing inside. The thief followed, sniffing at the aroma of death within my cabin.

"You ain't him. You ain't."

I shook my head, backing further into the cabin. "No. I am not."

The man drew his weapon, a blade curved much like a snake. A ceremonial kris, and a better weapon for close-quarter fighting, but I didn't dare draw my sword anyway. This man could lead me to the book.

Dazed or not the man moved fast, rushing forward, bringing the blade up then down again. I dodged to one side, but not by much.

The advantage of distance gone, I retreated, skirting the table. The tall man swung his blade again and I deflected it with my cane, though the blow was staggering. I scrambled to get the table between us.

He launched forward and I took another step away, my back pressing against the wall. The blade swept down with savage ferocity and sunk deep into the wood tabletop. He worked the kris, trying to free it.

Seizing the advantage, I swung my heavy cane around, the arc finishing in a meaty thud against the side of his head. It didn't have near the force hoped for, but it was everything I could muster, and it was enough. The thief's eyes rolled up and he dropped like a poleaxed cow, tumbling to the floor. The kris, now free, clattered next to him.

I watched this unconscious man, expecting him to jump up and continue the attack.

Now what? I had no rope to bind him. In my doctor's bag was a hammer but no nails.

The man groaned.

Soon, this opportunity would be gone, but inspiration struck as I looked at the bed.

Would it work?

I threw the blanket off the top and pulled the sheet underneath from the bed. Laying it flat on the floor next to the unconscious man, I flipped him onto the sheet and started rolling, making the package as tight as possible. His arms needed to be pinned. When the job was done, he lay facedown, and I gave him one final roll.

Open eyes stared back at me.

He thrashed against his bindings, which were not near as tight as I'd hoped. I bolted to the table, grabbed his kris and returned to place the cold metal against the skin at his throat. He calmed, the disconcerting grin of a man dedicated to his cause creeping across his face.

Lucidity floated in those eyes for the moment. It wouldn't last.

The man's smile widened, revealing missing teeth. "You're him. The hider."

"Yes, I kept that damned book hidden."

"The blasphemer. The heretic."

The thought of that *god* I blasphemed gave me a cold shiver of repulsion.

"The *Ripper*," he whispered.

"Enough! Where is it?" I demanded.

The thief giggled, his sanity wavering again now that he was fully conscious. I added pressure to the knife in warning.

"Safe from you," the man said.

"Who is the man you were looking for?"

More gap-toothed grinning, nothing less than expected. Questioning this man could take hours, but I knew I could get the information I wanted. I thought of the second-largest scalpel inside my doctor's bag.

What to put inside his mouth to muffle the screams?

"Cthuuuuuuuuuulhuuuuuuuuuuuuuu," the man whispered in an eerie echo of Stephen's wail from last night.

I pressed the knife still harder against his throat in warning, a bead of blood appearing under the metal. It was sharp as any scalpel and I fought the urge to just be done with this.

The thief giggled, then shoved his head forward, pressing the blade more forcibly into the skin of his neck. He jerked his head quickly left, sawing through his throat and the artery there before I could react.

A jet of blood spurted from the wound, covering me, the sheet and a good portion of the opposite wall, adding to the gore with each heartbeat.

"Damn it!"

Using the table's edge I pulled myself up and collapsed onto one of the chairs.

"What a waste."

I could have drawn so much more information from him.

His dead eyes and lunatic grin mocked me. I felt seized with the urge to kick him, but that seemed like too much effort.

"Stupid old man!" I said, slapping the table with both hands.

So what information *had* I found out?

The thieves were not alone in this. Someone in first class was their contact. Someone who had boarded in Queenstown? Maybe. This man would not be uneducated or psychotic. What else? Without this second thief it would complicate the two sides coming together. Both would wonder what had happened to him, assuming he was with the other. Would that give me time?

I got to my feet and approached the thief, grabbed the sodden mess of sheet that tied him and cut it free with his own blade. Inside the jacket pocket was a scrap of paper soaked through with blood. I unfolded it, frowning at the now mostly obscured words.

Mr. W—

Cabin—

A Dec

Mr. W? Was this his first name or last? And how many men had boarded with names fitting either? No, there wasn't enough information, and this Mr. W didn't have the book anyway. Not yet.

This left me where I started, needing to get to the remaining thief in steerage.

———

After jamming this second body into my wardrobe and cleaning myself and the cabin, I took a bottle of rubbing alcohol from my bag and poured half on the thief's remains, the other half on Stephen. That would mask the growing smell for now.

I returned to the closest gate leading to second class and stood at a nearby rail, watching. This steward was most attentive to his duties. One couple who had taken a wrong turn, perhaps on purpose, arrived at the opposite side of the locked gate. The steward spoke with them pleasantly, explaining where they needed to go.

If they'd arrived dressed in first-class clothing would the gate have been opened for them? Had the thief made his way through this way?

Hours of watching, wandering from one entrance to another, I came to the conclusion that there was no simple way to get past those gates. There would be *some* way to get past that gate, but did I have the luxury of time to discover it? It was as expected, but I still returned to my cabin in a foul humor to change into dinner clothes.

The dining room was a sea of tables on two levels, made all the wider by mirrors lining two opposing walls. The captain's table was foremost. Serving staff weaved their way around tables, chairs, and passengers, bringing food, filling glasses and being as unobtrusive as possible.

Seated on Captain Smith's left, I made idle chitchat throughout the many courses. The captain's affable manner lulled me into relaxation and I found myself enjoying our conversation when he wasn't engaging the other guests.

"Mr. Wainright," he said to a man who had done no more

than push food around his plate since sitting down, "are you unwell?"

Wainright? Mr. W?

"Hmm? Oh, yes Captain. I'm fine, thank you," he responded, glancing up. "My first cruise. I suspect being on a ship takes getting used to."

The captain smiled, understanding, comforting.

"I didn't sleep well last night," Wainright continued. "Strange dreams and all that."

Smith's smile faltered and he stared at the man, nodding mechanically. I noticed around the table other guests had halted conversation mid-word at the mention of the dreams.

"Yes," the captain said finally. "Just need to get your sea legs, I'm sure. It will be better tomorrow."

Wainright seemed to accept this, though he didn't eat more than he already had. This would not be the Mr. W associated with the thieves. That man wouldn't have suffered under the weight of nightmares.

The captain steered the conversation away from the topic and the meal ran its course without further mention of dreams. After dessert the captain excused himself, needing to attend to duties of the ship.

Before leaving myself, I made a quick tour of the room, over-hearing conversations with three different Williams and a Wilson. Too many names starting with W to be of any use.

The circuitous route back to my cabin took me past each of the gates once again. As expected, they were still well attended by the stewards. No plan presented itself for getting through, other than the desperate one of killing ship's crew.

Annoyed, I returned to my cabin, turning possibilities over in my head and discarding them as quickly. There would be some way below that wouldn't lead to my incarceration. I just needed to find it.

April 12

The sound of knocking woke me, an insistent quality to it saying it had been going on for some time.

"One moment," I said, voice too low for anyone to hear.

The deep slumber of morphine had left me with dry throat, as well as a certain fuzzy-headedness. Both would clear soon enough.

"One moment," I tried again, louder.

The knocking ceased.

With a muted groan I pushed my feet from under the covers, reaching out for my cane. Crossing the cabin provided enough time for my head to clear, and on opening the door found a ship's crewman I didn't recognize. The man shifted from foot to foot.

"Good morning, sir," he said in a quick, clipped tone. "The captain asks for your presence at his cabin."

"Now?"

"Yes, sir. I've been asked to escort you personally."

Why would the man be sending for me?

"I'll need time to dress," I said.

The man opened his mouth to reply, then took in my night-clothes and gave a nod. He stood, hands behind his back as the door closed on him.

"Damn it," I whispered.

This was the sort of attention I was trying to avoid. How did Smith know which cabin I was in, anyway? No, forget that. The man was resourceful, and if the ship's register had a different name assigned to the room, he would assume I had taken it from a friend.

Quickly I dressed in dayclothes, sparing a glance at the clock. A few minutes before nine. A longer sleep than expected, more than I'd been able to get in years.

I opened the door. "Ready."

The crewman started up the passageway and I tried my best to match his brisk pace but soon fell back.

"I apologize, Doctor," he said, embarrassment sliding over his face as he slowed. "I'm anxious to get you to the captain."

"Has something happened?"

"The captain is ... distraught."

We continued on in silence another ten paces before he spoke again. "There is something about this voyage ..." He shook his head, perhaps unsure how to complete the thought. This time his silence held until leading me into the crew's section of the vast ship.

A knock on one door was answered by it opening a crack, one eye filling the gap.

"It's Johnson, sir," my guide said. "I've brought the Doctor, as requested."

The door opened and Captain Smith appeared, gaze shooting left and right. The quiet dignity and affable demeanor were gone. What word had the crewman used? Distraught?

"Doctor, come in. Come in," Smith said, stepping aside to allow entry, then pulled himself to full height and settled his gaze on Johnson. "Thank you, Ensign. That will be all."

The command in his voice was unmistakable. Johnson snapped off a salute which the captain returned before closing the door. Smith deflated into a chair, waving an arm toward a matching seat across from him. I sat.

"What has happened since last night?" I asked.

"Doctor, I fear I am going mad. You heard Wainright at dinner. Dreams. Nightmares."

"You've had nightmares?"

Of course he had.

"No!" Smith laughed, a sound I didn't like. It was too close to the lunatic giggle of the dead man in my wardrobe. "Calling them nightmares is like calling this ship a raft."

"And you want my opinion on these nightmares?"

"Yes," the captain said without making eye contact.

I weighed the options. If the captain were incapacitated, would the ship return to England? No, more likely we would continue on with a new man in command. The attention on me would be gone at least, but was that the wrong way of thinking? This man could be a source of information.

"Often dreams are the hidden topics of our subconscious, our desires," I said.

Smith jumped up with a cry and paced.

"However," I continued, "more often they are influenced by outside stimulus which we are unaware of."

Closer to the actual truth than Captain Smith would ever be aware. His romantic view of the ocean and sailing life made him more susceptible to this evil influence.

"A rich dinner, for example," I added, "can provide a night of vivid dreaming."

Smith came to a stop in front of the cabin's one small window, watching the ocean outside pass by. Two full minutes passed while he, hopefully, absorbed the concept. He nodded once. Another minute passed before he would nod again and turn toward me.

"You are telling me there is more of gravy than of grave about these dreams," he said.

Dickens has always been a favorite author of mine. The fact that Smith had been able to make a joke, as much as the joke itself, gave me hope for the man. The captain took a deep breath and exhaled the hold of last night's dreams.

"What does your ship's doctor say on the subject?" I asked.

I knew the answer already. The captain would not have brought this up with a member of his crew for fear of losing their confidence. It was why a passenger had been escorted to this cabin. The other man focused on me with such intensity that I was sure I'd asked the wrong question.

Smith said, "Of our two doctors, one is asleep and will not wake."

"Won't wake?"

"He sleeps, fitfully, thrashing and mumbling, but nothing rouses him."

And nothing will, not during this voyage at least. "And your second doctor?"

"We have no idea." The captain returned to his seat. "He disappeared in the night."

Disappeared. Three of the most important men onboard affected by the book's influence.

"Captain, given present circumstances, I recommend a return to England."

Anger flashed in the man's eyes, his mouth becoming a slit. For a moment I feared being struck, then the storm passed and Smith shook his head. "I can't do that. The shipping strikes at home have caused too much difficulty. I have my duty to the company and crew."

"How can you continue without a ship's doctor?"

"Yes, quite right." The captain drummed his fingers against the arm of his chair. "Doctor Shaw, I know it's an imposition and you are here to enjoy the voyage, but would you consider filling in until we reach New York?"

Refusal perched on my tongue, but then an image of the gates flitted through my mind. I closed my mouth with a sharp *clack*. "Of course, Captain. We all do what we must."

A sigh of relief. "My thanks."

"I would need a note from you," I continued, "to pass to any section of the ship where I am needed … unless you have a uniform in my size."

At that Smith laughed again, but a genuine thing this time that broke the last of the nightmare's grip on him. He went to his desk and wrote a hasty note which he handed to me. "This will do."

I opened it and read:

To whom it may concern,

Dr. Shaw will be acting as ship's doctor until further notice. Please convey every courtesy to him and allow access to any area of the ship he deems necessary.

Sincerely,

Captain Edward Smith

I tucked it into the inside pocket of my jacket. "Now, my first duty is to prescribe something for you to sleep."

"Nonsense. I'm fine."

"And the ship needs you to stay that way."

The captain mulled this over before throwing his hands up in surrender, mumbling. "Never argue with the ship's doctor."

"Quite right. When are you due on the bridge?"

A look at the clock and he jumped to his feet. "I should be there now."

"And when will you return?"

"Before dinner, but I need to be at my table."

"Fine. I can give you something after dinner to sleep through the night."

I headed for the nearest gate in high spirits.

The captain's letter turned the impossible task of getting through into a simple one. Each of the stewards read it then rushed to open their barrier.

Now I stood at the base of the stairs in third class, eyes closed and listening for the book.

"Damn it."

My mood plummeted in the span between heartbeats.

The book was indeed nearby, that much was obvious. It should have been simple to pinpoint now that we were on the same level. It wasn't. Unlike first class where the location had a constant downward sensation to it, now it felt to be everywhere.

Its power was growing.

"God damn it to hell."

All around me were people who had spent their every penny for this voyage, full of hope for a better life, but one of them was not what he appeared to be.

Would he be recognizable when I saw him? Would the book call to me when I got closer?

I had to hope so.

Announcing myself as ship's doctor I started talking to the nearest people. These third-class passengers expressed surprise that any attention was being paid to them by the ship's crew. They knew their place on the ladder of society.

Word of a doctor in third class would precede me, and that should offset the surprise of a first-class passenger being down here. I didn't want to alarm the thief.

Many complained of general ill-feelings, lack of energy, and, of course, the expected nightmares. One passenger who had boarded in Ireland muttered that the voyage was cursed and there was no arguing against that.

The rest of the morning and all that afternoon was spent in a slow circuit through third class, eliminating many as suspects but nowhere near enough. Too many had a natural distrust of the upper class, which matched how the thief could be expected to react. There was no sudden recognition with any passenger, and no pull from the book.

Calling to the damned thing might knock me into another coma or destroy my mind completely.

Was I desperate enough to try it?

No. Not yet.

In the end, I made my way back to first class, tired and frustrated, ready for a meal and knowing that finding the book was no closer than it had been when I first boarded the ship.

The dining room was three-quarters full at most. Every table held one empty seat at least, and those present were more subdued than the previous night. Captain Smith spoke with his table guests but it was forced, the man exhausted.

After dinner I accompanied him to his cabin as promised and shared some of my stock of morphine. There had been precious little in the ship's stores and it had already been added to my own. Keeping the captain in dreamless sleep would mean exhausting these supplies faster than expected, but I needed him in his right mind, both to keep this ship on schedule and to retain my ability to get through those gates.

April 13

The next morning, I found myself summoned to the captain's cabin once again.

Captain Smith stood erect, commanding, and in control. The perfect image of an experienced sea captain. He sipped a cup of tea. "Good morning, Doctor."

"You slept well?"

"Can't let a few dreams stop me. I have a job to do."

"Glad to hear it."

Smith sat and gestured toward the other chair and the tea. I poured myself a cup.

"Last night, three first-class passengers needed confining to their cabins," he said.

The crewman, Johnson, had filled me in. "People who were trying to harm themselves or others, as I understand it."

It would only get worse.

The captain sighed. "Our sleeping doctor is gone as well."

This was new information. "Gone?"

"He woke and scrawled a message on his wall, in blood no less, presumably his own."

"What did it say?"

"Insanity. Voices speaking to him. Sleeping things waiting to rise. Nightmares." The captain shuddered without noticing. "He concluded by saying he would fling himself off the ship."

"Did he?"

"I would say so," Smith shrugged. "Apparently he went from his cabin to wherever he ended up without a soul seeing him."

We sat in silence a moment before he spoke again. "The crew is calling this 'The Ravings.' Doctor, what is happening on my ship?"

Nightmares notwithstanding, I doubted this man was ready to hear that the doctor's wall scrawlings were true. I could be confined to my cabin, if I tried.

"The Ravings is as fitting a name as any," I began. "I've seen a similar illness before. It attacks the mind, affecting it with a temporary alienation."

"Temporary?"

"Yes, until patient is removed from the cause. In this case, the ship—or something on it."

The captain mulled this over before replying. "Very well. We'll need to keep these people confined to cabin until we reach New York then, and keep an eye out for any other strange behavior."

"Unless you are willing to turn back."

Smith shook his head. "Even if I could, it would be a moot point. We have reached the point of no return. We are closer to our destination now."

The captain put his cup down and got to his feet. "Doctor, please look in on these affected first-class passengers before doing anything else."

"Of course."

Leaving the captain's cabin, I headed straight for steerage.

The first-class passengers were a waste of time. There was little I could do other than sedate them, and I wasn't about to waste morphine on overly sensitive, easily influenced people. My time was better spent with continuing my search.

Smith's words rang in my ears as I walked: *We're closer to our destination now.*

While I was no closer to finding the book.

"Where the hell is it?" I said, stepping into second class. "Where?"

The book's presence hammered into me, pulling a groan from my throat. It was everywhere on this level, as it had been yesterday in third class.

"No! No, no, no."

I rushed for the gate leading to steerage. This sensation in second class *could* mean the thief was on the move, or ...

I flashed my letter at the steward. "Let me through."

"Are you well, Doctor?" he asked. "You seem ..."

"Yes, yes, yes. Just open the damn gate."

The man complied and I started to the next level.

"No. God damn it, no."

The thief *wasn't* on the move, but the influence of the book *was*. It had spread like a pestilence, covering the lower two levels. Soon it would occupy the entire ship.

Time was running out.

Like diving deeper into water the pressure of evil was greater down here, and the effect on the passengers was evident. Many were lethargic, eyes haunted by visions only they saw. One man leaned over his gathered family speaking in hissing whispers, warning them. Another stood in a corner, back to the wall and eyes darting, ensuring nothing could sneak up on him.

All stared at me with trepidation.

How had none of the ship's crew noticed this?

"I'm here to help," I managed.

Those that would speak to me told me about their night-mares. I knew what those visions would hold and moved on, searching for the one who would be less affected.

Some asked if I was well, as if I were acting in a demented manner.

Insanity.

I spent fruitless hours searching for the thief in this way, but there were too many people, and missing one in that crowd was easy.

"Where is it?"

Would finding the book be enough? There were still two more days at sea.

Two more days under this influence.

A ghost ship would arrive in New York.

I laughed, without knowing the reason why.

Could I throw the book overboard?

"It wouldn't stay there though, would it? No, it needs to be hidden. Guarded. This ship full of people is fair exchange."

There! That man was suspicious.

"You!" I rushed at him, drawing the knife the first thief had carried. "Where is it?"

I had the man pressed against the wall, knife in one hand.

"Where is that damned book?"

"What? I ..."

"Daddy?"

I turned to see the terrified face of a five-year-old boy. He hid behind the doorway, staring up at us.

"Go back inside, Jamie," the man said.

No. That wasn't right. The thief wouldn't be traveling with a child, wouldn't care about his safety.

I backed away from the man, seeing the terror in his eyes matching his child's.

"No, you aren't him. You aren't."

I turned and headed down the hall, making it ten steps before men were on me. They wrestled me to the floor, taking my knife away.

"No! I must find it. Can't you feel the evil?"

"Someone get the steward."

I lay there, under the weight of all these people, warning of the danger surrounding them. Couldn't they feel it for themselves?

"Doctor!" The gate steward shouted. Three other men in ship's uniform stood behind him.

"The Ravings," one muttered.

A second one added. "Another doctor affected."

They pulled me to my feet, my arms held fast.

"Help me find the book! Help me find the thief!"

"Yes, of course, Doctor."

They said they would help, yet they herded me toward the stairs.

"No. You don't understand."

"Easy with him," one of the crew said. "He's a friend of the captain."

The next I knew I was being eased onto my bed.

Then I started screaming.

Dreams of blood, death, and destruction. The entire world and everyone I'd ever cared for destroyed and defiled.

Archibald Shaw reveled in it.

Piled before me were all the bodies of those Whitechapel women, and many more that had only been possibilities. All of the men who had gone into that part of London with him were there, too, torn apart, eyes vacant and mad.

And Singh. The boy I had rescued. He lay, disemboweled on an altar.

In my hand, the long ceremonial blade of the thief, dripping with redness, my mind dripping with madness.

NO!

This was everything I'd fought against, everything I'd dedicated my life to preventing. This was not me. I rejected it.

I am not the Ripper.

Not anymore.

April ??

In my desperation to find the book, I had called to it, and it had answered. I saw this now that I was awake again, now that the madness had passed.

How long had I been unconscious?

I retrieved my cane from the floor and hurried to the cabin's one window.

Still at sea, and the sun only starting to set. I'd regained my senses before it was too late.

The clock on the table said 6:00 PM. Beside it sat a meal, lunch by the look of it. Cold to the touch.

The door to the cabin was locked, which was no surprise. People with The Ravings were being confined to cabin.

I shook my head, trying to clear the lingering fog, and paced the confined space. My body screamed in complaint and reminded me about the morphine.

Did I still have my bag?

Yes. On the trunk where I'd left it. Luckily the stewards had ignored that when they'd dropped me here. I crossed the cabin and opened the bag, pulling out a syringe.

For five minutes I gazed at it, wanting it, before sliding the drug into my jacket pocket with a regretful sigh.

No, I needed my wits.

What I needed more was to get out of here.

How though? I lacked the strength to break the door down, and the window was no exit.

Until someone came I was trapped in here.

While waiting, I changed my shirt and pants, the current ones being soaked in the sweat of madness. In the end I sat in the reading chair, facing it toward the door and eating the cold lunch, though I had little appetite. My cane laid across my leg in a casual manner.

A little over an hour later, the handle twitched as someone unlocked it from the other side. A deep breath and a mental reminder to be calm and unthreatening.

The steward, Thompkins, entered, a platter of food to replace my hours-old lunch balanced on one hand. When he saw me out of bed, he stopped, then turned to leave.

"I'm fine now, Thompkins," I said. "The fever, or whatever it was, has left me."

Thompkins nodded, coming no closer. "I'm happy to hear that, Doctor."

After another moment's indecision, he stepped forward to place the meal on my table, not picking up what remained of the previous one. He wanted to keep his hands free around me. Sensible.

"Can I get you anything, Doctor?"

"Just some news if you would."

"News?"

"Yes." I tried to keep any impatience from showing. "What has been happening on the ship in the hours I've been locked away?"

"Hours? Doctor, I'm sorry, but ... you've been in here since yesterday morning."

I'd lost an entire day? "No. God damn it."

Thompkins took a step back and I forced a calming expression to my face.

"Sorry. I was thinking of all the people I could have helped in that time."

The steward relaxed, somewhat.

"Have there been many more afflicted?" I asked.

"Yes, sir. I'm not sure on the number, but quite a few. Both passengers and crew."

"The captain?"

"Oh no, sir! Captain Smith is rock steady."

"Good," I said. "That's good."

The captain had slept through the night without relapsing into his nightmares. Perhaps he'd found something in the ship's pharmacy to help.

I leaned on my cane and got to my feet, suffering at least half of the effort I let Thompkins see. The man took another step back toward the door but looked embarrassed for doing so.

"Obviously you can't let me out," I said, "but would you take a message to Captain Smith for me?"

"Of course, Doctor. Is it urgent? I have other meals to deliver."

"After will be fine."

I crossed to my nightstand and scribbled on one of the papers there, then folded it into four. Turning back I headed for Thompkins, the paper held out in two fingers of my free hand. As he reached for the note I dropped it.

"So sorry," I muttered. "Must still be weak."

"Quite all right, Doctor."

Thompkins bent to retrieve the paper.

"*So* sorry," I repeated.

I took a step back, pulling the sword from my cane. Thompkins must have heard the soft whisk of metal on metal, but gave no sign of understanding its meaning. As he rose, innocent, unsuspecting smile on his face, I lunged forward and skewered him through the heart.

This time, I did not miss the killing stroke. Thompkins pitched forward and collapsed at my feet. Dead.

I waited.

No angry ghost. No wailing.

Thompkins had followed a different path into the afterlife than Stephen.

"Rest in peace," I muttered, not sure what that even meant.

No sense in hiding this body. Unlike the other two, Thompkins would be missed in time. I had to hope that, with the amount of people experiencing madness, the crew would be too busy to bother with one missing steward anytime soon.

The hallway outside was empty except for a cart of meals, which I wheeled into my overcrowded cabin.

"Now what?"

I locked the door behind me, picked a direction, and started walking. In motion I could think.

The captain's letter allowing me run of the ship was gone. Even if I did still have it, the crew would know by now what had happened to me. An alarm would be raised if I approached any of the gates. I couldn't be sure the book was still in steerage anyway. Stopping to sense, it told me it was everywhere.

The decks were now mostly empty, and those that were around gave signs they would also rather be left alone. I took up residence in one of the more secluded deck chairs, staring at the ocean.

"Now what?" I repeated.

After sunset, I worried less about being recognized and moved to the rail, chill night air pushing at me as I continued contemplating my next move. The last option of killing my way to the book was still available, and might be my *only* option now. If only I knew for certain where it was.

Lacking any better ideas, I decided to return to the gate, see if anything had changed. Two steps into that direction, my mind was assaulted and my body hammered to the wooden deck.

"Evil. Evil. The evil. The horror. The sleeping death. Cthul—"

I stopped myself. My words had grown from chant to near frantic scream.

"No. No."

I wouldn't allow that. Not again.

Between rail and cane I was able to get back to my feet.

Waves of hate and evil assaulted me, but I was ready.

"They're reading the book again. Reading the words. Reading ..."

Stop it!

Yes, they were reading it again, but this time they weren't stopping at a word or two. Oh god, they kept reading and my head felt like it would burst.

"No! Oh, sleeping gods of ancient death ..."

The morphine! I fumbled the syringe from my pocket, stripping my arm bare and injecting the needle. Fear and desperation said to depress the syringe the entire way, but I stopped at just enough to dull the assault.

The attack eased, my brain feeling less like it was being squeezed in a giant fist.

And I knew.

They were on this deck now.

Following the sensation back to them was simple. Two men, standing at the extreme bow of the ship.

The first was one of the people from steerage who refused to speak with me. He had been suspicious, but no more so than any of the others in steerage had been. The other, holding the book open in both hands, wore the splendid clothing of someone who had come from formal dinner, completely incongruous next to the thief. He was familiar too. Weston? No, Wilson.

Both had their backs to me, Wilson reading from the book.

Ph'nglui mglw'nafh Cthulhu R'lyeh wgah'nagl fhtagn.

"No!" I yelled, not thinking.

Wilson paused in his chants, turning first to me then the thief. "Get him."

The thief pulled a blade from inside his jacket and started toward me. I allowed him to advance, thinking I had the advantage of reach on the open deck. When I drew the sword from my cane the thief stopped and looked down, as if comparing his blade to mine, then he grinned and started forward again.

The man feinted left then went right. I kept my sword trained on him through both movements, then committed to an attack when an opening presented itself. I thrust forward and he dodged around my sword to swing his knife. Whether through luck or providence I still held the cane in my free hand and managed to get it in the way of the stroke so only the tip of it cut me. Even so it hurt like fire as the blade raked a shallow furrow along my left arm. I swung the cane up and slammed it across the thief's face.

Wilson continued chanting. What the hell was he trying to do?

Ph'nglui mglw'nafh Cthulhu R'lyeh wgah'nagl fhtagn.

Wind increased, chilling me to the bone, making my hands tight and frozen. My fingers wanted to open, to drop the sword, but that meant death and worse.

The thief's mouth widened into a grin more toothless than his friend in my wardrobe. He knew all he needed to win was to keep me from his master. The advantage was his.

The ship rocked to one side, throwing us all with it. Wilson kept his balance, leaning against the rails and grasping the book. I used my cane as a third leg, though without the head it *was* more of an effort. Only the thief lost his balance and stumbled, his hand opening involuntarily and dropping the knife to clatter against the boards of the deck.

Without a thought, I thrust forward with the sword and ran

the man through, the tip of the blade entering the man's stomach, though I'd been aiming for the heart. He screamed and twisted, dragging the sword from my grasp and staggering back toward his master.

"Damn it, you fool," Wilson said. "Kill him."

He resumed chanting and the thief rushed me. The man was dead, but a stomach wound could take hours and I didn't have that much time. The fire of a fanatic was in his eyes as he rushed forward. Blood trickled from his mouth and sprayed with each exhale. We collided and he drove me back against the wall, hands reaching for my face and thumbs digging for my eyes.

I screamed.

Something dug painfully against my own stomach and I grasped blindly, knowing what it must be. The sword's hilt, now sitting flush against him. Thumbs pressed against my eyes, pushing them into my skull.

Finding the sword hilt, I twisted it one full circle.

A gasp and the pressure against my eyes relaxed.

I pushed the hilt downward, like a lever, then reversed the action. I'd intended to go left and right next, but the thief staggered away. Fanatic he might be, but the human brain still fought to avoid death.

Through blurry vision I watched him retreat toward the rail.

The ship rocked again, this time to the other side and more violently. Wilson took one step back before pushing himself into the rail once again. The thief, in his desire to get away, toppled over the edge and into the freezing water below, taking my sword with him.

I tried using the remaining cane half for balance again, planting it against the deck, but the slickness of blood on my hands made it too difficult to hold onto. I slipped, losing my grip on the cane and watched it skitter across the deck.

The lunatic words poured from Wilson's mouth. My mind

was under siege, pulled sideways into a state of thinking I did not want to return to.

I was on all fours now, crawling toward Wilson. Without the cane this was much faster, though the pain in my lame leg was legendary. Hands and knees pressed against the wooden deck in step after step until one touched metal. The discarded knife of the thief was under hand and I grabbed it, not slowing my progress.

The chants had become more frenzied. Wilson had lost his mind and I had no idea how he could continue standing, much less reading. I doubled my speed, needing to stop the words pouring from that man's mouth before my sanity left as well.

Reaching Wilson I rammed the knife into the meaty upper part of his right thigh. He gave a short hiss between two syllables but no other sign he had been hurt. I pulled myself up to my feet, reaching to stab him again. Still reading he swung one fist around and connected with the side of my head. Reeling, I watched the blade sail away across deck.

With no options left I attacked Wilson with my fists. Puny, ineffective things. I might as well have been a child. He laughed. I cried and stepped backward.

What could I …?

My hand darted into the jacket pocket and came out with the syringe, still more than three-quarters full of morphine. I swung around and stabbed it into the side of Wilson's neck, pressing on the plunger at the same time. The man sagged, whether from the drug or the wound I didn't care.

He dropped the book to the deck, still chanting.

Bracing myself, I reached down and grabbed Wilson by the lower legs, lifting the man and flipping him over the side of the ship and into the water below.

The book called to me, whispering, ordering me to finish what was begun.

I shook my head and looked down, seeing the pages. The

book was in my hands, face up, the words burning into my mind.

Had I been reading?

Had I said any of this aloud?

"No. It has to be over. Please."

The ship lurched again as, in front of me, a shape rose from the water. Immense, coursing with rivers of slimy, stagnant water. A rounded, bulbous head ending in tentacles. An ancient god, asleep no more.

"No! No, no, no, no, no, no."

Once again I looked at the book, at the words that were there, at the madness awaiting. The ceremony had not been completed. I could see the spot where I'd interrupted Wilson. It blazed in my mind like fiery letters written across the sky, spiking into my mind like a silver needle of agony. Nothing else occupied my world except for the words of the book and this waiting, ancient deity.

READ!

I heard the word inside his head, felt it inside my soul, to the core of my being and beyond. Nothing else.

Nothing!

"Please."

I closed my eyes.

The words filled my head. I saw them, saw what I was expected to say, commanded to read.

READ THE WORDS!

"Yes. Read the words."

Had I said that?

Yes. Yes, I had. And I saw it was true. I *did* need to read those words dancing in front of my eyes.

Fhtagn wgah'nagl R'lyeh Cthulhu mglw'nafh Ph'nglui.

I read them. Backward.

More tumbled from my mouth. Word after word until I was screaming myself hoarse and had lost all sense of who I was.

The ancient god raged at the reversal of ceremony, thrashing as it returned to the depths. One appendage—A wing? An arm? —collided with the ship. The screech of rending, tearing steel filled the air.

I lost my balance as the ship was rocked sideways. That damned tome went overboard, following its god back to the ocean's bottom. A moment later I followed it, watching the freezing water rushing toward me.

The book was gone, my mission with it, and I welcomed death.

When my eyes opened I was lying in a lifeboat, cold and sodden, a blanket wrapped around me. Inside the rocking boat hunkered people with the haunted expressions of ones who had gone through war.

"Rest easy, Doctor. You're safe," a familiar voice said.

"Mrs. Hooper?"

"You're lucky the steward saw you."

"What happened?" I asked.

"Something hit the ship," the steward said. "Some sort of …"

I knew the word *monster* was on the man's lips, but he wouldn't allow himself to speak it. His mind didn't want to acknowledge it. None of these people did.

"Iceberg," I said. "Yes, I saw it."

Everyone in the lifeboat focused on me and I repeated the word several times. Iceberg. They were ready for any explanation but the truth of what they had seen.

"Iceberg," I repeated one final time.

There were murmurs of agreement and the repeating of my final words as I slipped away.

Iceberg.

ABOUT THE AUTHOR

John Haas is a Canadian author, born and raised in Montreal before moving to Calgary, where he lived for twelve wonderful years. Now he lives in Canada's capital, Ottawa, but still misses seeing those Rocky Mountains in the distance.

John has been writing for most of his life, but only became serious about being published in the last decade or so. In that time he has published twenty short stories in various venues, including *Writers of the Future Volume 35*. His first three novels have also been released—*The Reluctant Barbarian* (2017), *The Wayward Spider* (2019), and *The Unavoidable Quests* (2020), a fun and humorous fantasy trilogy.

Currently he is hard at work on the next novel of Shaw and Singh's struggles against the forces of darkness.

His goal is to become a full-time writer (rich and famous would be nice too, but not the main goal).

He lives with his two wonderful sons who continue to give him motivation, support, and time to write.

OTHER WORDFIRE PRESS TITLES BY JOHN HAAS

Arcana
by Paul Kane

Selected Stories: Horror and Dark Fantasy
by Kevin J. Anderson

Elements of Mind
by Walter H. Hunt

Our list of other WordFire Press authors and titles is always growing. To find out more and to see our selection of titles, visit us at:

wordfirepress.com

facebook.com/WordfireIncWordfirePress
twitter.com/WordFirePress
instagram.com/WordFirePress
bookbub.com/profile/4109784512

9 781680 572322